A Winter of Wonders

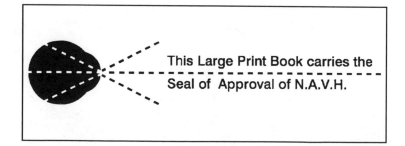

This Large Print Book carries the
Seal of Approval of N.A.V.H.

CIRCLE OF FRIENDS: JUST OFF MAIN
BOOK 2

A WINTER OF WONDERS

JENNIFER O'NEILL

THORNDIKE PRESS

An Imprint of Thomson Gale, a part of The Thomson Corporation

Detroit • New York • San Francisco • New Haven, Conn. • Waterville, Maine • London

LIBRARY OF CONGRESS CATALOGING-IN-PUBLICATION DATA

O'Neill, Jennifer, 1949–
    A winter of wonders / by Jennifer O'Neill.
        p. cm. — (Circle of friends, just off Main.) (Thorndike Press large print
    christian fiction)
    ISBN-13: 978-0-7862-9605-7 (lg. print : alk. paper)
    ISBN-10: 0-7862-9605-4 (lg. print : alk. paper)
    ISBN-13: 978-1-59415-187-3 (lg. print : pbk. : alk. paper)
    ISBN-10: 1-59415-187-3 (lg. print : pbk. : alk. paper)
    1. Female friendship — Fiction. 2. Spiritual life — Fiction. 3. Large type
books. I. Title.
PS3565.N4985W56 2007
813'.6—dc22   2007012898

Published in 2007 by arrangement with Broadman & Holman Publishers

Printed in the United States of America on permanent paper
10 9 8 7 6 5 4 3 2 1

We are designed to flourish and excel more fully when supported by the trustworthy, loving encouragement of others, which unfortunately is a rare experience. I praise and worship God in all things, and I thank him for blessing me with Dale. Her friendship and partnership surely have been heaven sent.

CHAPTER 1
-COMFORT ZONE-

Just off Main, Norros was buzzing with wall-to-wall patrons inhaling the unrivaled best food south of the Mason-Dixon line. Even Nashville's snooty restaurant menus paled next to Norros, where "busy" was normal fare.

Truth was, city dwellers didn't mind the relatively short drive to the outskirt town of Centennial when they had a hankering for southern cooking at its finest. And the local residents never minded the thirty- to forty-five-minute wait for a scat, even if that seat was at the counter of the fifties-styled diner; they'd simply gather in any available corner of the restaurant to exchange stories and updates until they could be seated.

Irene had recognized right off that being a transplant from New York City to Centennial had the potential to create its own calling card for the curious. Still, ever since her husband had died and she'd been arrested, the local-yokel scrutiny had been beyond merciless. And with every postponed trial date, the insanity multiplied.

No question, Irene was the talk of the town; and she, uncharacteristically, hated every moment of the attention. Where she was from, as long as they were talking about you, it was a good thing; but Irene quickly came to terms with the truism that in the South being talked about was not something to aspire to.

Stephanie skillfully navigated her way around the popular diner, taking orders and serving her customers with a smile and a professional manner. As the only waitress at Norros, she handled the task with aplomb.

She couldn't help but cringe at the barrage of critical words and speculation being bantered about by Norros loyal patrons concerning Irene Williams's personal affairs. Frankly, it raised the hair on the back of Stephanie's neck, and she wondered just how long she would be able to bite her own tongue so as not to speak out against such mean-spirited conversations. But then she calmed herself with the knowledge that not everyone from around those parts had a spiteful heart. In fact, since Stephanie had moved to Centennial, she had made the best circle of friends she'd ever known, and that knowledge held her at bay, at least for the moment.

It looked like a little girl's bed, one barely big enough to accommodate the worn, one-armed teddy bear nestled between a double set of pillows trimmed in lace. The hand-stitched pink quilt came just short of covering the down comforter, its corner turned back as an invitation to crawl under and rest without reserve.

In the scheme of things, the twin bed appeared oddly out of place in the relatively large bedroom that boasted arched windows overlooking a concise garden of evergreens framed by a white picket fence. Stephanie always had a way with creating a gracious home, no matter her circumstances.

A few leaves hung onto a formidable branch of an oak tree defying the inevitable turn of season from fall to winter. This bark-encased monument of time marked the corner of Stephanie's yard, which was located in the center of the mobile home park where she and Trace lived.

It was Wednesday, November 14, 1996. Long shadows cast by a rising sun cut across the room where Stephanie knelt in prayer at the foot of her bed. There was something childlike about this lovely woman; dreams still filled her heart despite so many disappointments.

Her innocent qualities were never more evident than when she was in prayer, seeking God's forgiveness, healing, wisdom, restoration, and glorious presence. This was her quiet time; her habit was to be up well before dawn to nourish herself spiritually.

Stephanie always began her prayer time with some Scripture that would eventually move her heart and voice to song. Trace had grown up hearing his mother's melodic prayers called out to God early every morning, and this new day was no exception. In fact, these past years he had distinctly heard every lamenting word his mother uttered through the paper-thin, prefab walls that divided their bedrooms. Then, like clockwork, he would roll over, taking solace in the fact that he had at least an hour more of sleep before having to get up for school.

The seventeen-year-old's six-foot-four athletic frame sprawled sideways across the king-size bed he had inherited from his mom when they moved to Tennessee two years ago. He never quite understood why Stephanie had offered him her bed, and she never told him the *real* reason. All she said was, "I stopped growing years ago, . . . size wise." Then she'd wink. "Now it's your turn to have some unencumbered snooze space."

But the truth was, when Stephanie lost her husband in a horrific trucking accident in Alabama, she couldn't bear to spend even a single night alone in the bed that she and the love of her life had shared with such passion and commitment.

Trace was not even fifteen when his father died, and Stephanie, only thirty-nine, was suddenly a widow. She could relate to Trace's anger with God at such a loss; and soon after her husband's death, she found herself at a crossroads in her faith. That really frightened her!

She had heard stories about such loss, and she had read somewhere that "crossroads in faith" happen to most Christians at some juncture in their spiritual lives. Nonethcless, realizing that she was not alone in her questioning allowed her a bit more latitude in her dialogue with God; she finally let herself wail from the depths of her soul without the fear of losing her reverence for the Lord as she questioned the meaning of her plight.

During those first days of grieving, Stephanie decided her teenager's bed would suit her far better than the king because she was absolutely sure there would never be another man in her life. Besides, she just couldn't stand any physical empty space residing beside her empty heart.

And so it never failed: over the last several years when she would kneel at the foot of her son's little bed, she was somehow comforted by its size — or lack of it. It actually took her back to her youth, to her teddy bear and mounds of pillows that made her feel secure in the middle of the night despite the fact that she was surrounded by six older siblings in three separate sets of bunk beds.

Yes, she was the baby, and she liked it that way, even as she grew into a young woman. But the security of a large family was short-lived for Stephanie.

Aunt Reba tried to comfort the thirteen-year-old Stephanie when she came to live with her after the disaster. "God must have a mighty special plan for you, girl, to have spared you the fate of your family." The kind woman wrapped Stephanie in her arms, stroking her hair as she hummed an old-time hymn.

Stephanie battled with a bushel-load of mixed emotions while Aunt Reba's eight younger children gathered in the living room, settling into their favorite spots sprinkled around the family area of their modest homestead nestled in the backwoods of Alabama.

Stephanie remembered thinking that she'd never seen a TV with such big rabbit ears, extended by wire hangers and whatever else was necessary to get reception in the mountainous countryside. Everyone pulled their seats closer up to the set to watch the local news program about to report the story of Stephanie's loss.

An advertisement for Hoover vacuum cleaners filled the screen for what seemed an eternity, and although the family expected to see the interview with Stephanie, everyone was stunned when her likeness popped up on the little screen. Watching herself on camera, Stephanie remembered she was literally shaking in her boots during the interview.

The girl recalled wondering why the news anchor's lips didn't slide off her face since they were so rosy and shiny from lipstick and gloss.

"Stephanie, we're so sorry for your unthinkable loss but so thankful you're here with us. Tell us what you remember when you came home from your friend's house after Mother Nature's tool of destruction passed through your town."

Stephanie slowly started to answer, hemming and hawing at first. Her voice was barely audible as the news anchor shoved the microphone just inches from her mouth. "Well, I was at a friend's, and then we heard about the tornado. . . . But it didn't hit where I was staying."

The interviewer urged her on. "And then what happened? When you came home, what did you find?"

Stephanie was holding a teddy bear with one missing arm close to her chest. "Well, my friend's father brought me home in his truck, and there were all these police and ambulances around, but the farm was gone . . . just pieces left. And my mom and dad . . . and my brothers and sisters . . . they were already in the ambulance."

Stephanie choked up, unable to go on. Thankfully, the news anchor was compassionate enough not to press the issue, turning away from the girl toward the camera to finish her report. "Unfortunately, all of Stephanie's immediate family were lost to the incredible force of the tornado." She turned back to Stephanie. "Sweetheart, how old are you?"

Stephanie murmured in a wavering voice,

"Thirteen."

"Is that your teddy bear?"

Stephanie protectively reacted by squeezing the bear tighter, almost as if someone were going to make a move on her memories. "He's mine. He was in the tree. The policeman got him down for me." Her eyes shifted focus. "My kitty always sleeps next to my teddy bear, but we haven't found her yet."

Fighting tears, the news anchor turned back to the camera. "It's our understanding that Stephanie's aunt will be coming to pick her up soon." She turned back to Stephanie. "Is that right, sweetheart?" The girl nodded as the woman once again addressed the camera. "This is Eva Brown reporting for WNKT TV News, Tolly, Alabama. If anyone would like to know more about how to donate to the storm victims, please contact the TV station, WNKT TV News in your local listing."

The backdrop for the interview was a seemingly never-ending stream of medics, policemen, and firemen wading through the rubble; and as they wrapped the shoot, the young girl solemnly watched in disbelief as the ambulances drove away to take her family to the morgue.

15

■ ■ ■ ■

That winter morning, Stephanie could feel the Holy Spirit move in her. The moans and groans of a prayer language known only to God's children transported her.

Daily, Stephanie longed for the refilling of the Holy Spirit and the renewing of her mind. She always prayed for a hedge of protection around those she loved, which God so graciously supplied her upon request. But as she put on the armor of God (see Ephesians 6:11–17), the claiming of his Word never failed to beg the lingering question, Why hadn't her husband been protected the day of his death? Yet, as quickly as she asked, a peace surrounded her, and God's promise, *"I will never leave you or forsake you"* (Joshua 1:5), crossed her mind and heart, and she knew she was truly and completely adored by her Lord.

Yes, she had learned that abiding in God and trusting that he always had her best interests at heart, even when she didn't understand the why of his ways, was the way to go.

Stephanie prepared a hot bowl of oatmeal topped with bananas, three scrambled eggs, a stack of buttered toast, grits, fresh squeezed orange juice, and a granola bar for good measure every morning for Trace to fuel up on before school.

The boy took up most of the far side of the small kitchen table after he dropped his gym bag by the back door and greeted his mom. By habit, Stephanie's hand ran along her son's broad shoulders as she moved across the kitchen for another cup of coffee.

Just as Trace was about to chow down, Stephanie piped in, "Thank you, Lord, for this food and sanctify it for your use, in Jesus' name." Contrite, Trace glanced at his mom, recognizing that his appetite had, once again, sideswiped his thanksgiving.

"Big game tomorrow, Son?"

"They're all big." He took a moment to swallow before lifting his eyes. "Thanks, Mama, for cookin'."

Stephanie nodded, content that her son never took her efforts on his behalf for granted, even in his most rebellious moments. His father had instilled respect in the boy before he died, and Stephanie was thankful Trace's childhood lessons had not waned.

Sitting across from Trace, she observed her son through the steam rising from her coffee. After a beat, she noted that the gleam in his eye looked different from when he used to talk about playing college ball on a scholarship and going on to the pros. Lately sports didn't seem to be Trace's main interest. In fact, from the beginning of basketball season, this handsome young man had been off his game. On the other hand, his grades had improved.

Stephanie concluded that both changes had something to do with a young lady named Chelsea. Ever since the girl had moved to town at the beginning of the school year, she and Trace had become inseparable. Truth was, Stephanie was concerned about how close these two teenagers had become.

"Congratulations on getting that 'A' on your biology test."

Trace held his fork up in a little victory twirl while he continued to devour the breakfast before him.

"So Son, you haven't asked me for any help lately with your homework. I think it's wonderful you're doing so well, but . . ."

". . . Chelsea helps me. She's real smart, Mom."

Stephanie tried to maintain a casual demeanor. "That's good. She seems like a really nice girl. Must be, you sure are spending a lot of time with her."

Trace stared at his plate, avoiding his mother's glance. "Yeah, I like her."

Stephanie laughed. "I gathered. Your record with any of the other girls in town maxed-out at a week. You two have been going together, what . . . three months?"

Trace shoveled some more scrambled eggs in his mouth. "Yeah, I guess." He could feel her eyes on him, despite his avoidance.

"Trace, I feel like I'm talking to a wall here."

He looked up at the change of her tone. "Yes, ma'am?"

Now that she had his attention, she continued. "I wish your father was here to have some of these sit-downs with you. . . . You know, man-to-man talks."

Her comment instantly raised old feelings of bitterness in her boy. "Yeah, well, he's not here, is he, Mom?"

Stephanie was not going to let him go down that path. "No, he's not Trace, but that's not my point. I know you miss him, and I miss him, but that's not what I'm talking about right now."

Trace downed his orange juice in a couple of gulps. "We've talked about this a million times." He tried to adopt his mother's vocal lilt for emphasis. " 'There are consequences to every action.' 'You have to treat girls like ladies because you're a gentleman.' 'The only way to stay pure is by practicing abstinence.' 'If you really love somebody you'll want to save yourself, and so will she.' . . . I'm being careful, Mom. And I really like Chelsea."

Stephanie studied her son again. "Well that's good, Trace, that's good. But being 'careful' doesn't cut it. If you're treating the girl with respect and yourself with respect, you don't have to be careful. You just have to be trustworthy and caring. . . . I can tell you genuinely care for this girl, but I also have to tell you that my impression of Chelsea is that she's got some problems."

That comment did not sit well with Trace. "How do you know what she has? You've only said hello and good-bye to her."

"You're right. That wasn't fair. I guess I'm assuming some things. Maybe because her family's going through so much. . . . Her mom's having such a hard time in town with the court and all. It's not hard to imagine that Chelsea has some issues. Her aunt is part of our prayer group, you know."

Trace glared at her. "So what do you do? You all talk about Chelsea?"

Stephanie put her coffee cup down with authority. "No, absolutely not. We don't talk about people. I just know that the girl's in therapy with Pam. . . . I don't know any other details. It's none of my business. Her privacy is of utmost importance to everyone. But I'm not going to lie to you; we pray for her. . . . We pray for you too. We pray for all of our family and loved ones."

"We're not little kids, you know."

Stephanie didn't care for the edge in her son's voice; it was something new to her. "Please don't speak to me in that tone. I don't care if you're fifty, you're still going to be my son, and I'm always going to pray for you. . . . And I hope you do the same for me. That's what family's about. . . . That's what love's about, and that's what a hedge of protection is about. I've told you that since you were knee-high. There's nothing more powerful you can do for people than pray for them."

She waited for him to look her in the eyes. "You and Chelsea are spending every spare moment together. . . . And that may end up putting a strain between you two in an area that you might want to leave a little bit more space."

"Mom, we're studying and stuff."

"OK, your grades are better, but it's the 'stuff' I'm concerned about. Chelsea is one pretty young lady."

Trace was back looking at his plate.

21

"Son, I'm just trying to say that the decisions you make today make your tomorrows."

"I know that, Mom."

Stephanie poured herself another cup of coffee while Trace gobbled up the last morsels of his breakfast. He wanted to get out of that kitchen as fast as possible.

Trace stood up. "I gotta go."

"I know . . . Trace, I'm not saying that you should be single. I'm just asking you to slow down and know that while you're putting all your attention and focus on this girl, other things are going to suffer. You've always had dreams. . . . I'm just not seeing you following through like you used to."

The boy headed for the door, his demeanor indicating his frustration with his mother. "I don't want to be disrespectful, Mom, but that's my business. I'm almost eighteen and . . ."

Stephanie stopped him before he went any further. ". . . And clearly you've got someone else to talk to. I know you're not my little boy anymore. But I'm still your mom. You've been shut down lately, and that concerns me. I'm not talking about excluding Chelsea. I'm just asking you to put things in the right perspective."

Trace was about out the door. "Gotta go,

Mom, or I'll be late for school."

"OK. . . . Have a good . . ." But before she could finish the sentence, he was gone.

She sat there a moment as she wondered how she was ever going to get through this raising time without the help of Trace's father. It was all going by so fast.

She recalled the times she'd talked to her boy about God's plan for a man and a woman, about the fact that God had designed sex to be glorious and everlasting within marriage. She had even read the Song of Solomon in the Bible with him so he could see the intimacy God had in store for his people within the parameters of commitment and respect. And she was clear to point out that living in a manner outside of that plan brings only pain and disappointment in the end.

She had even asked Trace to think about all of God's creation, from animals to plants. Then she illustrated that God had only designed human beings anatomically to face one another when they made love. Invariably, Trace would blush when his mother talked to him about such things, but she would not be dissuaded. Her point was too important. She would tell him that people were designed to face each other so that they could look into each other's eyes when they made love in an intimate and trusting relationship.

"And how could that kind of relationship evolve?" she would ask. "One of trust only comes through commitment. And what is commitment but marriage?"

She was also quick to remind Trace that they served a God of second chances, and that if he were to stumble and fall, she didn't want him to feel that fidelity was lost for a lifetime. He could always repent and start fresh. Yes, Stephanie had laid a solid foundation for her son, but the question remained, would he heed her advice?

Stephanie took a deep breath. She thought about her circle of friends, her prayer partners, each in their own way having gone through so many tests in the last several months; Eleanor's bout with breast cancer, Tonya's waiting for a commitment from the father of their son, Pam's determination to help Chelsea in counseling and to open Hope School. And Lauren, their newest friend, struggling with her divorce and issues with her family.

Yes, they all had a lot to pray about, but Stephanie was encouraged knowing that at least they all had one another for support and accountability, and that was more than most people could claim. Trust was hard found in this world. Although, in God's economy, it was the emotional glue that held one together during life's storms.

CHAPTER 2
-WARFARE IN THE SPIRIT-

"Rene," as Lauren had always called Irene, "Dreams are just about things we don't get finished. . . . Then we try to fix them when we're sleeping."

That was Lauren's theory as a child concerning her older sister's nightmares, those bedtime battles that often led Irene literally screaming into the night as she ran to the safety of the girls' outdoor playhouse. And there she would hide until dawn when she'd be admonished by her dad and ordered to get ready for school.

Neither Sam nor Margaret had much patience when it came to their daughters' emotional dramas that intermittently plagued both girls. But then again, Sam and Margaret didn't have much patience or time for anyone but each other.

They had adopted a strict, old-fashioned approach to child rearing; "Children should be seen and not heard." And although they were caring parents, their love was displayed at arm's length, never spending the personal one-on-one time with their children necessary to develop and encourage esteem and individual talents. The end result was two daughters who grew up feeling invisible, which, in turn, led to their "looking for love in all the wrong places."

Yes, there were deep scars to be healed within the Patterson family.

At age eleven, Lauren shot up taller than her five-foot-seven-inch thirteen-year-old sister, all the while complaining of excruciating pains in her legs. In the late fifties, polio was still a concern, so Lauren's parents carted their youngest child to several doctors over a period of time only to be told that Lauren was experiencing a nonthreatening case of "hysterical growing pains." Although implied, the doctors didn't actually say outright that Lauren was exaggerating her suffering; they merely concurred that she had to "tough out" her growing spurt.

Despite the physicians' diagnosis, it was Lauren's conclusion that she had caught some mysterious disease because she knew she was tough, and if other growing kids hurt like she did, they'd be in the hospital under heavy sedation and wearing leg braces. But not Lauren, who prided herself on being brave and stoic; after all, she was the one who survived having her tonsils out without complaint, while Irene suffered through twenty thousand gallons of ice cream before she would even venture swallowing solid food.

And then there was the time the ambulance had to come in the middle of the night to take their mom away, leaving Irene and Lauren to stay with neighbors. Irene cowered, petrified she would never see Margaret again, while Lauren was totally calm, convinced their mom was merely having a bout with the same mysterious disease she'd been experiencing for well over a year.

Lauren fully expected the doctors to tell Margaret that she too would have to "tough it out" and go home to suffer. She was wrong. The fact that the siblings didn't see their mom for more than a week after her emergency appendectomy meant that the girls' respective nightmares and leg cramps would never be taken seriously in light of their mother's near-death experience. Not even when Irene broke her nose falling down the stairs after another one of her sleepwalking episodes was her condition considered serious.

Mercifully, the day finally came when Lauren's growing pains finally subsided, but not until after she physically shot up three and one-eighth inches in a thirteen-month time period. Yes, she outgrew her torture and grew up at the same time, finally getting her period and her first bra just a month apart. And suddenly, what seemed an eternity of suffering to this teenager became just a hateful chapter lodged in her past.

Unfortunately, Irene's angst persisted.

As sisters, Lauren and Irene were always close despite an occasional round of catfights.

They were also beautiful in their own right, never having to compete with each other for male attention. "Alluring" came naturally to both. Yet growing up looked different in each girl's case. Other than Irene's nightmares, she seemed to slide through puberty relatively unscathed by her changing body and hormone levels. Her torments were played out at night when she seemingly could not control her runaway emotions.

By day Irene was an in-charge, responsible, slightly aloof individual with creative juices coursing through her veins. So it was not a foreign concept to anyone when she grew up to become a respected writer and artist among the highbrow New York elite, even if being published and public sales from her private art shows had thus far eluded her. Besides, Irene, the crowned queen of society, was well taken care of by her international tycoon husband, Ford Williams. Or was she?

Mrs. Irene Williams had spent many double sessions with Dr. Stern, her Upper-East-side psychotherapist, over questions concerning her spouse. But when Irene found out that her husband had had an affair with her best friend and her shrink had been in Ford's pocket to make sure Irene stayed medicated and benign when it came to their marriage issues, she decided she'd had enough and finally opted for a divorce. Still, she was not privy to what extent diabolical behaviors by Ford had been acted out behind their swank Park Avenue apartment doors.

Whenever she walked into Dr. Stern's office, Irene couldn't help but think that the décor was reminiscent of his name. The furniture was stiff leather with masculine linear lines illuminated by sharp overhead lighting; nary a throw pillow to curl up with and certainly no couch to recline on in an effort to ease one's tensions and loosen one's tongue.

Irene always felt that she was somehow entering into an inquisition when her appointment time started. But despite his *stern* surroundings, the doctor was a consummate pro at delving into the subconscious of his patients. And within moments he would engage Irene in conversations that rerouted her concerns and discomforts of the day by taking her down a path that invariably left her, at the end of the session, with more on her plate to analyze than when she began.

His method of merry-go-round motivational thinking always referred back to events from her childhood, keeping Irene on the fast track to nowhere. Of course, if her frustration became too overwhelming, medications were adjusted causing her to become politely responsive to the doctor's leadings — once more the perfect patient, wealthy and unwise.

Irene often revisited a particular session with her doctor when she was in the mood to review her painful past.

". . . I'm trying to explain, Dr. Stern. . . . It's just a feeling. I can't back it up with any corroborative evidence. I feel I'm being cross-examined on the witness stand by you. Am I not allowed to have feelings?"

Dr. Stern leaned back in his chair with a knowing look and a slightly raised eyebrow. He was a small man with a generous face, conjuring up in Irene's imagination a picture of Humpty Dumpty. With that thought, she concluded that she was the one who was going to fall off the wall and break into a million pieces, not he.

"Feelings are important, Irene. But if they are founded solely on your insecurities, then they become something *you* have to deal with as opposed to confronting someone else about their behavior."

"So what you're saying is actually what Ford says. This is all coming from my 'menopause frame of mind.' "

"Not exactly, Irene. I'm not discounting your feelings. Whether your levels of hormones are not at their most harmonious during this period of your life doesn't discount how you feel. I'm here to help you sort out the realities as opposed to the emotional frustrations or fantasies borne of your female constitution."

Irene finally put down the oversized purse that she was holding tightly to her stomach and reached for a glass of water. "Dr. Stern, I just sense that my husband is seeing someone else. I don't know how to put it. . . . Maybe it's women's intuition. . . . Not constitution. Ford is just not the same. . . ."

Dr. Stern interrupted, ". . . The same as how?"

"The same as before. The same as yesterday. . . . No, not yesterday. The same as . . ."

"When?" Dr. Stern insisted.

"I don't know. . . . When we used to make love more often. When he used to come home before midnight. When we used to laugh. . . . Before there was so much tension in the house with my daughter."

Dr. Stern gave her a long look. "Well, perhaps therein lies a dynamic that is not particularly conducive to a relaxed marital relationship between husband and wife. Teenagers can be extremely disruptive in a household."

"Really. What exactly do you suggest I do, Doctor? Send her away to boarding school like all the other 'uptown' parents do?!"

"Certainly that's a consideration. How are her grades?"

"Her grades are fine, and she doesn't want to go away to boarding school. . . . Actually, she spends more time with my husband than I do. She likes living at home. They're very close. . . . And that's good since her dad is nowhere to be found." Irene was becoming increasingly uncomfortable. "I've told you before: that's one of the reasons I married Ford — because he and Chelsea got along so well."

"Then I take it the tension at home is not between her stepfather and your daughter, it's between *you* and your daughter."

"I suppose you could say that. It's not tension exactly. . . . A distance . . . It just feels . . . She feels almost . . . I don't know — it's crazy to say — but competitive with me somehow. I don't know. . . . That's insane. What's wrong with me? I must be overreacting. I sometimes catch her looking at my husband at the dinner table or walking around in a nightie, and she just seems . . . provocative. She and Ford are always going off somewhere having fun . . . to the zoo or shopping. . . ."

Dr. Stern handed Irene a tissue, a gesture that gave her permission to cry. And at his prompting, she did just that. "It's not unusual at all for preteen girls to begin to spread their wings. You shouldn't take it personally. It's the beginning of their right of passage into womanhood. I'm sure if you think back in your own adolescence, you'll find more understanding for the stage your daughter is currently experiencing. We can review in the next couple of sessions how you were feeling at Chelsea's age. It's important for you to recognize how upset you would be if Ford expressed no interest in his stepchild. It's natural for mothers and daughters to experience a chasm during the teen years. You had your sister to go through those times with, but Chelsea is a single child. And please remember your concerns about Ford's natural children being grown up and out of the house. You were worried that with his extensive business undertakings and travel he wouldn't have time or interest in taking a father role with your daughter."

Irene leaned back, defeated at the thought of having to revisit her past and embarrassed at not understanding her own family dynamic.

"Dr. Stern, I know how I felt at Chelsea's age. I just don't know how I feel at *my* age. Obviously I trust your judgment, but it appears I can't trust my own intuition. Everything I seem to be feeling, I've been imagining according to you and my husband. I just don't know what to think. I don't seem to have a sense of what's real and what's not real. It's very disconcerting. The nightmares are starting again, and I can't sleep. I just feel . . ."

Before she could finish her sentence, Dr.

Stern was leaning over the desk with some sample prescriptions in his hand. "Irene, everything is going to be fine. Why don't you just try these? I've found them to be effective. You can go ahead and take them with your other medications. There shouldn't be any negative reactions, but if there are, just call me and stop taking them immediately. I believe these will ease your mind, and they'll help you sleep until we can get to the bottom of your feelings. My advice is that we schedule triple sessions and go back to your core issues. Perhaps, in seeing from whence your feelings really were spawned, you'll be able to understand how they may be revisiting your life today. If you have a cancer, you want to get to the tumor before it spreads. Do you understand?"

Irene simply nodded, steeling herself for the loathsome task ahead; she was trapped, held fast in a fog of confusion and medication.

When Lauren picked Irene up for lunch after her morning session with Dr. Stern, she restlessly challenged her sister. "Rene, I've been in town for five days, and all you've talked about is that your husband is cheating on you. If you feel something is going on with Ford, you should investigate. Hire someone. You're not crazy. What about women's intuition?"

"Dr. Stern says I'm an unappreciative hormonal blob of insecurities and crazy thoughts."

"I'm going to punch that man. That's rude!"

"Hey, I was kidding . . . sort of."

"Well don't. I was about to kill him and mount him on a wall. Look, Rene, you've only been married a few years to Ford, and the man seems to have you mesmerized, wrapped around his finger. You do everything he says like some robot. That's not you."

Irene suddenly turned on Lauren with sarcasm. "Ah, out of the mouths of babes. Here's my little sister giving me advice on relationships. Your answer to any problem is divorce and then run away to California."

"Now that's mean, Rene. You and I are one for one in the divorce department. Besides, I'm not saying that you should leave Ford. I'm saying that you should find out what the real deal is. Don't deny your feelings. I've never seen you so unsure of yourself."

Irene sagged as they entered Ford's stretch limousine. The two sat in silence while Irene tried to renew her strength. "Lauren, what is happening to me? You were always the fanciful, renegade wild child with me constantly galloping in for the rescue. Whatever it took, I always made sure that you were safe. And now, it's all slowly changing. . . ."

"I found Jesus, Rene."

Irene shot her hand up like a traffic cop. "Stop! I can't take your 'born-again' bit right now. I'm sorry, but the last thing I need is a lecture about what I need. OK?"

Lauren acquiesced, realizing her sister was on the edge and clearly not in the mood to hear more about her new and meaningful faith experiences. "OK . . . sorry, sorry. I just want you to be as happy as I am."

"*Happy* may come later. . . . Right now I just want to sidestep the loony bin."

Irene crumbled into a pile of tears as Lauren covered her with hugs of comfort.

It was no surprise that by 1996, after several more years of Dr. Stern's wisdom and Ford's deception, Irene's nightmares had escalated with a vengeance. Reminiscent of an opening newsreel in a 1940s movie theatre, scathing reports of her personal war zones and headlines filled the screen of Irene's never vacant mind.

Disturbing, and out of control, her recent slumbering image reruns covered in detail the last years of her life with ruthless accuracy accompanied with a splash of the macabre. What Irene was experiencing in her sleep state was exhausting and threatening; and while she was driven to escape the distorted memories, she just couldn't seem to pull herself away from the persistent subconscious whipping post to which she was emotionally tied.

No doubt, Irene had come up against some seriously unsettling events lately, not the least of which was her second husband Ford's infidelity, an impending divorce, and then his shocking and untimely death.

But all that was a walk in the park compared to the excruciating knowledge that her now seventeen-year-old daughter's rebellious behavior aimed squarely at Irene over the last several years was fueled by Chelsea's having been sexually abused by her stepfather, the very same Ford Williams. That discovery haunted Irene and lay bare her feelings of helplessness, deep-seated fury, and suicidal fantasies.

Well before Irene took her nightly sleeping pill in an attempt to get even a sliver of rest, she knew she was doomed, completely filled with despair. And as she would lay her head back on the pillow with trepidation, she always hoped that her exhaustion would override her overactive mind. Unfortunately, that never happened. It seemed that Irene would barely close her eyes when a parade of full-blown color pictures began to carve out the terrain of her ensuing dreams.

As Irene's sleep patterns took over, images splashed across the available spaces of her imagination. And then, as suddenly as they appeared, they would spiral into a never-ending succession of visual threats. This particular evening, the first barrage was a review of newspaper headlines; the compilation of real images and events were followed by feelings on her part of shock and righteous indignation. The disturbing montage appeared in chronological order at first, but then her emotional frustrations would pop up with no rhyme or reason between the newspaper headlines that always, in some fashion, starred Irene.

Tonight's show began with the recent and ridiculous photograph of Irene and Lauren splashed across the front page of Centennial's journal. This less-than-kind, small southern town was where Lauren had decided to relocate the entire Patterson family. Seemingly, an unfortunate choice. Irene's dreamscape now focused on the newspaper's headline:

The Search for Ford Williams's Widow
Ends Here in Centennial

Underneath the headline was a private school junior-high picture of Chelsea from her New York days, and next to it was a photo of Irene spying on Chelsea, scrunched down in the front seat of her BMW station wagon. She was obviously yelling at Lauren, who was standing beside the car smashing out Irene's flicked-lit cigarette on the sidewalk. The caption under the picture read:

Irene Williams and her sister Lauren Patterson across from Franklin Café on the first day of school.

Then Irene's visual editing scanned down to reveal more of the newspaper's written word:

Irene Williams, fifty-two years old and widow of the recently deceased shipping magnate, Ford Williams, moved to Centennial last weekend. It is reported that she is looking to buy a home locally, but in the meanwhile, Irene Williams and daughter Chelsea are living with Mrs. Williams's sister, Lauren Patterson, her son, Tucker, and their parents, Sam and Margaret

Patterson. Tucker is attending first grade at our very own public elementary school in Centennial, while Mrs. Williams's daughter, Chelsea, is part of the senior class at Greystone High. Irene Patterson married Ford Williams in New York City in 1984, where they resided on Fifth Avenue with their daughter Chelsea, born in 1979. Presently, Mrs. Williams and Chelsea reside at 1815 Linden Street in Centennial, Tennessee.

Suddenly, the ethereal image was shattered by the haunting, distant echo of Lauren's voice screaming at the top of her lungs into a phone, "Rene, I don't believe it! Did you hear me? They gave out our address! They talked about Tucker! They had pictures! They said that Chelsea was yours and Ford's daughter! That's terrible! They may just as well have said that she was the *illegitimate* daughter of . . . Oooh, how could they get their facts wrong like that? How could they do this? How could they put us on the front page of the newspaper?"

As the voice faded, the next newspaper headline invaded the dream:

Irene Williams Arrested in Centennial

In and out of focus at first, the additional

information all of a sudden took shape as it carved out the following newspaper article:

Irene Williams, a recent resident of Centennial, was arrested by officer Chet Monty and arraigned by Judge Baxter this morning at two thirty a.m., allegedly charged with assault of an officer, resisting arrest, and public intoxication. Bail was set for fifteen hundred dollars. Mrs. Williams was released into the custody of her sister, Lauren Patterson. A preliminary hearing was set for one week from today where Mrs. Williams will have an opportunity to make her plea.

Covered in perspiration, Irene sat bolt upright in bed at the first ring of her alarm clock. A pained expression responded to the trite saying that popped into her mind, "saved by the bell."

It had been over three months since that "preliminary hearing" was put on the docket, and it quickly became evident to all the family that Irene was facing a legal dilemma that was well beyond any of their control.

Caught in the tangled details of court procedures, good-ol'-boy politics, and curiosity seekers that would rival major world gossip columnists, Irene remembered that it was within the first week of living in Centennial that her deep resentment formed toward the two-faced town she had moved to at Lauren's behest. Yes, her little sister's ever-uplifting vision of reconciliation for the Patterson clan had instantly turned into Southern *Dis*-Comfort meets Peyton Place.

Irene fumed as she pulled one of the curlers off the top of her head; she had bigger fish to fry than to rerun all this insanity. Today she needed to consult once again with her lawyers. Not one, mind you, but *two* were representing her — one from the city of Nashville and the other from the ever-so-sweet suburb known as Centennial.

Irene's dynamic duo of legal muscle was supposed to fan the furrowed southern politician's brows while setting Irene free in the speed of a horsetail. But over the last three months their efforts simply to get Irene's case to trial had failed dismally. For one reason or another, once Irene had pleaded "not guilty" to all charges and asked for a speedy trial, the judicial and political process seemed to grind to an agonizing halt. Yes, she wanted her day in court, but Irene couldn't seem to get her foot in the door — lawyers or no lawyers.

The madness of the one-after-the-other

postponed trial dates was enough to drive even the most patient person into a stress level worthy of a heart attack. Irene was fighting not only for her reputation but for her health. And every time her trial was reset to be heard, all the lurid details of her arrest were, once again, spread all over local and international news, just to be set aside one more time when the arresting/testifying officer would come down with the flu, or was called to another county court, or had "family matters to attend to." The delays boggled the mind, and yet, as all efforts to close the matter failed, the negative press thrived.

Sadly, feeling totally out of control for Irene was not a new experience. There was the issue of Ford having cheated on her for years with her best friend *in her bedroom.* And worse, for years she thought she was losing her mind when Ford, a consummate verbal batterer, was able to convince her that all of her suspicions were merely a figment of her imagination, insecurities, and menopause.

"Oh no!" Irene hissed as she slammed the bedsheets back. She wasn't going to revisit all that craziness, not while her eyes were open. Maybe she couldn't stop the nightmares, but she simply refused to go there wide awake. She had to pull herself together, which was becoming more of an arduous task day by day.

Gathering herself up, she slowly headed for the bathroom. Once inside, she stared at herself in the mirror over the sink with a disbelieving expression of dismay. She could no longer deny that her circumstances had actually taken a visual toll on her appearance.

Formerly a compelling figure of a woman with eyes that danced with intrigue, desire, and passion, Irene now stared back at herself with eyes that were all but vacant. "I hate this . . ." she whined as she leaned in for a closer look. Suddenly, she wagged her finger at the mirror with a vengeance, "No! Stop being such a wimp!" she muttered, taking a breath for control.

And with that her thoughts took a rare turn for the positive. She told herself that things were looking up with Chelsea lately, and that's what really mattered. She needed not to focus on the frustrating battle for her deserved inheritance from Ford's estate, or some stupid, bogus charges from a few pipsqueak people in what was an otherwise perfectly decent place to live.

Irene had actually seen glimmers of hope in her daughter's demeanor since she'd been counseling with Lauren's friend, Pam. The sexual abuse Chelsea had endured from Ford was finally being addressed, even if healing was still a matter for the future. And at least there had been some civil dialogue between Chelsea and Irene. *It was a start, a good start,* Irene thought as she splashed some water on her face.

Still, she knew deep in her heart that darkness lurked at every turn. Irene felt her daughter believed she must have known something was going on between Ford and her, so in Chelsea's mind, Irene hadn't protected her. Irene's eyes suddenly flooded with tears. How could her daughter think such a horrible thing!?

Whenever Irene expressed some of her fears to Lauren, her sister would always talk about God's take on forgiveness. "Rene, both you and Chelsea need to choose to forgive Ford and each other for whatever has pulled you apart. The details will reveal themselves. Please, just leave the retribution to God so you all can truly heal. Ford is dead, and God doesn't want any of us stuck in our past pains through our unforgiveness. If we ask him to, God empowers us to forgive because he knows that in the end we're the only ones whose lives are robbed by not doing so."

That was about the time Irene would lose it. "Lauren, that's sweet but stupid! You're right, Ford is dead, and I hope he rots in his grave. He got away with the whole sick thing! What can God do about that!?"

"Oh, Rene, you have no idea. *Everyone* has to answer to God. Real healing only comes when you connect your head with your heart. When I realized that Jesus died for *all* of my sins, I could forgive anything because I've been forgiven of everything. God sees us whole and healed through his Son's sacrifice. Rene, Jesus is our intercessor!"

"I don't want an intercessor. I want a good lawyer and justice so these Southern snakes with their own code of *non*-ethics can crawl back under their rocks where they make their self-serving deals at the expense of others. All they care about is covering their backs and selling newspapers!" Irene was steaming. "And I want Ford resurrected so I can kill him myself for what he's done to Chelsea . . . and to me! I don't want to know a God who can let such horrors happen."

"Rene, you don't understand. I know life's taken us both on quite a ride, but . . ."

". . . No, *you* don't understand. I know

48

you're trying to help, but bet on it, you're not!"

Irene shook off the memory as she stared back at her image in the mirror — at the little girl she now saw herself, curled up in a corner, betrayed and unprotected. She knew in her heart that her disappointment did not come from Chelsea. It was her husband's pedophilia and incomprehensible behavior that had slain Irene's heart. Trust, oh yes, that was a big issue for Irene — one that began with a disengaged dad, then the abandonment of her first husband, and recently life being strangled out of her with lies upon lies.

No, she could find no relief, not even in her drinks, pills, or cigarettes. And how could she possibly trust God, as Lauren suggested, if every male in her adult life had hurt her so horrifically and let her down so consistently?

CHAPTER 3
-TESTING THE WATERS-

If not for me, for who? Lauren wondered as she slid into a steaming hot bath, waving her disposable razor around in the air as if it were a baton before she started shaving her legs.

Giggling, she cautioned herself to be careful as she had not shaved since she moved to Centennial. "Oooh, you're disgusting!" she chided. "There's no excuse for being a female Neanderthal."

She had reasoned for months now that she had no man in her life, so why bother shaving her legs? And the fact that she never wore skirts, only boots and jeans, made the decision even easier.

Still, she had to recognize that slowly but surely she was taking less pride in her appearance; something she had concluded was a work of the enemy whose only desire was to tear her down. Even though she was going to spend eternity with Jesus, Satan just loved to rob her on a daily basis, tugging at her vulnerable areas and insecurities. And yes, she knew that looks were fleeting and superficial at best, but every time she would accept and recognize how much God truly loved her, how patient he had been with her, and how he had waited years for her to turn to him, she'd melt into a marvelous sense of well-being.

If she had learned anything else over the last ten years of her faith, it was knowing that it was imperative to have a solid foundation in Christ. And once that was there, she could put on the makeup, do her hair, and knock everyone's socks off.

OK, fine. So what was it lately that bothered her about the fact that she wasn't caring for herself as she used to? She thought of Irene, who wouldn't come out of her bedroom without full makeup, let alone consider going to the store or out in public without having every hair in place and every head turning her way. Yes, Irene was exquisite, but Lauren felt insecurity, not ego, was the reason her sister always needed to look so perfect. And that wasn't a criticism, mind you. Lauren absolutely adored Irene. In fact, she admired her in many ways even though they had radically different styles. Lauren had always been much more of a tomboy, and although she could dress up with the best of the girls, she didn't hold her looks in such high esteem.

"But that's different from not caring," she told herself. Maybe her sloppy attitude was born of time constraint. After all, just putting on makeup seemed like such a waste of precious moments, especially with all the demands of her work and family.

Nicking herself, she slowed her leg-shaving down a notch, reminding herself that she could take a minute or two longer and not commit hara-kiri with the razor blade.

She actually had gotten up half an hour earlier that morning so she could enjoy a long bath, put on her makeup, and still have breakfast ready for Tucker before she headed out for work. This was going to be an exciting day, and she wanted to look the part. The building inspector was scheduled to make his final rounds at the shelter, and once it passed, she could actually open up on Monday!

Lauren sank deeper into the bath, thinking over the last months and all the amazing changes that had come about — not all necessarily for the good, but certainly all intense.

It seemed like just yesterday that the entire

family had moved into Centennial and she had stepped into Dr. Burke's veterinary factory to begin her job as the newest local small-animal veterinarian. Shaking her head, she recalled how horrified she was standing in front of that butcher's office staring at the chute for animal drop-offs — cats, dogs, chickens, whatever, all thrown down a hole to be held overnight until Dr. Burke gathered the poor creatures up to euthanize them. It was beyond cruel; it was criminal. The disgust Lauren expressed in the editorial she wrote managed to get published in the local newspaper the following Sunday. To her joy, it ignited a controversy in the town that quickly ended Dr. Burke's career.

Just days after Lauren's editorial blew the lid off of the truth of how the county was handling their animal overflow, she met Mrs. Strickland. This lovely woman was a great-grand-dame, old-line Nashvillian with oodles of money and generations of gentle behavior to back her sweet spirit. Not only that, but Mrs. Strickland was also an animal lover and immediately took up for Lauren's cause.

She thought back on the time she sat in the midst of one of Nashville's more refined country clubs having a luncheon with Mrs.

Strickland. Lauren felt like she was reading some novel where the main character's circumstances were transported magically by some fairy godmother. Yes, there she was with this delightful woman who seemed amazingly interested in all that Lauren had to say.

"After reading your article, Ms. Lauren, I must admit that I was impressed with your bold review and at the same time horrified by the facts you were recounting. I called some of my family members and had them look into the situation well before I decided to give you a call. And I found that all you portrayed was purely true. So how can I be of service to you?"

Lauren was flabbergasted. "Well, Mrs. Strickland, I haven't thought out in detail how to rectify the situation at Dr. Burke's. Frankly, I barely have the broad strokes down as yet. First, I wanted to expose the problem. The answer, of course, would be to shut Dr. Burke's torture chamber down completely and remove his license. But more importantly, we must replace the service — if you could even call what he provided a service — with a humane, life-giving shelter. Unfortunately, I have not been in the area long enough to cohesively investigate that possibility."

Mrs. Strickland waved her gloved hand to the waiter who was by their side before her arm dropped. "Yes ma'am?"

"We'll have two sweet teas and the chef's special."

"Yes ma'am." He was off in a shot.

Mrs. Strickland smiled at Lauren. "I hope you don't mind my ordering for you, but there's nothing that comes through those portholes that's not beyond delicious. Of course if you don't care for whatever the chef serves, we can order you something of your preference."

"No, no. Please, whatever you're having is fine with me."

"Lovely."

"I have to admit that I was taken aback by your call. . . . Thrilled, thrilled beyond words, but surprised. So, if I don't seem prepared, it's because I'm not. I do know that it's delightful to meet you and confer with another animal lover."

A little gleam crossed Mrs. Strickland's face. "Do you remember a TV show years ago called *The Millionaire?*"

Lauren thought for a moment, then shook her head. "I don't believe so."

"Well, it was a marvelous show. It was about a wealthy man named John Beres Fortipton, who, by the way, you never saw on screen. You see, he sent his emissary out on missions to help common people whom he had researched. Mr. Fortipton would benefit these individuals with a gift of one million dollars, hence the series title *The Millionaire.* It was a marvelous show of hope and generosity. Its theme gave every one of its viewers the sense that at any moment someone could bang on their door and their lives would completely change."

Lauren was enthralled with the concept. "Oooh, what fun."

"Also popular around that same time, or perhaps a few years earlier, was a show called *Queen for a Day.* That was a nasty series, in my opinion, because on one hand it appeared to be generous and uplifting, but in fact the undercurrent of the show's theme played off of individuals' misfortunes. It featured women with pathetic lives and displayed them as if they were in sideshows at a circus. Perhaps the secondary purpose of the show was to have the audience realize that their fare in life was not so bad compared to these women, but compassion was clearly not the series's calling card. Humiliation was. And although they gave the contestants gifts, it was really only after they pitted each against the other to draw out the most pathetic story. The show's producers were not humanitarians or bene-factors; they were greedy individuals who preyed on the less fortunate."

"That sounds flat-out mean-spirited," Lauren offered.

"Precisely. Then there was 'follow the bouncing ball,' an advertising campaign well before your time. . . ."

"Oh, Mrs. Strickland, I bet we're not even a decade apart. You look absolutely glori-ous. I just turned fifty, by the way." Sud-denly embarrassed, Lauren flushed. "Not that I'm asking you how old you are. That would be rude, and I'm not rude. Trust me, you don't know me, and I would never ask that of a lady. Although personally, I am thrilled to have made it to the fifty mark. The truth is, I usually add a year onto my age because I'm so amazed that I've made it this far. I know that many women are extremely sensitive about their age, espe-cially from where I came from near Holly-wood. Oh my gosh, the nip-and-tuck center of the world." And then Lauren realized she'd gone off on one of her tangents and had cut off Mrs. Strickland's conversational flow. But instead of being offended, Mrs. Strickland simply waited for Lauren to fin-ish, amused by her passion and childlike approach to life. "Sorry to interrupt."

"No, you're fine darlin'. By the way, I just turned seventy, and I'm happy for every day God gives me here on Earth." Despite her shimmering white hair, she did have a face of a much younger woman with dancing blue eyes and flawless, iridescent skin. "But, as I was saying, 'follow the bouncing ball' was a little ball that bounced on the words that came up at the bottom of the screen during commercials to get your attention by annoying the viewer. Conversely, another strength in advertising is to appeal. All that to say, *annoying* is not my style; *appeal* is. And my trademark is to spring to action once I'm inspired. I realize you have recently moved here and don't know the lay of the land, so, if you'll allow me, I'll walk you through the underbrush. The way to approach our overflow pet problem, of course, is to spay and neuter anything that walks — animal-wise that is. Although there are a few individuals I'd like to see at the top of that list."

Mrs. Strickland delicately patted her mouth with her napkin, then winked at Lauren before she continued. "We must take in the strays, evaluate them, train them, and then find good homes for each one. We will have a no-kill policy unless the poor things have a fatal illness, or they are suffering, or

I'm not interested in helping. Do you agree?"

Lauren practically fell off her chair. "Of course. Exactly."

"So I have a plan that I'll lay out for you, step-by-step, and if you agree, from this day forward I'd be honored to call you my partner. I'll offer you full financial and political assistance to open a new county shelter . . . one that will compete with the best in the country not only on a humane level but a service level as well. For your part, you will oversee the endeavor, its staff, and come on board as chief veterinarian. Needless to say, I have already reviewed all your credentials. I also want to talk to you about field service, but we'll get to that later."

Lauren bounced in her chair like a little girl. "Partners, absolutely. No following the bouncing ball for us unless we're playing fetch. Thank you. . . . Thank you!"

The rest of that afternoon was spent sharing a whirlwind of information and visions. Lauren learned that living in Nashville proper, as Mrs. Strickland always had, meant she'd never been privy to the animal chutes used for pet disposal prior to seeing Lauren's editorial in the Sunday paper which read:

City-Sanctioned Child Abuse in Centennial?

What if you're a small child and someone grabs you up by the arm, throws you into the car, drives across town, and takes you to a smelly building. Then they drop you down a dark chute into a cage full of people of all ages and types. Some are killers; some are foreigners that speak strange languages; many are diseased and undernourished. There is fierce fighting throughout the dark night, and you are alone to fend for yourself.

Sounds like some dark fantasy from the age of Communist Russia? Well, if you're an unwanted animal in Centennial, this could be your fate! It must be a dark secret in such a southern jewel of a town; the local animal dump at Dr. Burke's office, where unwanted critters of all kinds can be conveniently disposed of down a drop chute with no more effort than returning a late movie rental in the middle of the night to avoid extra charges. The real irony in this story is that the address of Dr. Burke's nightmare is not on Elm Street but rather on Church Street!

Stop by any day of the week and watch your tax dollars at work. One must wonder who is worse among the offenders in this all-too-real scenario. Is it the heartless citizens who, in a selfish attempt to rid themselves of unwanted animals, simply drop them off like their garbage and drive away? Or is it an elected city government so caught up in backroom deals and good-ol'-boy politics that they have no time to consider the well-being of these defense-less creatures?

As a citizen of Centennial and a licensed veterinarian, I hold them both accountable for these atrocities. How about you?

Lauren had to admit she was pretty proud of her penned expressions, but never in her wildest dreams did she think that in just a short three months her concerns for the animals and Dr. Burke's office of horrors would propel her into the position of head veterinarian at the county's new animal shelter.

She smiled to herself later that night as she muttered, "God, I don't know why I'm always so amazed by you. After all, you are God . . . and this has definitely been a God appointment-time. Thank you, Lord; thank you, Lord; and all the little animals thank you too. You created them for us, and we're to be good stewards for them."

Lauren recalled that when she first became a Christian she felt confused about her passion for animals. Not confusion exactly — she knew confusion was not of God. It was more about trying to align her priorities properly so that they would be pleasing to God.

At first she went through a period of mourning; now that God came first in her life, where did that leave her passion and deep attachment to her furry friends? She had to admit, they, not people, had actually given her the most joy in life. But in his time, God took care of that question too; the recent gift of the clinic was clearly his stamp of approval — and here Lauren was as the head veterinarian only a decade after beginning this profession. Yes, she was allowed to adore her animals; they weren't competition for God but his gift, and Lauren melted like a popsicle in a heat wave at his favor.

Although circumstances were changing for the better for Lauren, she remained concerned about Irene and her niece, Chelsea. She found it difficult to contain the excitement she felt for the new opportunities that lay before her, but at the same time they were hard to enjoy when Irene was struggling so profoundly with her trials and tribulations.

As a mother, Lauren couldn't imagine what it would be like to have a teenager like Chelsea in such a threatened state. If anything ever happened to Tucker, she'd lose her mind if she couldn't fix it all immediately. "But some things just take time," she told herself, ever the impatient one. Fortunately, Tucker was a thriving five-year-old doing well in school; even her ex-husband Brian seemed to be stepping up to the plate more consistently as a dad.

Whenever Lauren thought about Brian, it never failed to give her pause as she tried to reason why their relationship hadn't worked in the long run. But then she'd remind herself that there had never really been any surprises in the people she'd chosen to be around, especially the two men she had married. The truth was, from childhood, Lauren had invented just about all of her friendships, and when it came to picking a husband, all she saw was what she wanted to see or decided to fix later.

Yes, she had made the same mistake with

Brian that she had with her first husband, Steven, even after she had become a Christian. Her need to be loved, at least until recently, had always overridden her discernment; and it was a looming bad habit that was mighty hard to break. She knew, by God's Word, that if she was ever going to have a successful marriage, she would need to wait on God to bring her a godly man. She also had learned that no person could fill the hole in her heart she'd carried all her life — not until she met Jesus Christ.

So for now, thankfully, the need of a husband was not even on her radar screen. Getting on with her life had become an all-consuming process that left zero time for romantic wanderings. . . . At least that's what she kept telling herself.

Lauren made her way down the hall to Tucker's room, as she did every morning, flanked by William, her ever loyal yet not terribly bright doggy, and Bingo, her ever-opinionated yet lovable calico kitty.

Lauren praised her two buddies as they pranced about, showing off their most effusive twirls and tail wagging. She thought about what incredible companions these animals had been for her, and as much as they might squabble like kids, she preferred to believe that at the end of the day, they would cover each other.

Lauren laughed at the memory of both her dog and cat looking embarrassed when she had come home early one stormy afternoon from her veterinary practice to find the two huddled together in William's bed, each more scared by the thunder than the other.

"Ooooh, too cute," she reminisced. And then, as she neared Tucker's door, Lauren broke out in song, "This is the day the Lord has made and in it I will be glad, glad, glad, glad, glaaaaaad! . . . Not a Glad-bag. . . . OK, I'm a Glad-bag, I'm an old bag, . . . but I'm still glad!"

Lauren knocked lightly on the door, then burst into Tucker's room with enthusiasm. This was her favorite time of the day. Her boy was already sitting up in his bed, shaking his head at his mother's silliness. Then, as always, he jumped up and announced that he had to go potty.

As he passed her, decked out in his Superman pajamas, Lauren imagined what the day would be like when she couldn't just knock on her son's door, walk in, and have him give her that glorious child-smile. She knew that day would come all too soon. Still, there was hope that her relationship with Tucker would miraculously sidestep the angst and division so common during teen years. "Why does it seem that young adults so often need to turn tail on their parents during their process of gaining independence?" Lauren prayed that she would be wise enough to rewrite those potentially difficult days ahead and remain close to her son as he transitioned into adulthood. She was also painfully aware that hers was not a unique desire — and surely one rarely attained.

Lauren flattened Tucker's collar after his head popped through his crew-neck sweater. Giving him the once-over, she thought he looked like a miniature Yale man. "Hey Tuck, do you know why a dog has so many friends?"

"Because he brushes his teeth?" The five-year-old slayed his mom with another wide grin.

"Close, but no cigar. . . . Because he wags his tail instead of his tongue!"

Tucker headed for the door giving William a quick scratch behind the ears. "That's silly, Mom," he countered as he disappeared around the corner.

Lauren decided then and there that no one had ever invented words to describe how much she loved her little boy.

By the time Tucker, Lauren, and the four-pawed duo entered the kitchen, Irene already had coffee brewing and cereal on the table.

Lauren was a bit surprised to see her sister up and dressed to the nines by 6:45 a.m., but lately Irene had displayed a bevy of unusual behavior. Lauren thought back on the morning just last week when Irene was sitting in the middle of the kitchen floor in a lotus position meditating. She wouldn't stop "ooooommmming" until Lauren knocked her over on her side and covered her mouth with a piece of bread.

"Hey!" Irene glared at Lauren. "You were the one who taught me my mantra!!"

"Hello . . . twenty years ago! . . . Before I knew the truth."

"What's a mantra, Mom?" Tucker piped in.

Now Lauren glared at Irene. "See what you're doing? Filling Tucker's head with nonsense. Now come on, let's call a spade a pick!"

Irene rolled her eyes at another one of Lauren's misspoken quotes she was famous for. "It's, 'Let's call a spade a *spade!*'" Irene hoisted herself onto a chair, taking a moment to rub her aching legs.

"I don't care if it's a bulldozer. I don't want Tucker thinking New Age is the answer to anything."

"Eastern philosophy has stood the test of time, Lauren. Don't be so narrow-minded. What's wrong with communing with the higher power?"

"Because Eastern philosophy encourages you to come closer and closer to the higher power."

"And what's wrong with that?"

"Irene, they teach that eventually you can become *one* with the higher power, and therefore, eventually you *are* the higher power."

"Exactly my point."

"The best lie is the closest to the truth. I don't know about you, but *I am not God. . . .* And I don't believe in reincarnation. I'm not going to evolve from a rock to becoming God, no matter how many lifetimes I'm allowed to try. I need a Savior, and I need grace, not sorcery and astro flight!"

Tucker's curiosity peeked. "What's astro flight?"

Lauren threw her sister another nasty look. "Astro flight is believing you can actually transport your consciousness outside of your physical body."

"Cool, Mom!"

"It's not cool, Tuck, when people believe they can become God!"

"God doesn't have a body, and we do," Tucker simply pointed out.

"Exactly. . . . Except when he sent his Son to earth to die for all our sins."

Irene snickered, "Talk about confusing the kid."

"I am not," Lauren shot back. "Remember, Mark Twain said a light can travel halfway around the world while the truth is putting on its shoes. And God says the truth will set you free."

"What on earth do shoes have to do with God?" Irene threw her head back for added drama.

The moment was broken by William's bark. He was totally out of sorts since he hadn't been fed yet — an oversight he simply refused to accept, despite his normally congenial personality.

"Mom, I'm going to miss my bus," Tucker stated matter-of-factly.

"Ooops, . . . sorry, sorry." Lauren hated when her little boy had to be the voice of reason.

"Mom, the toast is burning," Tucker now

observed, pulling Lauren back from her memory to the present.

"Ooops, . . . sorry, sorry." Lauren lunged at the toaster while smoke began to fill the room. Looking sheepish, she casually tried to scrape the burnt crusts into the garbage and offered up the first mutilated piece to Tucker.

"It's OK, I'm having cereal, Mom."

"Sure, . . ." she then offered some of the wheat crisps to Irene, who just shook her head.

"Maybe Chelsea wants some. What do you think, Rene?"

"I think she already left for school with Trace. No matter how early I get up, I miss the worm!"

"Where's the worm?" Tucker picked the raisins out of his cereal to nibble on first.

Lauren fidgeted, "Auntie Irene was just making a joke, Tuck. No worms here, right Rene?"

After a beat Irene gave her nephew a thumbs-up. "Nope, no worms allowed. Only monster ticklers." She lunged at Tucker, rubbing his rib cage until he squealed in delight, but not before he knocked over his cereal bowl.

"Ooops, . . . sorry, sorry." Irene mimicked Lauren, who grabbed at some paper towels to mop up. Despite her quick response, William and Bingo beat her to the mess, diving in for an unscheduled treat.

Surprised, Tucker pointed at William charging through the spilled cereal. "I didn't know dogs ate raisins. . . . I thought they didn't like fruit."

Lauren meticulously wiped the milk splatters off the table leg. "William likes anything that falls under the category of food. Hey, don't you remember how my horse Gracie loved bananas?"

"Oh yeah!" Tucker squealed again. "She looked like she was smoking a yellow cigar."

"You're silly, Tuck."

"I know. Daddy says I get it from you."

"Silly is a good thing," Lauren sounded slightly defensive.

"Sure, . . ." Irene picked up the plastic cereal bowl and put it in the sink, ". . . but only if you're under ten years old."

Tucker thought for a moment. "So if you're grumpy like you, Aunt Irene, it means you're old?"

Lauren roared, "Oh my, that was sweet!"

Now Irene grabbed the bowl out of the sink and threw it at her sister Frisbee style, bonking William in the head in the process. The dog didn't skip a beat on his clean-up mission.

Lauren jumped to William's rescue. "Rene, you hurt him!"

"Clearly not!"

"Mom, I'm going to miss my bus!" Tucker insisted.

"Oooh, . . . sorry, sorry," Irene and Lauren said in unison.

What a family . . .

CHAPTER 4
-TENDER TOUCHES-

Hamilton watched his wife toss and turn for most of the night, and now that the sun had finally risen, he stroked her hair in a subtle effort to awaken her.

Eleanor never had difficulty sleeping — not until she had undergone the radical double-mastectomy a few months ago at age forty-seven. And since then, most of her waking and sleeping moments were fraught with trepidation, physical pain, and longings for emotional and spiritual relief. Yet, as much as Eleanor was going through, so was her diligent husband of thirty years.

He watched her in silence until she began to groan. Facing a new day brought its own set of new issues for Eleanor since her surgery. Hamilton glanced down at his "bride," as he always called her, love pouring from his eyes. His concern for his woman was all consuming — this woman he had deeply longed for, for a lifetime. He thought back to their wedding day when the pastor asked, *"Hamilton Walton Robert James III, do you take Eleanor Grace Jackson to be your lawfully wedded wife, in sickness and in health. . . ."* The memory trailed off as he considered his affirmative answer to the question, "in sickness and in health." He knew in every fiber of his being that no matter what the future might hold for him, Eleanor would in all ways forever be by his side. And there he would be for her as well — staunch, reliable, sensitive, and yet a powerhouse of a godly man.

No one would say that "Ham," as he was affectionately referred to by all who loved and respected him, was big in stature; but the effect this man had on just about everyone who crossed his path was nothing short of life changing.

As basketball coach at Centennial High, Ham had tidbits of wisdom for the kids not only on the court but for all occasions of growing up amid personal dilemmas and curiosities. And Eleanor, the school nurse, perfectly rounded out the male versus female advice concerning relationships, balancing her husband's forthright wisdom with her feminine perspective, sensitivity, and grace.

Hamilton had been reevaluating whether he would support his and Eleanor's decision to continue to live in the black projects known to the locals as "The Bucket of Blood." Heretofore, it had been their decision to stay there, not due to lack of financial means but so they would easily be available to some of the local kids who appeared to be most needy. Ham and Eleanor were not just a black couple in a black neighborhood where they had lived the better part of both their lives; they were healers of the heart and soul with credentials of having been there and survived.

Actually, their son Mark brought up the idea of moving. This up-and-coming lawyer in the nation's capital was one brilliant yet caring individual. Anyone would have been proud to have Mark as their child, and Ham and Eleanor were shameless about the pride they took in their offspring. People found it easy to take the James's advice about child-rearing since they had had such a successful turn in doing so with Mark.

As a teen Mark had campaigned hard to have the family "move on up to the East

Side" when he realized his parents could afford to buy a decent home in one of the better neighborhoods/developments in Centennial. But after some lengthy lectures about sacrifice from Eleanor and Ham, Mark reluctantly understood why they wanted their family to stay put.

It helped that Mark was a church-going boy, not because his parents made him go, but because he saw how God worked in his parents' lives. He observed firsthand how their being the "real deal" as believers affected others.

Growing up, he had also heard second-hand from family members about his dad's problems after serving in Vietnam, although Mark never experienced the repercussions of Ham's wartime horrors. It seemed they had all but healed before he was born. Mark was told that his mother had insisted, "No child of mine will be born into a house of stress and anger." And with that credo in place, Mark grew up with parents who rarely did, thought, or condoned anything without considering eternal consequences.

The James family would actually have family celebrations every time they heard of someone accepting Christ as their Savior. And on those occasions, as a child well into adulthood, Mark would do a little jig around the table to the beat of a lively song sung by his mom. Eleanor's exquisite voice was known to penetrate the walls of their house, heard all around the neighborhood heralding the good news of salvation. This family of few with a heart for many might as well have put a flag up on their front porch in their zeal for each and every saved soul's proclamation.

Despite the fact that just about every kid from the high school, most of their parents, and all of Ham and Eleanor's neighbors visited her in the hospital while she was launching her battle against cancer, Mark still felt that a change for his mom was in order. He was convinced that the little bit of luxury she'd never asked for would be just what her spiritual doctor would order during these trying times. And to that end, Mark attempted to talk his parents into finally moving out of the projects.

In response, Ham repeatedly told his son that the decision was totally up to his mother, and whatever she chose to do, he would be happy to follow. So after much deliberation Eleanor decided to live right where she was, comforted by the windows she'd looked through for oh so many years. She opted to be surrounded by the walls that displayed her pictures hung exactly in the spots and order she wanted them to be so she could review her past as her body repaired and her spirit refreshed.

That Thursday morning, Ham glanced over to the bedroom door on which there were two sets of reports from felt-tip pens — the first, celebrating every three inches Mark had grown over the years; the second, Eleanor's heroic record of recovery from her surgery.

Baby Mark's memories were never to be wiped away, nor was the set of marks above to the right where Eleanor was still struggling in her physical therapy to raise her arms ever so slowly, higher and higher as her body allowed after the excruciating intrusion of the doctor's scalpels. Yes, Eleanor had been plagued by a particularly intense and invasive case of cancer, a kind so fast traveling that a double mastectomy was not just suggested; it was firmly ordered.

Eleanor's circle of friends — Pam, Stephanie, Tonya, and now Lauren — had prayed for hours before, during, and following Eleanor's surgery. And during the nights, although reservedly, Eleanor allowed herself to be held by her husband who showered her with affection and covered her in prayer. But at the end of all the caring and concern, it was going to be Eleanor's decision as to how she wanted to handle her medical threat.

She sought the Lord's leadings, coming to the conclusion that the surgery was going to be lifesaving, so she opted to proceed. The localized radiation treatments that followed, she also recognized, were a must. But her bold decision not to have chemotherapy was based on intense medical research from her point of view as a registered nurse. Eleanor was no dummy, and she concluded that, in her case, chemotherapy would hurt her body more than help it. She also believed that if she took all the reasonable physical steps for full and complete healing, God would take care of the rest. This is what she told her husband, and this is what the couple had been standing in agreement on ever since the surgery.

Hamilton came home early that evening with bags full of takeout from Norros that Stephanie had prepared specifically with Eleanor in mind. All of her favorites — an array of entrees and a variety of desserts befitting a queen, which is exactly how Hamilton always treated his bride.

Although the sun had not yet set, Eleanor pulled the curtains closed around the dining area and lit some candles. And there she sat with her husband, heads bowed as he said grace over their meal. "Father God, we thank you for all that you do in our lives. Please sanctify this food for the nourishment of our bodies and service to you. We remain in awe of your ability to work wonders in our hearts, bodies, and spirits. You could have come to this earth in any way you saw fit, but you sent your Son as a sacrifice for each and every one of us, and we thank you and praise you for the love that we have not earned but you give so freely to us. And Father God, we thank you that you say we can speak Eleanor's healing into being and that whatever is your will, it is well with our souls. In Jesus' mighty name, Amen."

Ham leaned over and gave his wife a kiss on her forehead, then began to serve the feast before them. Now Eleanor knew Ham always had a definite purpose for all he did and said, so she recognized that this afternoon's delight and surprise was her husband's way of broaching a difficult subject, one that she had thus far refused to discuss.

"Darling, I talked to Dr. Logan again today. I'd really like it if you would allow me into your thoughts about the reconstructive surgery."

For an instant Eleanor felt that she had been duped, replacing her napkin on the table in a gesture of displeasure. "Hamilton, if this is what all this is about, I told you, I am not prepared to talk about that yet."

Before she could remove her hand from her napkin, he lovingly put his over hers. "Please, I know that is your decision. I'm just here to support whatever it is you decide. But putting it off, in itself, is a decision to make no decision, and I don't feel that is healthy for you. There is a time of healing, digesting, and reviewing . . . but after that, it turns into procrastination, which opens the door for the enemy."

Eleanor turned her head slightly, unable to discount what he was saying as the truth. Suddenly she felt like she was ten years old, at a loss for words without the wherewithal to overcome the flood of emotions she was feeling. Insecurities rushed through her that were unfamiliar. "I'm listenin'," she said in a small voice.

"Thank you. You know that we made a vow years ago, 'in sickness and in health,' and that meant, of course, just that. I could not be sitting here without the endless love and support you've given me over the years, especially at certain crucial times in my personal life. Please don't shut me out now that it's about you. Please allow me the honor of doing the same for you that you've always done for me . . . by letting you know that I love you unconditionally." He watched her expression for a moment before continuing. "I can't even pretend to know what it feels like as a woman to have had the operation you've endured, but I know that you know who you are as a woman, and who you are as a child of God. . . . And that has nothing to do with what you look like or what you think you look like."

"Hamilton, you're sweet, and you're right. You have no idea, so please don't try to tell me how I'm supposed to feel or what I'm supposed to know right now. I'm just not ready to address this issue."

"Eleanor, it makes no-never-mind to me whether you have reconstructive surgery or not. Whatever works for you, whatever makes you feel like you need to feel. But I just can't sit by and watch my wife vanish. Dear, I want to hold you. I want to be close to you. And whether you're aware of it or not, you're pulling away more and more. I know the doctors say that this is normal and typical and to be expected. But they don't know my Eleanor. You're not normal or typical. You are the unexpected, and I can't stand not being close to you. Give me a time frame. I'll wait as long as you want, but all I need to know today is that, at some juncture, you will allow me to hold you again, to be close to you, intimate with you like it's always been. I'm suffocating without you, and that is not easy to say because I don't want to put even the slightest pressure on you. I'm absolutely fine, but I just need to know that we're going down the road to recovery here, not the road to nowhere."

Eleanor slowly pulled her chair away from the table, got up, walked over to the dining room windows, and opened the curtains. She needed all of the time each of her movements took to gather her thoughts. And the words that finally came out of her mouth surprised her as much as they did her husband.

Her voice was low, angry, and hurt as she finally expressed everything she had been feeling, starting with the betrayal of her own body against itself. She was enraged at the notion of a disease within her that could threaten her life and threaten her happiness. A disease that was not of God but was there merely to siphon the life out of her, rob her of her time with her husband and her vocations as a mother, a nurse, a wife, and as a woman.

She finally admitted it all, with words slow and deliberate. "I feel . . . abandoned by God. In my entire life, I have never felt like this. I know I can't put God in a box, but I expected that he would spare me this. And I know that that is not how I should feel, and that is not wise, and that is not 'together' spiritually. But that's how I feel! And I also know that I'll get over it, at least I pray I will. It's not about the surgery. It's about this reconstruction bit. No one can just insert some medical replacement to my body like getting my tires changed. Yes, my body was invaded, but it's much deeper than that Ham, and I'm more surprised than you are that sometimes I simply don't want to 'handle it.' Sometimes, I have to admit, I just don't want to go on. And I know that's crazy, but that's how I feel. And I know that feelin's are unreliable and so easily used to taunt us. And I keep tryin' to get back to the land, to the solid ground, to a foundation I can count on, but I'm floun-derin' out in the water, paddlin' around in circles, goin' down and strugglin' to come up for air, and it's takin' all I can muster to get up out of the bed. And frankly, I do that more for others than for myself."

When she finally turned to him, tears were streaming down her face. And she also knew that once she let the floodgates go, her face would begin to swell like she'd just been stung by a hive of bees. But she didn't care right then.

Hamilton started to get up to soothe her, but she stopped him. "No, please. I'm goin' to stop cryin' now so I don't look like I was hit by a Mack truck. And I'm goin' to wash my face with cold water and I'll be back, and we're goin' to have our beautiful dinner. I'm goin' to be alright, Ham, but I'm still grievin', and I got some more of it to do. There's a difference between feelin' sorry for myself and just grievin' a loss. I hope that once I allow myself to grieve, once I allow myself to really feel and not want to be just numb, then the healin' will come. I don't want to talk about it again unless I bring it up, alright?"

"Of course." He got up and held the bedroom door open for her, daring to trail his hand along her back as she left to wash her face.

Eleanor's intimacy with her husband had always been nothing less than spectacular based on their dedication and commitment to each other. And their commitment carried them through the years following their insatiable physical attraction for each other from first sight as teenagers, a passion for each other that had grown in ways far more important than just the physical.

Yes, they had a marriage any would desire; that was why they were so compelling as a couple for relationship counseling, especially considering their victory over Ham's issues after Vietnam. Love showed through their lives as partners in such an attractive fashion. God surely was pleased with their ability to call others to him by example. And although they had had some difficult scenarios to conquer in their past, they always considered themselves extremely blessed, having enjoyed a path of favor when it came to the issues that really count in the long run.

So what now? This threatening turn of events with Eleanor had surprised both her and Ham. "Caught off guard" sounded corny but true — not that they felt they were invincible, surely not. But still, this latest hit was a biggie, and it had left Eleanor in a place of confusion that she'd never experienced before.

The doctors told Ham that it was normal for his wife to withdraw from his love and touch for a period of time. They said he should just let her feel her way while she sought out new footings for her life. But Hamilton Walton Robert James III never expected his bride to be "gone" for so long. Not that the time frame had been that extensive; the truth was, he was used to Eleanor's resiliency, her never-say-die attitude, and her complete comfort zone with herself as a woman.

Yes, Ham could certainly understand her uneasiness after the mastectomy. But he knew, as surely as he lived, that she remained the most beautiful female picture of perfection to him, no matter the years, her weight, or, now, her surgery. He also understood why she wouldn't undress in front of him anymore and wouldn't allow him to hold her in ways that he had always held her. Yes, he understood, but he just didn't want to lose this jewel of a female that he absolutely cherished.

What could he do? The doctors had no concrete answers, so he prayed for a word from God. He prayed that the Holy Spirit would envelope Eleanor. He prayed that she would remember how much God loved and cared for her and how much he, Hamilton, as a man wanted and missed his wife. He bought her flowers, wrote her cards, put love notes on the "welcome sign" of the school where his words of *amore* were displayed for all to read.

Yes, it had been echoed since their teens as they engraved on the local oak tree: Ham loves Eleanor — Eleanor loves Ham — xo Forever xo. So this man waited for his wife to return to him, and he prayed it would be sooner than later that they could be one again.

Eleanor had refused to go to therapy or counseling about her cancer as suggested by all her caretakers, insisting that her God was the Great Physician and her counselor. And then there was Ham, and her son, and her circle of friends, and her church family who would also support and sustain her. So, as slowly as the marks on the door were rising heralding her physical healing, Ham could see her sass return — the beginning of a smile, a step to her stride that reminded him that his beloved girl/woman/wife Eleanor was coming back to him on the road of recovery. He rejoiced at the mere thought of such a gift!

And with all of that improvement, he considered that, just perhaps, this would be the morning he could actually hold her close. He had been praying all through the early morning that it would be; but as she turned to him and her eyes opened, he could see that it was not yet time. He simply smiled at her and told her to stay there until he brought her breakfast in bed before they started their day, and a slight smile crossed her beautiful face.

Tonya had her hands full, what with her four-year-old, wiggly worm tank of a tot on one hip and a hefty set of school books on the other. This African-American twenty-year-old beauty had it coming and going 24-7 between her college classes and raising a son ostensively single-handed.

Single was the operative word in Tonya's life since she'd become pregnant in love, but out of wedlock. Her little boy Bobbie's dad, Shooter, had been Tonya's main man since he was thirteen and she fifteen. Unfortunately, the inappropriate nature of their youthful relationship was not that unusual between kids from the projects (not that the upper-crust cultural offspring didn't entertain more than their share of trouble and scandals).

At the behest of Tonya's broken family, Eleanor placed the pregnant teen under her wing and in her church, while Ham had some serious man-to-man chats with

89

Shooter about his parenting and partnering responsibilities, despite the boy's tender age of fatherhood at fourteen.

Although this early-bloomer basketball team captain had a heart of gold, he also had aspirations to play pro ball. Still, Shooter wanted to do right by his girl, whom he honestly loved, so he accepted being a father with nary a complaint. The only thing the young man wouldn't agree to do was to marry Tonya — not until he graduated high school and his future in sports was set in stone.

Tonya's response to her boyfriend's plan was straightforward. What was set in stone was, they were already parents, so Shooter needed to make things right with her in God's eyes, not by his own code of ethics or timing. Despite her insistence Shooter wouldn't budge on the issue. Although kindly put, he made clear that he would always be Bobbie's dad, and he would always be there for Tonya, but he needed to call the shots as "the man."

Shooter, like a lot of people around those parts, had suffered the old-time church upbringing laced with brimstone and wrath that branded fear in the hearts of young and old alike. "Judgmental, graceless religion," Ham called it. Of course, there was the matter of Shooter's daddy holding a belt and the Bible in one hand, and a bottle of whiskey and his mistress's key in the other that ultimately turned the boy away from church. And "Bible thumping," as Shooter called it, surely hadn't held his mama in good stead. She was hardened and worn to the bone by thirty-five. Her only hope for the future was for Shooter to make it big in sports, and the boy was determined not to let her down.

Shooter told Tonya that he was going to carve out his own way of life before he'd give it up for God's way. His attitude concerning the issue of faith broke Tonya's heart, but not as much as leaving this one-of-a-kind guy she'd been lifting up in prayer for five years now.

However, that did not mean that Tonya watered down her own set of boundaries that were also etched in stone when it came to Shooter. Supported by her circle of friends, Tonya and Shooter dated strictly "outside of the bedroom" while spending more time than most parents do together with their son. Thus far, the relationship had worked alright since neither of the young couple had ever strayed. But lately, Tonya confided to Pam, "being together alone" was starting to get old, no matter how much she loved Shooter.

And then there was the issue of their being unequally yoked, which Tonya and her friends had prayed over for years. Tonya would insist that Shooter did believe in Jesus, just in his own way. That point always stirred much discussion among the group about God's Word on the matter: religion and salvation are two different things, they would debate. But no doubt, there was only one way to be saved, and that was not "Shooter's way," they would conclude.

Then Eleanor would remind her charge, Tonya, "According to the Word, the only way to God is through the blood of his Son Jesus, no matter what 'church' someone does or does not attend." She would also comfort her young friend, reassuring Tonya how much God loves Shooter to have surrounded him with those who also love him enough not to compromise the truth of God's eternal invitation. And so it had been.

No one could ever say that Tonya wasn't extremely bright, keeping her own dreams alive by attending the community college until she knew where Shooter ultimately stood concerning their wedding. Her take was, if he doesn't come through after graduation and marry her, she was off to New

York City with Bobbie to model.

The local advertising and modeling agencies had been courting this bronzed-skinned, blue-eyed beauty with a runway figure and a smile that could stop a bus. But despite the temptation for instant fame, Tonya had enough patience and foresight to know she would still have time for that career after she secured her education. Surprisingly, she did not buy into the worldly sales pitch that she'd be over the hill by twenty-one. Tonya's beauty was beyond skin deep; her hypnotic glow came from her inner spirit, not her bone structure.

But despite the confidence she'd gleaned under Eleanor's tutelage over the last half decade, she'd complain to her buddy Pam that she was so exhausted being a single mom, she was going to need to retire before she turned legal age.

Pam called Tonya a "sorry sap." "You should follow me around for a day to see what *hectic* really means. . . . And I've got ten years on you, girl."

Tugging on Pam's waist-length blonde hair, Tonya countered, "Hey, don't forget I've got eight inches on you, little one, so you better show this girl the respect I deserve. . . ."

". . . And let you cry on my teeny-weeny

shoulder?"

Tonya giggled at the image. "Long as you don't blow away with the next gust of wind."

Yes, Pam was a petite one. Yet these two women were a picture-perfect study in physical and rearing contradictions. Pam had been brought up on the better side of town, Tonya in the projects. Still, they were bound inexplicably by friendship and faith.

When a wave of cold air entered through the door that morning, Pam gave Tonya some extra support, grabbing Bobbie so he could join the other kids at the day care center she ran at the back of her church.

"What are you feeding this boy? Rocks?" Pam strained as she hoisted Bobbie over to his locker area.

"Dry cement with raisins. . . . You know he doesn't like to chew his food." Tonya laughed, joining Pam who already had Bobbie's coat off and hung up. "All I have to do is give him a big glass of water after he eats, and he gains his fifty pounds for the day."

"And to think I put you up for 'Mother of the Year.' " Pam always amused Tonya, even on her most frustrating days. The young mother gave her son a quick hug and kiss, making sure to take the time for a moment of loving eye contact before she headed for the door.

Since the dozen or so children of various ethnic backgrounds, ages, and energy levels were enjoying their free playtime, the background sound-level caused Pam and Tonya to converse in controlled screams. "Bobbie's going home with Jason today so I can make our prayer time."

Pam nodded, "His mom already told me. Hey, and if I'm a little late, just start without me. I have a counseling session with Chelsea, and they sometimes run over."

"How's it going with her?"

"I can't really discuss . . ."

". . . I know that. I just wondered if you're making any breakthroughs." Tonya was sincerely concerned.

"Well, we seem to get to a point and then Chelsea shuts down. . . . But that's no surprise. I don't know how anyone can begin to forgive and heal without Christ, and Chelsea tells me that she's not there. Matter of fact, she's furious and sarcastic when I even talk about Jesus. . . . So," Pam winked at Tonya, ". . . she must be getting close."

"Amen, Sister. . . ." Tonya knew how right-on her friend's words were. The spiritual battle over eternal life was real, and the truth concerning forgiving and healing was at the core of everything Pam was about. Her collaborative dream with Eleanor and Ham to open the Hope School was all about accepting Christ and healing generations of pain and division while offering all the community's children an excellent education. And all that could not be accomplished without dispelling racial hatred, tensions, and separation.

Yes, Pam had a big vision. Taking on the founding of Hope School was an enormous task that required megafunds that, as yet, had not fallen in place despite Pam's tireless efforts. Tonya referred to Pam as a miniature pit bull who simply would not let go of the dream. But only when her circle of friends echoed the need for Pam to lay the financial support of God's work through the school at the foot of the cross did Pam back off a bit.

Clearly she was going to have to "let go and let God," which, interestingly, was just about the same place all her prayer partners presently found themselves in their own lives. And although each of the women was intermittently frustrated, they all knew that "at the foot of the cross" meant total reliance on God's Word and power in their circumstances; and that's precisely where their Lord wanted them.

The group was slowly embracing the fact that at the end of themselves they would find their God, and only in him all things were possible. Yes, they had been standing in agreement, and they had been watching God work miracles in each of their lives — in his time and by his might, not theirs. So this phrase was added to the end of their prayers, "The absence of fear means the presence of God! Amen, in Jesus' mighty name."

And then Eleanor would remind them, yet again, "Growing old is inevitable; growing up is optional."

That November morning a daily double of Ham's "tidbits of wisdom" adorned Greystone's welcome poster outside the front of the brick high school:

If you're the smartest one in your group, move on.
Don't blame God when you lose something.
Thank God when you haven't lost everything.
— Ham

The students poured in for morning classes while Hamilton escorted Eleanor to the side door of the building where they came upon Chelsea and Trace. The teenagers were making a weak effort to hide behind a bush while locked in a kiss when they were interrupted by Ham's firm hand on the boy's shoulder. Chelsea bit Trace's lip from the impact of Ham's intrusion. "Boy, one more act of disobedience and disrespect for your young lady here, and you're off the team." Ham's expression left no room for discussion.

Trace paled, standing at attention. "I'm sorry, sir." The boy had learned the hard way not to mess with his basketball coach.

"Don't apologize to me, Son. . . ."

". . . Yes sir." Trace knew the drill from an earlier altercation just a week ago. He turned to Chelsea who stood frozen in place, finding it difficult to divert her attention from Trace's now bleeding lip. "I apologize for disrespecting you, Chelsea. Will you forgive me?"

The girl looked like a deer in headlights. Her voice caught in her throat out of abject fear. Finally she was able to squeak out, "Sure."

"Now you both get to class and stay out of trouble. I won't be warning you again, Trace. I hold you responsible and accountable, and I will be talking to both your mothers if you two don't have a change of heart and ways."

With eyes fixed on the ground, Chelsea and Trace muttered, "Yes sir" in unison before disappearing into the side entrance of the school.

Eleanor had been observing the three from the hallway window when Ham joined her. "I feel young-love trouble comin' on with those two. I believe it's time for some serious intervention for their own good."

Ham wrapped his arm tightly around his wife's shoulders. "I believe you're correct, my love."

He adored the fact that Eleanor still put her concern for others first, despite her circumstances. He'd never forget the effect her personal sacrifice and direction had on him when he returned from military service and they were first married. Bottom line, Eleanor was the only influence that sustained him through the destructive toll from which so many Vietnam vets still suffered. The aftermath of what Ham experienced during that brutal and unsupported war had left him with post-traumatic stress disorder that reared its ugly head in the form of verbal battery, rages, an array of destructive behavior, and an inability to have an intimate and personal relationship not only with Eleanor but in his faith.

To have witnessed the healing power of prayer and the grace and patience God held out for Ham was nothing short of miraculous. Hamilton Walton Robert James III prospered as a husband, father, and community leader while so many of his comrades were left behind in the clutches of evil. And for Ham's personal experiences with the dark recesses of his mind and the struggle for freedom, God gave him a voice that could reach others in pain. He worked as diligently with his fellow servicemen at the local veteran's hospital and after-care meetings as he did with the town's youth.

Yes, the hand-tooled sign above the James's dining room was particularly appropriate when it came to Hamilton and his family:

GOD TURNS ALL THINGS FOR GOOD FOR THOSE WHO LOVE HIM AND ARE IN HIS PURPOSE. (ROMANS 8:28)

CHAPTER 5
-TREADING WATER-

Lauren fidgeted at the corner waiting for the light to change in front of the Jiffy Lube on the outskirts of town. She spotted Irene across the street in her BMW after having circled the block to find a place to park while Lauren dropped her truck off for service.

Lauren's mind wandered from the blinking red stoplight before her to the bare winter trees framing the background that suddenly transported in time to full summer bloom. This prompted one of Lauren's visits down memory lane, and with that, she heard an odd rendition of the nursery song "Pop Goes the Weasel" playing in the distance. As she glanced in the direction of the music, Lauren saw an ice cream truck coming up the street in slow motion with a herd of children running behind in pursuit of its delicious treats.

Lauren's flashback wasn't from her childhood, but from just a few months earlier when she and her family had first moved to town. Lauren remembered thinking what a sweet sound the ice cream truck made, invoking recollections of her youth and the piles of soft ice cream in cones that spilled over and ran down her.

Last fall Lauren had introduced Tucker to the ice cream man in the truck playing "Pop Goes the Weasel" on the very corner where she now stood. During those first days in Centennial before all the craziness began, Lauren experienced such a sense of peace with her new lot in life. She was so looking forward to the relief and repair southern gentility promised to bring her family who had been fraught with tension and discord for as long as she could remember.

But her sense of well-being was shattered in short order, and now so was her ice-cream-truck memory at the intrusion of a honking horn which rudely broke into her serene image. The traffic light had changed, and Irene, ever the impatient one, was urging her sister to cross the street and, "Get in the car!"

Sprinting to beat the light, Lauren smiled sheepishly as she slammed the door behind her. Irene just shook her head as she pulled into traffic, smashing her half-smoked cigarette into the ashtray. "Day dreaming again? Do you realize a school bus almost hit you?"

"Well, I sleep better than you do," Lauren said matter-of-factly.

"What's that supposed to mean?"

"It means I get most of my memory-go-rounds reviewed during the day. Just a different style, Rene. You were always a night person, I'm the daydreamer."

Irene groaned. "I'll trade you any time."

Lauren looked at her, concerned. "You still haven't slept, have you?"

Immediately self-conscious, Irene glanced at her weary eyes in the rearview mirror. "I look a mess, don't I? . . . Kind of like a defeated criminal before the enemy has even passed judgment." She was visibly overwhelmed. "Oh Lauren, I can't stand this anymore!"

Lauren put her arm around her sister with such impact it almost caused Irene to run the car off the road.

"Easy!" Her eyes widened in fear.

"OK, . . . sorry, sorry." Lauren pulled away, gently realigning Irene's shoulder pad to its proper position. After a moment of silence, Lauren burst out laughing. "Ooooh, I can just see it now. . . . A front-page picture of us hugging while swerving down the street with copy stating:

> And it was just before the demise of the two crazy sisters in Centennial that we suspected they had . . .

Irene screeched, "Stop! Don't even kid about that! You're always telling me to 'speak things into being'. . . . Well, that's the last thing we need. Next they'll be saying that we're lesbians because you can't keep your hands off of me, *even in public!*"

Lauren adored teasing her sister, "Of course, Rene. . . . Don't you know that's why we all live together. . . ."

". . . Don't go there. I swear, this all has to stop soon, or I'm going to lose my mind." Irene raised her fist in warning.

Backing down, Lauren adopted a softer tone. "I know, Rene. They've got to get you to court soon. . . . The truth will set you free, . . . and it will be over. . . ."

"Lauren, don't placate me. . . . Try another tack."

"OK, how about we just change the subject?" Before Irene could agree, Lauren fast-forwarded to her next thought. "Thank you for taking me to drop my truck off."

"You're welcome," Irene answered by rote.

"So, when I drop you at the lawyers' office, I'll run over to the shelter and be back in a flash." Suddenly, Lauren's face exploded, "Oh, Rene, I am so excited! Can you believe this is *finally* happening?! Not really *finally*. . . . It's actually happened so fast. It seems like years, but it's really not been that long. . . . Ooooh, the shelter's going to open and we're going to be able to help animals and . . ."

Irene starred blankly ahead. "Maybe you've got a nice big cage you can put me in so I don't hurt somebody."

"Come on, Rene. You've got two great lawyers. And the nice, cute one from Nashville hasn't even asked you for a retainer."

"Lawyers are never cute, nor are they stupid. He knows that I'm good for it . . . at least if I ever get Ford's will straightened out." Irene sank farther down behind the wheel of the car as if she could completely disappear from view. "I just can't seem to get ahead of the game."

"I'm sure tomorrow will be your day in court."

Irene bristled, "*Days* in court! I'm *sure* they'll drag the trial out just as long as they're taking to get it started!"

"Rene, they simply can't keep postponing you indefinitely. It's illegal."

Irene threw her head back in frustration.

"It seems they can do anything they want around here. Whatever happened to a citizen's right to a speedy trial? Honestly, I don't think I can take this much longer."

Lauren was about to comfort Irene with another hug when she noticed her sister had two sets of reading glasses hanging around her neck. "Ahh, Rene, . . . I know you decided to dress down for the trial look, but I don't get the double glasses. 'School marmish' doesn't suit you."

Irene regarded her chest, then snapped back. "See, I told you I can't take any more! I'm totally distracted. . . . And I'm *hot*. . . . I'm broiling. . . . And then all my makeup runs down my face like I'm in the shower, and it's the middle of winter! And I can't go out in 'cotton sleeveless,' so I try on half my closet, and I take a hit of hormones and start all over. . . . And by that time, I don't even realize I'm wearing *two sets of glasses instead of a necklace!*" Screaming by now, Irene started waving her hands about in an attempt to ward off a full-fledged hot-flash attack as Lauren grabbed for the steering wheel.

"Whoa now, Rene!"

"I'm not a horse!" Irene was hyperventilating.

"Sorry. . . . Just tell your lawyers that

you've got a different set of 'readers' for each of their legal fine print." Lauren beamed at her joke.

Irene took a beat to digest the concept, then the two sisters chuckled at such silliness.

Finally pulling herself slightly together, Irene wiped away the tears still streaming down her face. "Now they're going to *know* that I've lost my mind, not just think it." She mercilessly tugged at one of the pairs of glasses hanging on a bejeweled chain around her neck, finally ripping it over her head. "There, that should make all things right with the world. . . . My goodness, what would *Vogue* say about such a designer faux pas?" Irene took a few deep breaths.

"They'd say you look grand." Lauren gathered up the pair of glasses before she could sit on them while she considered how important appearances were to Irene. With all of her out-of-control behavior, this woman was still spectacular.

Lauren also considered that her sister was beyond overwrought, even if no one else had been able to note her diminishing condition. Lauren hated to see the waning glimmer in Irene's eyes and slight droop in her countenance. *Yes, all of this does have to end soon,* she thought. But the way things had been going, Lauren wasn't sure it would.

Then she wondered if her zeal concerning her own newfound fortuitous circumstances might have caused her to overlook some of her sister's needs. She regarded Irene, her eyes filling with tears. "I'm an idiot. . . . Do you want me to go in with you today? I just thought you were going to have a quick meeting with your lawyers, but if you want me there, I can call Mrs. Strickland and see her later."

Finessing the traffic, Irene opened the car window, gasping for an infusion of fresh air just to continue breathing. "Thanks, I can do this. I can handle this. But tomorrow . . . Yes, will you come with me to court tomorrow?" She suddenly sounded like a child.

"What do you think? Of course! We're all coming, the whole family. And I've got the girls marching around the court building praying like Jeremiah . . ."

". . . As in the bullfrog?" Irene cracked a tiny smile.

Lauren didn't appreciate Irene's humor. "As in the Bible. . . . I'm serious, Rene."

". . . So am I. While they're messing with me in the papers and postponing court dates, I'm losing opportunities to protect my interests in New York. It's insane!" She started breathing heavily again. "I have no big funds to fight the big guns in New York. My stepchildren, who remind me of Attila the Hun and his sister Ulga, are out for blood and have a fleet of dream-team legal weasels. And . . . I've already had to give 50 percent of Chelsea's and my potential inheritance away to that slime lawyer who took over my case on contingency!"

"Please don't get in a flurry, Rene." Lauren patted her sister's shoulder. "You told me that Ford was so wealthy that if you got just 1 percent of his worth, you and Chelsea would be set for life. So 50 percent of everything is better than 1 percent of anyone."

Irene stared straight ahead. "No, Lauren, you mean '50 percent of something is better than 100 percent of nothing.' "

"Exactly my point."

Exhausted, Irene was in no mood to argue.

Just as they were nearing the legal offices to drop Irene off, Lauren had another one of her bursts of energy. "Oh Rene, wait just a second. I had this vision the last time I took you to the airport that I forgot to tell you about. . . . I was going back to get the car out of the parking lot, and I was sitting in one of those buses, you know, that take you there, and I was staring at two signs in front of me. One said, 'Don't push the doors, they open automatically.' " With that Lauren simply offered her best Cheshire-cat grin as if her statement should prompt some profound revelation in Irene.

She pulled the car to the curb and stared back blankly at Lauren. "So? . . ."

". . . So then the sign underneath it said, 'Don't sit on the baggage, and hold onto the railing tight.' "

Irene was getting annoyed. "Tightly, not tight."

"That's not the point, Rene. We're not in English class on a bus."

"I'm not on a bus at all."

"Fine," Lauren huffed. "I hate when you make fun of me."

"OK, . . . sorry, sorry," Irene giggled, then glanced at her watch, noting that she had two minutes to get to her appointment on time. "Go on."

Lauren bounced up and down on the seat like a kid. "Well, don't you get it? Don't you get what God's trying to tell us?"

Irene took a deep breath.

"Rene, get it. . . . 'Don't push the doors, they open automatically.' In other words, just be patient and God will make the way. Every time I try to do something in my own way and in my own time, it's like bashing my head against the wall . . . and then boom! All of a sudden, I'm in God's will, and it's God's way and his timing, and it works like butter! Look what happened with Mrs. Strickland. In just three months time we're about to open the shelter, we've gotten rid of that disgusting chute thing at Dr. Burke's, and the animals are going to be saved. . . . And . . . I got a job, and my whole world has turned around. How's that for not pushing the FedEx envelope?"

Irene leaned farther back in her seat. "I am truly happy for you. I really am. You deserve it all and *more*. . . . And by the way, I'm not as mean as Tucker thinks I am. I'm just under a lot of pressure, and I'm glad you don't have it, but it's still on me. I have to push some doors open, or I'll get run over. . . . And what is this about 'Don't sit on the baggage'? I get the part about hold onto the railing so you don't fall on your head. What's the baggage riddle?"

"It's a metaphor, don't you see? You just have to open your eyes and look around for the good and not the bad. 'Don't sit on the baggage' means don't bring all your old baggage into your today, into your *now*. Not that we don't have to deal with our old baggage. . . . Of course we do. Otherwise it will affect how we are with other people. . . . It will ruin future relationships, and make us oversensitive, angry, or sad. . . . Sad is really bad."

If daggers could shoot from a person's eyes, Irene was pitching them right at her sister. Her voice was low and intense. "Lauren, you sound like you're in a commune in the 70s. . . . Now I'm just going to go in, take this meeting, and see if they have me on the docket for tomorrow. Then the legal eagles and I are going to go over our strategy for the ten millionth time. . . . Meanwhile, you go on and check out your shelter and your benefactor, and I'll see you later, OK? I've got my cell phone; you've got your cell phone. . . . If anything comes up, I can always take a cab back home." Irene finally inhaled. "So, feel free to use the car, and please don't talk to me anymore about automatic doors and baggage because I will strangle you, and then they can arrest me for something I really did."

"OK, . . . sorry, sorry." Lauren slid over to take the driver's seat as Irene exited the car. "Call me if you need anything, Rene. And if it's early enough when you finish, we can go out and have a wild, crazy lunch. You always like to do that. I don't think you've eaten in days."

Irene handed Lauren the car keys through

the open window. "That sounds wonderful. But unless we can get a charter plane to New York, I refuse to sit in any restaurant in this town. I'm tired of being starred at, pointed to, and recorded."

"Ooooh, Rene, I don't think they would actually bug us, . . . do you?"

"I meant photographed. But no, I wouldn't put 'recording us' beyond them, . . . would you?"

Lauren couldn't argue with the fact that Irene had been treated in a ruthless fashion of late. She gave her sister a weak smile. "Hey sweetie, you look absolutely gorgeous. Just put on your 'do not disturb' sign. Don't let anyone get to you. Just keep remembering that you didn't do anything. They're wrong, and you will prevail. OK? I mean, unless it's against the law around these parts to be upset, and you had every reason to be upset. . . ."

Irene stood back. "I've got to go. You know they bill by the millisecond. I'll call you later. Love you."

"Love you, too." Lauren watched her sister disappear into the law offices. Her mind raced trying to figure if there was anything she could do to ease Irene's overwhelming pain. And then she thought of the statement her pastor had said at church:

"Isn't it funny how people always say, 'Well, I've tried everything, so all I can do now is pray.' " Lauren laughed. For so long prayer had been her last resort. But she believed in her heart that since prayer had become first and foremost for her, it was the sole reason her life had turned around so radically. Still, it was hard for Lauren to embrace the joy she was feeling when others she loved hurt so deeply. Yes, she was just going to keep praying, and then she'd pray some more — incessantly, in fact.

As Lauren proceeded across town and up a highway exit to her meeting, she reviewed some of the outrageous events that had happened to her family since moving to Centennial. Irene's soon-to-be ex-husband's unexpected death just days before her final divorce decree was to be signed paled next to the fact that Chelsea had been sexually abused by Ford, according to Chelsea. Suddenly a horrible thought flashed across Lauren's mind: What if this girl was making it up? No, that's not possible, Lauren checked herself. Why would anyone do such a thing? For attention? Teenage discontent? Anger? No, no. It all fit — the girl's behavior, her withdrawal from her mother, her major mood swings. And once Chelsea had heard about her stepfather's death, her response was so real. Lauren remembered looking into her niece's scared eyes. No, it was all real — a real nightmare.

As she approached the Grace Animal Shelter, Lauren was taken aback by the metamorphosis the building had undergone entirely due to the tender heart, financial support, and direction of Mrs. Strickland. What's more, to have a new job was a lifesaver since Lauren still remained the only breadwinner in her family for the time being.

Pulling her car to a stop before parking, Lauren thought back on the joy she felt having her parents living in the same house with Irene, Chelsea, Tucker, William, and Bingo; and her heart sang. Despite all the stress that was going on, she had high hopes, just like the song's refrain. Lauren had been so ecstatic lately that she'd even written a rap song for Pam to perform for the kids in the day care.

WWW.GOD.CALM

The peace of God transcends all understanding.
Lift up our holy hands in prayer (yeah)!

The very hairs of our heads are all num-
   bered.
God wants us unencumbered, not scared
   (oh yes).
Do good and share with one another
As brothers and sisters in Christ (go on)!
Resist the devil, and he'll flee,
And the truth will set us free (ah ha).

W-W-W dot G-O-D dot C-A-L-M
God dot . . . caaaaaaaaaalm.

The Word says if we believe, we'll receive
Whatever we ask in prayer (wow).
Faith is being sure of what we hope for;
So do what's right, just, and fair (cool).
All of you share in God's grace with me.
It's more blessed to give than receive (hee
   hee).
When I was in need, he saved me.
Yes, the Lord sets prisoners free (whoop-
   ee).

W-W-W dot G-O-D dot C-A-L-M
God dot . . . caaaaaaaaaalm.

Fight the good fight, finish the race.
Keep the faith in our righteous Judge
   (that's it).
Now these three remain — faith, hope,

and love;
But the greatest of these is love (amazing).
God is true, righteous, and holy.
In Jesus there's rest for my soul (uh huh).
Test the spirits, fear is not of the Lord.
God will wipe away all of our tears! (We
hear you.)

Lauren laughed out loud when she thought of the time all the gals in her circle of friends were dancing around in the diner trying to get a beat going for her rap song. Surprisingly, it wasn't Eleanor's or Stephanie's amazing vocal talents that owned the tune; rather the rendition evolved out of Pam's innate rhythm and hip style. And when she threw in the "handshake from the hood" at the end of her rap/dance, everyone went wild.

As an adult, Pam had spent most of her time in the projects working with the kids and families she hoped would be Hope School's first graduating class, so "cool" came second nature to the young woman. Even Tonya had to admit that Pam could outsnaz her on the dance floor, and that was saying something for a "white girl."

Mrs. Strickland stood triumphantly on the top step of the renovated building she so thoughtfully had named "Grace Animal Shelter" after the horse Lauren was forced to leave behind in California.

The petite lady leaned at a slight angle supported by her great-great-granddaddy's silver-tipped, carved ivory cane. Yes, this woman of means was ever elegant but always understated. Her antique jewelry dripped with history surrounding each stone and facet, family heirlooms that were subtly worn as an expression of respect for her heritage rather than badges of monetary trophies.

Lauren marveled at the time she had been blessed to spend with this amazing woman who shared, in few words, quite a bit of her life with her new protégé. Strickland's countenance and upbringing fascinated Lauren, who quickly realized she was in the company of a rare individual.

Although seventy, she had flawless skin and, Lauren was quick to note, fewer lines in her face than Lauren sported at ten-plus years her junior. Of course, Lauren gave herself the excuse that she was an outdoor girl, an equestrian, so the sun had taken its toll on her complexion. But it was beyond the wear-and-tear issue that was so unusual about Mrs. Strickland; there was something almost opaque about her, physically and spiritually. And although she did rely on the support of her cane due to a car accident years before, Lauren could only think at first that that mishap must have been the worst thing that ever happened to the woman. Lauren was to find out that that was not so.

Unlike so many self-centered individuals who are blessed from birth with wealth and position, Mrs. Strickland possessed a strong and unwavering spiritual lineage with a personal devotion to the Holy Trinity. And although her fairy-tale upbringing was compelling, what was truly unique about Mrs. Strickland was that she gave away more monetarily and emotionally than she ever kept for herself. And when she did, her spirit soared from the experience of being such a good steward of what she had always considered God's provision.

She did admit to Lauren that generosity was something she was taught from the time she was a little girl. Her parents would often tell her to go over and speak to some person in church who had just walked in and obviously felt uncomfortable or to approach an indigent on the street with a kind word and a donation.

Her elders never sent her on missions that carried a condescending tone. Emmy Strickland was simply encouraged from the time she was a beautiful young girl to think of others before herself and to break through her barrier of shyness for the sake of others. It was not uncommon to find Emmy at the tender age of ten holding a door for an elderly woman in a wheelchair at the grocery store, never looking at the woman's legs that remained frail and motionless in the chair but rather making eye contact as she took real interest in the person, even if for only a brief moment.

And so had gone the raising of Mrs. Strickland. Yes, private boarding schools. "The best education is required to do the most with your abilities as an ambassador of God," her family had told her as long as she could remember.

Lauren also learned some other details about Mrs. Strickland's background. She'd been married once yet was never blessed with children. Her husband had died early on, so Lauren realized that she too had suffered as most people do in the details of life despite her Pollyanna upbringing. And after so many afternoons of storytelling, Lauren wished she had had the opportunity to meet Mrs. Strickland's parents, who also had passed on not long before. Perhaps that's why these two women had become fast friends; they had both experienced lost loves, and they shared a common bond in the enjoyment of caring for the needs of God's creatures. Often they found themselves giggling over tea at the excitement they felt when it came to creating Grace Animal Shelter, a safe haven for furry friends of all shapes and sizes.

That winter morning shone brightly for these cohorts. They proudly stood on the steps of what used to be a home for the elderly. In fact, the building had originally been constructed by the Strickland family to aid the homeless in the Nashville area. Since then, they had moved that center to a bigger, medically equipped facility, and with the speed of lightning and a lot of financial backing, Mrs. Strickland was able to turn the original building into an animal shelter of top-notch quality.

As the two women stepped through the doors of the shelter, Lauren could almost hear the sounds of the kennels chock-full of cats, dogs, and, she suspected at times, a raccoon or two, some ducks or birds, and perhaps a squirrel every so often. Yes, they were about to be open for business for any animal that needed help, and their motto was to place every single critter either in a loving home or back out in the wild. And if that quest required rehabilitation, training, patience, and good old-fashioned match-making, so be it.

To that end, Mrs. Strickland had already acquired an extensive kennel just outside the city limits that encompassed twenty prime real estate acres with a beautiful barn and a riding ring to boot.

Lauren was in seventh heaven. And although she didn't want to take advantage of the situation, Lauren surely could see down the line opening a riding stable for the handicapped as well as the underprivileged. OK, "down the line" never set well with Lauren, so she'd already planted that seed in Mrs. Strickland's heart. Over lunch just last week, Lauren couldn't put a harness on her enthusiasm. "What a great program!" she bellowed over the noisy downtown restaurant. "Oooh, just imagine bringing some of the inner-city kids out into the fresh air to have an opportunity to pet some horses, tickle their whiskers, groom and tack them, and take a ride for the first time in their lives."

Lauren was sure she could find qualified trainers to run the entire facility. On a roll, she added that the program wouldn't be just for the handicapped, physically or mentally, but also for children who had been emotionally mistreated or just never had an opportunity to enjoy the simplest things of life. About that time Mrs. Strickland waved her cane at Lauren with a sweet smile to back it up.

Lauren moved off the edge of her seat. "Too much vision at one time, huh?" But before waiting for a response, she continued in her inimitable style. "OK, . . . sorry, sorry. I always put too many square holes in round baskets. I got it."

Mrs. Strickland was amused as well as impressed with Lauren as a godly woman, talented veterinarian, responsible mother, loving family member, and with her charming supply of childlike energy that simply would not be quenched. There definitely was a mutual admiration going on between this unlikely pair of formidable females.

Over the last several months, Pam was practically jumping out of her skin at the prospect of talking to Mrs. Strickland about Hope School. And although Lauren couldn't wait to introduce the two, it was Eleanor's suggestion that Pam and Lauren simmer down and let the generous lady conclude her work at the shelter. "Once up and runnin', maybe she'll consider movin' on to other needs."

Although solid advice, Eleanor felt like she was telling a couple of children to sit in the middle of FAO Schwarz amidst every toy imaginable without touching a single one until Christmas.

Eleanor had also suggested that Lauren ask if Mrs. Strickland would like to join them in their prayer group. Pumped as always, Lauren extended the invitation at their next meeting, but Mrs. Strickland's response was surprisingly reserved.

Lauren was concerned she had somehow insulted her friend, or overstepped a boundary, but Mrs. Strickland explained that she had been brought up in the Episcopal church in downtown Nashville and was rather formal in her worship. Nonetheless, Lauren and she agreed wholeheartedly that they both loved the same God, believed that Jesus is his Son, and believed in the Trinity — the Father, Son, and Holy Spirit.

Mrs. Strickland called the Holy Spirit the Holy Ghost, but Lauren didn't care because, at the end of the day, all that mattered was that they both were born-again believers. In fact, at that very meeting Mrs. Strickland spoke boldly, contrary to her usual quiet style, about the division in the body of Christ, while opening the door for Lauren to share how she'd come to her faith late in life.

Then suddenly Lauren's breath was taken away when Mrs. Strickland innocently mentioned that she happened to have met Lauren's ex-husband, Brian, at her church's early morning service last Sunday.

"Brian . . . my . . . Bri . . . my, my . . . you say church?" Lauren tried not to let her jaw drop in surprise while she wrestled with conflicting flashes of emotions.

Mrs. Strickland was curious about Lauren's reaction. "Darlin', I believe this is the first time I've ever seen you speechless. Brian seemed quite the charmer, I might add." She studied Lauren for a moment. "Are you on good terms?"

"Yes . . . Well, we . . . Of course . . . Why not try to be decent?" Lauren blubbered.

"Surely, . . . for your son's sake."

"Absolutely. In fact, that's why we're all here. Brian's company transferred him to Nashville, and I followed, not wanting Tucker far from his dad. It was a scary move at first since I had to leave my practice and friends. . . . But hey, look how well things turned out."

Lauren flashed an enthusiastic grin but still couldn't ignore the arrows of jealousy that instantly pierced her heart at the news about Brian. She remembered thinking, *Why didn't he ever attend church with me? . . . With our son! And why couldn't our marriage have been saved?* The same old questions that had been going around and around in her head for years. But then, thankfully, when she was able to take those thoughts captive and reroute them to a better spiritual place, albeit fleeting, she experienced a sense of relief and gratitude that Brian may well be coming more acquainted with his faith and his personal relationship with Jesus. *That's all that matters,* she told herself. After all, Brian was Tucker's father, and she had loved him once as a husband, and . . . Nope, she was not ready to finish that sentence.

Mrs. Strickland tapped Lauren on the shoulder with her cane, heralding the entrance of Bennington, the building inspector.

Mumbling, the man said something about having been around back with the contractor to check the water heater one last time. This rather terse individual seemed to dislike everyone. He did, however, enjoy making everyone jump through circus hoops to get the building up to code. Moreover, Bennington was not impressed in the least with who Mrs. Strickland was in terms of her standing in Nashville society or her clout with the city planning board. He was all about himself — one of those people who, given a minuscule amount of authority over others, punished them with his need to be in control.

Yes, Bennington loved to watch people squirm, but for some reason, today he seemed almost amiable. Maybe his wife had made him a good breakfast, or traffic had been easy, or better yet, he just couldn't find anything to complain about in the building structure. Whatever the reason, he signed off on every checkpoint, proclaiming that the animals could start arriving on Monday. And he *actually* said congratulations.

Lauren was convinced this man's final approval of the job wasn't inspired by good weather or good food. She believed it was all about the consistency of Mrs. Strickland, who never lost her temper, never lost her patience, always treated Bennington like a gentleman (which he was not), and showed him great respect without placating the man. She just wore him down with goodness. And at the end of the day, he walked away from his chance meeting with this lady a better man than when he walked in.

And Lauren knew, as sure as she was standing in the gleaming hall of the shelter next to this grand dame of a woman, that

Mrs. Strickland was truly a gift from God, as was her other circle of friends.

CHAPTER 6
-FILL IN THE BLANKS-

It was early afternoon before Irene and Lauren connected on their cell phones to set a rendezvous. While Irene waited outside on Main Street for her sister, she couldn't help but note how quaint the village's stores were and pristine their landscaping, picture perfect in fact. The film *Stepford Wives* popped into her mind as her attention was pulled away to the façade of an old-time movie theatre.

She was surprised at the list of up-and-coming films that read more like a lineup of features playing at a movie complex at a mall rather than this small-town theatre.

Show time 1:30 p.m., she noted, *The English Patient.* For an instant, she considered vanishing like some disobedient little girl, disappearing into the theatre for the afternoon while everyone searched for her in a panic. What prompted her mental rebellion was the notion that she might learn something from this movie, *The English Patient,* even though she didn't know a thing about its theme. She was simply drawn to the title since she recently felt she'd been cast in some Fellini movie shot in a mental ward.

Irene scanned down to the next list of entertainment: *Jerry McGuire.* Yes, she should watch a comedy of sorts, something fetching to lift her spirits. Then her eyes fell onto the next option, *People vs. Larry Flynt.* Instantly disgusted, Irene pondered how they would play such a slimy movie in this so-called "family community."

Next on the list of "Coming Soon" was *Sling Blade.* Oh, she could give that story line a run for its money. Actually, she could star in the sequel! "Get a grip," she told herself as her eyes gazed up and down the street. She hated that she was relegated to standing in public. Checking her watch, she noted that Lauren was thirty-six seconds late; and as each second went by, she became more and more tense. Thankfully, her BMW pulled up to the curb within moments, and Irene literally jumped in.

"Wow, what a day!!" Lauren was her usual effusive self. "We passed! We're opening on Monday. The first private shelter in the area, ever!" She pulled out into the street, making a bold U-turn. "So, how'd it go, Rene?"

Irene snatched a cigarette out of her purse and lit it with a vengeance, dragging on it so deeply Lauren thought smoke would come out of her sister's ears. "You're going to get a ticket if you keep playing stunt driver in the middle of town."

"I looked both ways. Come on, Rene, it was a broken yellow line. . . . So tell me how it went."

"It went swimmingly. I've decided I'm going to charge my lawyers for *my* time. We kept getting interrupted. Your 'cute' counselor from Nashville was on a conference call half the time, and the other one kept having to run over to court about various traffic violations. . . . Which is why I don't want you to make any more U-turns or I'll drive!"

"Sorry, Rene. . . . Go on."

Irene took another drag on her cigarette to calm herself before continuing. "Meanwhile, I'm sitting there like a bump on a log, and I couldn't even go out for a smoke. . . ." Sarcasm and frustration framed her every word. ". . . Heavens no! No one is allowed to see me smoking publicly in this sweet little town that plays smut on Main Street where my daughter could buy popcorn and a soda and learn how to pose for *Playboy* before her senior prom!" By the time Irene finished her sentence, she was one decibel short of screaming. For once Lauren decided to be silent.

Irene stared out the side window for a beat. "We're on the docket, . . ." Irene said flatly, ". . . yet again. Tomorrow, eight a.m. We need to 'circle the wagons' in the office first, and then we'll know by nine whether the hearing is actually going to happen."

"Oh that's super!" Lauren honked the horn in excitement.

"Stop that! You're just determined to get us pulled over, aren't you?" Irene hissed.

"No. I was just excited about tomorrow. We'll all be there with bells on, Rene."

"Well, 'bells on' should get some serious attention with the press."

Lauren giggled, "You're silly, Rene. Hey, you want to hear a story about a frog that reminds me of smoking?" Knowing that there was nothing she could do but listen, Irene puffed away on her cigarette and settled in for one of Lauren's tales.

"So, did you know that if you put a frog in a pot of water on the stove and slowly turn the heat up, the frog doesn't even realize it's about to boil to death. . . . His demise sneaks up on him."

Irene glared at her sister. "I thought you were a veterinarian. I thought you loved

132

animals. That's disgusting. . . . I don't get your point."

"My point is, smoking seems soothing like a nice warm bath at first; but before you know it, it will kill you. Don't forget, I used to smoke."

"And there's nothing worse than a reformed anything." Irene complained. "Besides, my 'slow demise' is already underway. I feel like I've been knocked out, and I haven't even gotten into the ring."

"You have to stop being so negative. You know what I always say, 'When can you throw in the towel?' . . ." They both answered in unison: ". . . When you're dead."

"Go, Rene! Now just get your hackles up, and you'll be fine. You know, there's a wonderful thing about 'God's Court of Appeals'. You can keep going back and back until you're *exonerated of everything*. It's called forgiveness. God wants us to put all our negative past in an unmarked grave."

"I think you should write a column, . . . 'Dear person from another planet.' Honestly, I've known you all my life, and I just don't know where you come up with all your . . . whatever it is you're saying."

"Hey remember, we haven't really talked that much in the last ten years." Lauren refused to take offense. "Think of me as the water off a duck's feather. . . ." With that, she was off on another tangent. ". . . Oh, speaking of a column, thanks for reminding me!" Suddenly, Lauren started to rifle through her purse, practically running a red light in the process.

"Column?"

"Writing, a column." Lauren continued to rummage, causing Irene to grab the steering wheel for safety.

"Stop it. You're going to kill us." Irene snatched the purse from Lauren. "What exactly are you looking for?"

"A letter. . . . I want you to read it first before I give it to Chelsea. I couldn't believe I found it when I was unpacking. It just seemed so appropriate for the moment. But of course, I wouldn't give it to her unless you gave me permission first. I wanted your opinion so . . ."

". . . You're babbling, Lauren." Finally Irene pulled out a tattered, handwritten letter and waved it in the air like a flag. "Is this it?"

"Yes. And you know what's amazing? Before I moved here, I threw just about everything out. Poof. I let all of it go up in smoke. I didn't want anything from my past, *especially* my old love letters. By the way,

Mrs. Strickland said that Brian was going to the Episcopal church in town! Can you believe that?"

"Whoa, wait a minute. Let's stick with one scenario at a time. What's in the letter?"

Lauren refocused. "Right. Well, it's about hope. I composed it and then copied it for her when she was about ten. Then I wrote a new note of encouragement to her now. I thought I'd throw the spaghetti against the wall and see what peels the paper. Go on, read it."

As Irene reviewed the letter, Lauren watched her out of the corner of her eye to see if she could discern Irene's reaction. And as stoic as her sister had been lately in regard to anything tender, there was something in the letter reminiscent of youthful enthusiasm that clearly touched Irene's heart:

Dear Chelsea, I came across this letter I copied for you a few years after I moved to California. I missed you so much, and now I'm thrilled we're all together again. I know these have been tough times, but they will get better. Promise. You are so loved! (Proverbs 23:18) "There is surely a future *hope* for you."

- Hope -

When I was a little girl, not only did I know I could fly, but I was absolutely positive that I was going to dance across the waves of my life surrounded by my best imagined friends — horses, cats, and dogs. They would lavish me with unconditional love. I, in turn, would spoil them forever, and in my heart of hearts, I knew I would even die for them. By the way, my parents didn't have a clue what made me tick or what inspired me. Nonetheless, I was determined to maintain my love affair with my four-legged friends.

Carefree and unencumbered, I was full of colorful dreams that held zero potential of not coming true or fading into gray. I was innocent of misgivings or disappointments. In short, I had blind faith that everything was possible — most of all, the visions I hoped for. Cool plan, but unfortunately not meant for me. From age six I begged my parents for a kitten, but when I finally succeeded in my quest, Kitty was run over shortly after her arrival. Then when I was twelve we moved to a new town where I never was accepted into the clique, and worst of all, getting a pony was not even up for discussion. . . . Have you ever had hope turn hopeless? I hope not.

Even in my pre-preteen years, I knew that some kids had it a lot easier than I did, and somehow I knew that some kids had it a lot harder. The problem was, my world was all I knew, and it suddenly didn't seem so rosy. Do you know what I mean?

Don't forget to let your feelings out. Write them down and leave them around where you can check out how you're doing. Checklist some, and then share the ones you can with people who care, especially when life doesn't seem fair. Don't hold anything in. . . . But when your thoughts are too private, God always hears you, so you won't have too many tears.

Love you sooooo much!

Auntie Lauren

Irene slowly folded the letter with great care. Looking out the window again, she extinguished her cigarette as she tried to keep from crying. Lauren allowed her the moment but then couldn't stand it any longer. "Well, what do you think? Should I give it to her?" Irene finally nodded. "Really?" Lauren bounced up and down in the driver's seat. "Yes!"

After a beat Irene confessed in a small voice, "Lauren, . . . it just hit me that I've been running out of hope." Then she sighed slightly. "I probably needed to read that more than Chelsea does!" Irene looked at her sister, her eyes welling again. "It's sweet, Lauren; it really is sweet. Yes, absolutely, you should give it to Chelsea."

Once Lauren picked up her truck and made sure Irene was alright, she decided to head back to the shelter to prepare for Monday's opening; she had a zillion things to do before her meeting at the diner with her circle of friends later that afternoon.

As for Irene, she'd convinced herself and Lauren that she just needed to get home, close her bedroom door and shades, and rest. But her private plan was to go home and have a big glass of wine or two, take a sleeping pill, and zonk out for a long nap. She was totally spent.

Once again the lawyers had grilled Irene all morning about the details of her arrest. With only one eyewitness to the events, Irene hoped that her sister's account of the evening would be consistent with hers. Still, Irene knew she remembered everything from *her* perspective, one of high anxiety

138

mixed with anger and a little too much to drink.

As far as Lauren's credibility on the witness stand, all were a bit concerned about her "style," as they cited her propensity to ramble on when she spoke. But aside from those and a few other stumbling blocks, the lawyers were encouraged that Irene's story would invoke great compassion *if* she took their advice in her testimony; she needed to tell the jury that she had just gotten off an airplane, that she wasn't driving the car because her sister had picked her up. Further, she was under undue stress because just two days prior she had heard the news concerning the death of her husband followed by the startling discovery of her daughter's sexual abuse. And that's where everything got muddied up in the defense case.

The problem that her representatives were having with Irene was that she flat out refused to allow them to bring the circumstances of Chelsea's sexual abuse into the public arena even though it was the reason Lauren and Irene ended up on the side of the highway that fateful night. Irene had become hysterical when her sister informed her of Chelsea's account of abuse at the hands of her stepfather. And yes, that latest news proved to be too much for Irene.

It was then that the policeman pulled up behind Irene's car that was parked on the embankment of the highway. The officer began by assessing the situation before him; one ranting out-of-control woman in the company of another who claimed to be her sister.

Everything from there escalated with alarming speed as the policeman treated Irene like a drunk driver, insisting she had been behind the wheel simply because the car was registered in her name. Lauren adamantly objected, stating that she, in fact, had been driving. She told the officer that her sister was simply upset about some personal matters. But what sent Irene over the top was when the officer tried to have her take a breathalyzer test, shoving a plastic object her way. Horrified and insulted, Irene smacked it out of his hand, a reaction she believed was perfectly warranted. The concept that she had assaulted a police officer was completely insane, Irene had told her lawyers. And when Irene refused to take the sobriety test, everything really went south in a matter of moments.

Irene was whisked away in the police car, arrested, arraigned, and spent the night in jail despite Lauren's fervent objections. And once she was bailed out at six the next morning by her sister, the whole press package of Irene had already made the local news and, by the end of the day, the national news.

Irene pulled up to the house on Linden and sat in the driveway for a minute to ponder her fate or, more importantly, her lack of control over her fate. "I never thought that a frog being executed in a pot of boiling water would almost sound appealing," she mumbled to herself. She was interrupted by tapping on her car; she whipped around to find her dad staring through the window.

"Come on out. Your mom and I have been waiting for you," Sam said in an uncharacteristically sweet tone.

"Thanks, Dad." She paused for a moment, noting that this was the first time in her memory that her parents had actually sought her out in an attempt to comfort her. No, their reaching out of late had not gone unnoticed by Irene or Lauren, for that matter. Maybe their parents were just mellowing in their senior years, but whatever it was, it felt good.

Irene slowly got out of the car, then gave her dad a long hug. And as she did, she checked herself. Had she been remiss in her appreciation of what everyone was doing for her? *Yes, . . . you better snap out of the sappy, self-centered pity party you've been on for months now,* she decided. And by the time their embrace broke, Irene seemed to have a new sense of resolve.

She wondered, as she climbed the front steps of the house with her dad's hand on the small of her back to steady her, *Is that all it takes? . . . A simple gesture of caring, a word of support, the recognition of pain, . . . love?*

As Irene and Sam ascended, her mother Margaret stood at the front door with her arms outstretched. Irene paused again. Was she having some sort of dream — a sweet dream but a dream nonetheless — because nothing felt familiar?

"Hello, darling," Margaret beamed. "How did everything go? I've got some dinner on if you want an early one. We can sit down and have a cocktail and catch up."

Irene nodded. "Court's on for tomorrow."

"Good. We'll be there."

"Thanks, Mom," she heard herself say. Although feeling rather numb at the moment, Irene had an instant wake-up call when William and Bingo sped through the kitchen and galloped toward the threesome. Sam quickly slammed the front door to avoid a pet escape, catching his pant leg in the process. He pointed Margaret and Irene toward their apartment.

"Let's go in here. No one's home. Tucker's with Brian." The two women headed off when Sam stumbled, unable to release his pants from the grips of the door. Trapped, he looked up for assistance, but Margaret and Irene were about to disappear into the apartment. As they went, Margaret put her arm around Irene's waist while her daughter lay her head ever so briefly on her mother's shoulder.

"Mom, Chelsea has her counseling this afternoon. Just don't let me get too maudlin, OK. I have to go pick her up in a little while."

"OK, darling. We'll watch the clock." Without looking back, Margaret called for her husband. "Come on, Sam. . . . And don't let William in."

Sam tugged on his trousers that finally released but not before receiving a full-face love lick and wash from William during the process. "Be right there . . . And don't you worry, Irene." Sam strained as he gathered himself up. "I'll pick up Chelsea. You just relax. Your mother made your favorite tonight . . . leg of lamb and strawberry tarts."

At the sound of the bell, school let out; and the students poured from the exit doors like bees from a hive.

Trace and Chelsea made their way to his Volkswagen, his arm ever attached about her shoulder. These two were definitely an item. And although some of the kids waved or nodded at them as they went, Chelsea and Trace seemed to be in a world of their own.

Once they entered the privacy of his car, the boy maneuvered into the stream of traffic heading out of the parking lot; Chelsea started rubbing his leg. "So you'll pick me up after practice, right? I'm supposed to have a double session with Pam, but I don't know if I can handle it. If practice goes too long, I'll just be waiting on the steps, OK?"

Trace nodded. "I'll be there. I'll cut out early and pick you up by five."

"Cool." Chelsea gave him one of her most seductive glances, something that had become normal fare between the two. "Do you have to go to the JV game tonight?"

"I'm supposed to . . ." Mesmerized by her, Trace almost ran into the car in front of him. "Are you sure your mom said it's OK for me to pick you up?"

"Yeah, I called after my last class, and she was home. I told her I wanted to go to the game with you. She sounded pretty wrecked. . . . So did my grandfather. He said he'd come get me, but I guess they figured he'd better not. Anyway, her court thing is up again in the morning, and it makes her crazy, so I think everyone was happy I had a ride. Course, I got the third degree and the long-version lecture on behaving myself . . . blah, blah, blah. Pretty soon, they'll all just have to leave us alone, right?"

She leaned over and blew in Trace's ear before he had a chance to answer. She knew exactly how to get to him. Trace stroked her hair in response, settling into the driver's seat. Yes, this girl made him feel like a real man.

"Mom's cool as long as I keep up the counseling thing with Pam. It's stupid, but at least everyone leaves me alone." Chelsea took some gum out of her book bag, offering some to Trace. Content she had everything under control, she leaned back for the ride.

Combing downtown Centennial for a dried-flower store to furnish the finishing touches on the reception area at the shelter, Lauren's truck passed Trace's VW just off Main. The chance drive-by went unnoticed by Lauren, who was in the middle of an intense phone conversation with Brian.

"Oh, . . . I was just concerned there might be traffic." Lauren fidgeted at the wheel. ". . . I know you're never late. I was just checking. And I won't be late picking Tuck up either. Seven sharp . . . because I'm always on time too."

Brian's Jeep moved along the open highway toward Centennial with only a single truck in view about a mile ahead. His hair whipped around his chiseled face as he sported the winter elements with all four of his windows locked down. This was a rugged man, much younger looking than his forty-eight years.

He yelled into his cell phone to be heard over the wind tunnel. "Lauren, what's up?"

"Nothing. I was just checking. Oh, by the way, I was talking to Mrs. Strickland . . ."

". . . Who?"

"Mrs. Strickland, . . . the lady who's backing the shelter. Apparently you met her last Sunday at her Episcopal church." Lauren slowed her words for emphasis over the *"Episcopal church."*

"So?"

"So, . . . since when are you going to church?"

Brian was amused by Lauren's interest. "I don't mean to be rude, but since when is what I do your business?"

Lauren was caught short, but she quickly reclaimed her composure. "Since you never went when we were married, and now you're going to church. Since you're Tucker's father, and I'm Tucker's mother. . . . And since I've always been interested in your eternal salvation. Since . . ."

Interrupting, Brian overrode Lauren's soon-to-become monologue. ". . . *Since* we're divorced, Lauren, it's really none of your business. But, if you must know, I've been going to church for a while now. And I've taken Tucker a couple of times on our weekends. He seems to like it although he always tells me that 'it's more cool at your church' because the kids dance in the aisles when everyone is singing before they have to go into Sunday school."

Lauren noted a bit of sarcasm in his voice. "And what's wrong with the children dancing in praise to the Lord?"

"It's fine, Lauren. It's not a problem; it's just not my style. You know I came from a Catholic background, so Mrs. Strickland's church feels mid-range to me as far as formality goes. Point is, it works for me, that's all."

"But you hated the Catholic ways. . . . You said everyone was a hypocrite. You said it was all based on fear of going to hell. You said . . ."

"That was then; this is now. I've made some friends here who took me to their church, and I liked it. And just imagine, they don't have rulers to hit my knuckles, and I'm enjoying my steak on Friday without guilt. So if it's OK with you, where I worship is my choice."

Lauren was flabbergasted. "Worship?" she whispered, mostly to herself. Then there was a long pause, a dead zone in the conversation.

Lauren spied a JoAnn's fabric and crafts decorating shop on her right and pulled in, while she tried to adopt a casual tone. "Hold on, Brian, I'm about to crash into a parking lot." The truth was she needed to gather her thoughts again. "Anyway, I'm in, I'm OK. I think that's great. I think that's super. I think that's good. Sometime we should chat about God, . . . you know."

"You never fail to confuse me. I thought going to church would make you happy. . . . Not that I'm doing it for you."

"No, no! You shouldn't do it for anybody.

You should do it for yourself. . . . That's good. Mrs. Strickland is a wonderful lady. Actually, we asked her into our prayer circle, but, well, obviously you all attend a bit more formal church. . . . But that's just super. Praise God! Anyway, I'm getting ready to open the shelter on Monday, so I'm getting out . . . of the car, that is."

"That's great, Lauren . . . The part about the shelter, not getting out of the car." Brian was sincerely pleased for her. "You've worked really hard."

Lauren melted at his words. Just the sound of a little caring from this man had always turned her into mush in about a second and a half.

"Thanks, Bri . . . Brian. OK, well, I'll see you later. Thanks for getting Tuck. . . . Right, bye-bye."

Lauren hung up without waiting for his response as she pulled into a handicapped parking space right in front of the store. Since she was in such a dither about her conversation with Brian, she didn't even notice where she had lighted, but the moment she started to get out of the car, she noticed the sign. Sighing, she got back in and reparked, all the while rerunning their conversation over and over in her mind.

"Friends . . . took me to church. . . . Worship?"

CHAPTER 7
-MOVING TARGETS-

The air that hung over the basketball court in the gymnasium was thick during practice that afternoon. A big varsity game was scheduled for Friday night, and Ham was relentless in his drive for excellence from his team.

More than a handful of parents always gathered around to watch practice along with clusters of flirtatious female students and girlfriends of the team members ready to protect their interests.

The Junior Varsity team hovered in the bleachers, taking in every move of the varsity team, before their own Thursday night game, hoping to pick up on a new move or be inspired by the notch-higher drills being played out before them.

Ham was ever on the move, up and down the court challenging the kids, calling out game plans and new strategies as he went. His muscles tensed with every pass, every jump shot, and every steal. No one could say that Ham asked any more of his players than he asked of himself. And at the end of every practice and every game, Ham was soaking wet and breathless as if he had actually played ball with his team. This man really cared — not just about winning but about pushing his kids to their limits set not against others, but rather against their own capabilities and talents.

Ham couldn't remember who had made the statement "It's not how you win the game; it's how you play it," but he had adopted that saying as one of his favorites because its sentiment rang so true to him.

Tonya was standing at the corner of the bleachers chatting with Eleanor, who had just entered the gym moments before. They were both about to head over to Norros for their prayer group, but as always, they had stopped by to give their men support.

Tonya watched Shooter move down the court like a panther. It always amazed her how incredibly graceful the six-foot-ten, two-hundred-fifty pounder was once he hit the boards and had a basketball in his hands. Yes, Shooter was liquid in his flow, and that was one of the things Tonya admired about him the most. At those times she especially loved being his woman.

Pride just oozed from her lips. "He's having a rockin' season, isn't he?" Tonya beamed.

Eleanor was duly impressed. "I hear the scouts are comin' tomorrow night."

"I have heard about that from Shooter for every waking, eating, talking, walking minute. It's all he's about. I think he's ready though. . . . Mmmm, he's looking gooooood!"

"Wrap him up and send him an invitation. I think he's on his way to the pros, Ms. Tonya." Eleanor applauded one of the boy's slam dunks.

Tonya's attention shifted to Trace on the court. He was one package of sinewy muscle and athleticism. Although not as tall or big as Shooter, both were vying for "star position" on the team. And yet Tonya wasn't the only one who had noticed that lately Trace wasn't such a potential threat to Shooter in terms of catching the scouts' eye.

She turned to Eleanor, lowering her voice so no one could hear. "Trace doesn't seem to be 'in his sneakers' as well as he's been. What's up?"

"Ms. High-heel Sneakers, Chelsea, I suspect." Eleanor studied Trace, clearly underwhelmed by his game.

Ham called a break, then jogged across the court to join the ladies. Instead of offering his wife a hug, he kissed her hand, maintaining a little distance between them. "A man in sweats dare not embrace such a damsel." Ham winked at Tonya, who giggled at his noble behavior while Eleanor glowed at the compliment.

"As long as this damsel does Sir Lance-a-laundry's bidding."

Ham was already heading back to his players. "Promises, promises. . . . It's a good thing I'm wash 'n' wear. . . . Easy maintenance. See you at home, Sweetheart. Have a wonderful meeting."

Oh my, Eleanor thought as she watched Ham spring back to action with the boys, *I surely am a blessed woman.*

About midway through their session, Pam handed Chelsea a soda out of the Styrofoam cooler under her desk centered in the small but organized church office. The room featured the worn, yet efficient desk behind which Pam sat, maintaining a posture of authority far beyond her years. Despite her professional demeanor, warmth exuded from her words and expressions, stamping her counseling style as effective yet compassionate.

Chelsea was curled up in a threadbare, overstuffed armchair, her feet tucked underneath her while her sneakers lay askew on the floor before her as per the rules. Pam had instructed Chelsea on their first session when the girl claimed the chair as if it were her own, "I don't ask you to leave your shoes at the door, but I do ask you to leave them on the floor when your feet go on *my* furniture. It may not be fancy digs, but it's the only chair I have."

Pam had thus far been successful in maintaining authority over Chelsea while mixing in a level of friendship. Still, this counselor was no pushover, and she was well aware that Chelsea was merely telling Pam what she thought she wanted to hear so Pam wouldn't probe into the girl's real and deeply hidden feelings.

Truth was, her ploy amused Pam. This teenager actually believed she was getting something over on everyone. Nonetheless, Pam did not make light of Chelsea's intellect or drive to be independent and secretive. Yes, she had gone through years of horror that included sexual abuse, but Chelsea was also not terribly interested in resolving any of those issues other than to say, "Ford is dead. I'm glad. He can't hurt me anymore, and I don't really want to think about it."

It seemed the only time Chelsea's eyes danced or her demeanor changed from sour to enthusiastic was when the subject of Trace came up. And Pam knew, although she believed Chelsea's affection for the boy was sincere, clearly he represented her "ticket to ride" out of her pain, transferring all her emotional needs and desires onto his broad yet immature shoulders.

Chelsea's acting out her painful past in her present was of most concern to Pam. Her biggest job was to keep the girl engaged in her healing process in an honest fashion. And to that end, Pam had not watered down the issue. She had come clean and clear with Chelsea about the fact that she was aware her coming for counseling was merely to please her family and hold conflict at bay.

Pam also let Chelsea know that if she was not even going to attempt to make real strides in her therapy, Pam would have to let Irene know that. And it was that point that finally got Chelsea's attention. So for approximately four weeks worth of sessions, the girl seemed focused and intent on working with Pam in a legitimate way. But then, for the last month, Chelsea's focus had waned; and Pam found herself, once again, receiving elusive answers along with an aloof attitude. Pam had to give Chelsea an A+ in creative sidestepping.

Pam's notes from her counseling sessions with Chelsea had become her lifeline for review since Chelsea had become such a challenge. Pam recognized that she was not educated as a therapist in terms of degrees. Her expertise in working with troubled kids came from years of firsthand experience on the streets.

There weren't too many situations where Pam hadn't been able to break through to help damaged, hurting kids. She knew that success rate was based on the love of Jesus; and she always relied completely on God's healing power when it came to physical, emotional, and spiritual matters. But in Chelsea's case Pam seemed to be speaking a different language from the girl, with no common denominator as a basis for the terms of reconciliation, forgiveness, and renewal on the heels of such damaging abuse.

It had been decided well before Irene took Chelsea to Pam that if a medically qualified psychiatrist was necessary for Chelsea's well-being, Irene would be quick to move her daughter from Pam's Christian counseling to more secular care for her daughter's psychological issues. Pam realized that Irene's attitude was totally understandable, given her personal experience of therapy over the years: "Medicate what hurts and analyze the past forever," was most often the game plan. Unfortunately, as Pam knew all too well, that kind of head therapy is not designed to connect with the heart and rarely translates into spiritual and emotional well-being and freedom for the patient even after years of analysis.

Pam had recently poured over her notes in review of Chelsea's treatment. Then she prayed for guidance. Yes, she had only been working with the girl for three months; and yet, although things appeared to be alright superficially, she knew deep down that Chelsea was not really interested in the kind of healing Pam had to offer from the Word of God.

She recalled talking with Chelsea early on about the fact that the opposite of love is not necessarily hate but indifference. Pam had offered the concept that perhaps Chelsea had grown up feeling unlovable or unheard, which made her particularly vulnerable to the kind of abuse she suffered. Pam was careful to explain the dynamic of a pedophile with a young girl when it came to her need of love and attention. She was also adamant that Chelsea recognize she was a victim. Although the girl was not tied up, locked in the closet, beaten, or forced during the sexual abuse, she had nonetheless been coerced by a pedophile; and that insidious behavior, although not her fault, could affect her ongoing life if not dealt with and healed.

Pam explained the importance of talking through Chelsea's past events so they would not taint her future. She stressed that what happens to young children when they are exposed to illicit, inappropriate affections from an adult when the youngsters are unable to assimilate those advances in a healthy fashion is devastating if left unresolved.

"Chelsea," Pam would lead her softly, "in some cases with children, you can see the bruises on their bodies. . . . You can actually see the evidence of physical abuse or mistreatment. But when we have bruises on our hearts, . . . they're just as real. And those are the kind of bruises so many of us suffer from but never deal with. These bruises end up robbing our lives on a daily basis because they're never recognized, understood, grieved, or healed."

Pam offered layers of ideas over the

months she'd worked with Chelsea: "Ignorance is not bliss. Simply pretending things didn't happen to you will not make them disappear, Chelsea. Every action and event in people's lives leaves a thumbprint on their soul. And if it's a negative imprint, it needs to be brought to light and exposed for what it is so the truth can be seen clearly. Only that truth can translate into a healthy life despite former offenses. Confusion actually is sustained by fear."

But Chelsea insisted she had no fear, that Ford was dead and she was safe. Conversely, Pam felt that Chelsea was driven by fear — fear of being alone, fear of not being loved. And the emotional neediness that made her such a target for a looming pedophile was engaging her now in her frantic desire to be loved by Trace, a desire to have a relationship where she was in control.

Pam tried to pull Chelsea out of her shell, explaining that when a moral code is broken, so are our hearts, and that healing must take place first before a pain can be replaced by other emotions. But every time she got close, Pam would hit a dead zone in Chelsea, a blank wall; and Pam had to confess, they were not really making any headway.

During intense prayer Pam asked the Lord to show her whether she was in over her head with this girl. Her conclusion rested on the fact that she and Chelsea did not share the common denominator of faith as a basis for healing, so Pam believed her hands were tied when it came to significantly impacting this damaged young lady.

Today's session seemed only to confirm Pam's deepest concerns. Chelsea offered increasingly superficial rationales concerning her feelings about everything unless it pertained to Trace. And although Pam tried to press that envelope, there was just so much Chelsea would reveal before she would withdraw once again. What she would talk about without reserve was the latest Garth Brooks hit or her aspirations after high school to become a country singing star. Of course, that all depended on where Trace was going to be.

". . . Yeah, so I don't know." Chelsea paused to blow a gigantic bubble, somehow managing not to explode the gum all over her face. "He says that he wants to go to college, but that depends on that stupid basketball scholarship. . . . So I don't know if that's going to happen. I hate that. . . . Whatever. All that matters is that we're going to be together and . . ."

Pam interrupted. ". . . Whatever? What does that mean, Chelsea? Don't you have any plans of your own? Do you have any desire to continue with school?"

Chelsea wiggled in her seat for a moment as she took a sip of her soda. "No. I desire to get out of this lame town and see the world, and I think that's what Trace wants to do too. Although he hasn't really *said* so, but . . . I'm pretty sure."

Pam studied her for a moment before making another stab at keeping her on track. "Chelsea, how much of your situation with Ford does Trace know about?"

Chelsea put her soda down and turned toward the window, a physical gesture she often made when she didn't like Pam's question. "I already told you. He knows about it. Everybody knows about it. We just don't talk about it."

Pam leaned across the desk. "Chelsea, why does everybody know about it unless you told them? I know your mom hasn't told anyone, or your aunt."

"Well, I figured everyone would just . . . They'd find out, OK! So I told a few people, and, you know, I figured we're on the front page of the newspapers, so . . . I don't know. Anyway, I don't care. I don't care that everybody knows. That man is dead, and so is what he did to me."

Pam proceeded with caution. "Do you

think it's possible you might have told people about it so they'd understand your pain? . . . Maybe they'd feel sympathy for you?"

Chelsea whipped around, suddenly exploding. Obviously Pam had hit a nerve. "What do you think? I'm trying to get attention? You think I'm making this up? You think I liked what happened? You keep telling me it's not my fault. . . . So it either is or it isn't. If it's not my fault, then who cares who knows?"

"Chelsea, why did you keep it a secret so long? Why couldn't you go to your mother?"

Chelsea laughed sarcastically. "My mother wouldn't have believed me. That man could have told her anything, and she would have believed him. No one would have believed me!"

"So now that he's dead, you think that they'll have to believe you because . . . ?"

Chelsea stood up. ". . . Because they have to believe me because it happened! I don't want to talk about it anymore. I just come here so people don't rag on me, but if you don't believe me . . ."

Pam stood. "Whoa, Chelsea, I *definitely* believe you. I'm not saying it didn't happen. I'm just trying to understand where you're putting it in your life right now."

By this time, Chelsea was full-out screaming. "I'm putting it out of my mind! I don't
want to think about it anymore, and I don't
want to talk about it anymore! I'm OK, I'm
happy, I'm fine! I'm going to be on my own
soon, and everything's OK. Just tell my
mother everything's fine."

"Why don't *you* tell her?" Pam said softly.
Chelsea started to pace the room. "How are
you and your mother doing?"

"Who knows? She's back and forth, here
and going to New York. . . . She's got her
own gig going. The court thing. It's all just
. . . never mind."

Pam urged her on. "No, it's all what? What
is it?"

"It's all stupid. It's stupid because everyone is just making fun of her. . . . And I
hate it. I hate *her.*"

"Chelsea, do you think your mother knew
what was going on with you and Ford?"

"I don't know. . . . She didn't do anything.
I knew she wouldn't believe me. Yes, I think
she knew."

Pam sat again as an invitation for the girl
to settle down, but Chelsea wasn't biting.
After a long beat, Pam offered, "Would it
be alright, Chelsea, if I spoke to your mom,
and maybe we could all talk together? I
think after this period of time it might be a

good thing if we could hear what your mom feels, what she's thinking, . . . what her experience was."

Chelsea took her seat again but only to put her sneakers on. She threw her words out like a Gatling gun. "I don't care what she thinks! I don't care what she went through! I don't care what happens in her stupid court case. . . . I just want her to leave me alone. We're getting along just fine. We're not arguing. She's letting me see Trace. . . . Everything's cool." She glared at Pam with raw panic and hatred. "And if you mess that up, I'm never coming back here!" And with that she stormed out of the room, leaving Pam to reconsider the fact that she might not be able to help the girl. And that broke Pam's heart.

The tail end of the lunch crowd at Norros was finally thinning out. All but two customers in the corner remained as Stephanie scurried about, cleaning the tables and preparing for the next onslaught of patrons due in just a few hours. She had a special spring to her step as she did every week when she was allowed to put the "Closed" sign on the diner's door.

Yes, this was the ladies' prayer meeting time, and one of Stephanie's stipulations when she applied for the waitress job was to work every shift from 6:30 a.m. to 9:30 p.m., be allowed Sunday off for worship, and one-half of one afternoon off a week to close the diner so the girls could come over and have some uninterrupted fellowship.

When this request was first brought up to Norro, the owner's greedy answer was, "No way." But Stephanie insisted he try her in the job for one week, no pay, so he could see that she'd handle all the shifts by herself instead of hiring two waitresses as he was expecting to do. After he saw how well she worked, she told him with a steady gaze that she was sure he'd accept her requests. And words were never so true. During that first week Stephanie had proven she could bring in more business and more turnover than Norro had ever experienced in the diner's ten years of existence.

Stephanie's circle of friends insisted she didn't have to make a stand about using the diner. They could meet at various locations every week, but Stephanie stood fast.

"I'll never be able to get to 'various locations' and get back to work on time. But more importantly, I need at least that level of respect from Norro, or I can't work for the warthog."

Her disdain for the man's personality was

well-founded; nonetheless, everyone knew that Stephanie's colorful array of nicknames for her boss were said in fun, not malice. And although it wasn't in Stephanie's nature to be mean, she was insistent about her time off. And so it had been for the last two years; the ladies' meeting place was secure at Norros every Thursday afternoon.

Stephanie was the first to admit that she could not do any of her fancy footwork in the diner without her great back-up team in the kitchen. At the helm was Bubba at the grill, who was nothing short of a gourmet chef adorned in a Southern short-order cook's chubby body and accent. His team was comprised of a dishwasher, Mario, and a prep boy, Lucas, and that was it.

To say that Stephanie and Bubba and his group were a well-oiled machine was an understatement. And yet Stephanie sensed that Norro was always lurking in the shadows somewhere, watching to see that no one was stealing an extra apple pie or a couple of bucks out of the till. He was untrusting and unappreciative of the quality of work that was going on in his diner, and that really annoyed Stephanie.

Still, she would always tell Trace when he complained about the hours his mother was putting in and how low her paycheck was,

"Son, that's why I take all the shifts, so I get all the tips. I'm doing just fine, and all is right in my particular world. You just wait and see; someday I'll have my own place. But until then I'm going to treat wherever I work as if it were my own, and I'm going to treat whoever I work for with respect . . . And now, if you'll excuse me, I'm going to take a bubble bath for about three hours and turn into a prune while I soothe my aching feet."

As the last two patrons were leaving the diner, Stephanie scanned the area with her eagle eye to make sure every napkin was in place; every fork setting was aligned; every glass, salt and pepper shaker, and bouquet of flowers were set just so before she took a deep sigh and grabbed herself a cup of coffee.

Enjoying a long moment of silence in a room constantly filled with chatter and clanging dishes, she suddenly felt the ugly presence of someone lurking in the building. Turning to check behind the counters, Stephanie gingerly entered the kitchen. "Bubba?" No answer. When she heard the little rattle and a noise on the far side of the refrigerator, she grabbed a broom from the closet and proceeded to check out the back area. Just as she was about to bring the broom down on the interloper, Norro stepped out of the shadows and squealed as he shoved something into his pocket. "Hold on now; it's me!"

She stepped back, taking a breath. "Oh, Mr. Norro, . . . I thought there was a big rat back here," she said with a touch of sarcasm.

"Yes, well I was just leaving. I have some meetings, and I'll be back later."

The lug of a man made his way through the back of the kitchen and out the door. As Stephanie watched him go, she swore she could see a grease spill trailing behind him. No, she did not like Norro, not even since he had finally stopped pursuing her for a date, which was an improvement over the "quick squeeze" he used to try and steal behind the soda machine. Only upon threats of death and Stephanie quitting her job did this lowlife control himself when it came to his lust for his waitress.

Stephanie observed Norro through the window as he got into his car, knowing right where he was going — to the E-Z Motel he owned, just off Main near the expressway, where his poker games and political shenanigans ran amuck. Yes, Stephanie knew somehow she was swimming in a tank with sharks when it came to her boss, but she figured as long as she acted like she had a bigger bite than he did, she'd be OK. Besides, in the recesses of her heart she knew if this man ever really got out of line, all she'd have to do is tell Trace, and he would make fast work of him. Actually, she shuddered at that thought, ruing the day her son would ever get in a tangle with such a lousy element of society.

Lauren was sitting cross-legged on the reception area floor in the middle of a semicircle comprised of her new employees: a heavyset black seventeen-year-old boy named Clive held hands with a nineteen-year-old redhead slip of a girl named Savannah. She held hands with Brenda, sixteen, also heavyset with bobbed, dark hair and a bad complexion in recovery, who held hands with Carla, twenty, the shelter's front receptionist.

Carla was a newly married, pretty blonde girl and the only ex-employee of Dr. Burke's mill. Her background was in kennel care and recovery, but Lauren decided to put her up front since she was as good with people as she was with hurting animals.

Carla held hands with Lauren on her left; and Lauren, finishing the circle, held Clive's right hand while concluding her prayer of covering. ". . . So we ask you, Father, because you say when two or more gather in your name, you promise to be present. And we come before you in all humility to request your hedge of protection around this shelter. I ask for favor for all who are involved . . . that we work as a team and be your Gideon's army for the animals. I ask for protection and covering for Mrs. Strickland and give thanksgiving for her generosity and heart that sings your praises. And for each and every one of these youngsters here, let them flourish and be of service, kind to the animals and kind to everyone who walks through these doors, no matter the circumstances. Let them have wisdom beyond their age and knowledge beyond their understanding, and allow us all to be good ambassadors for your glory. Father God, thank you for this blessing and your choreography of putting all of us together in your service. In Jesus' mighty name." And all said, "Amen."

The shelter's reception area looked like a bomb had exploded; it was a mess of fliers, papers, office supplies, and kennel equipment. Lauren told the kids that she had to leave, and they assured her that they would have everything in order, "spit and polished," by Monday. To that end, everyone was also aware that they'd be working tirelessly through the weekend. But despite the labor ahead, the excitement of this little troop was contagious.

Eleanor and Tonya were the first to arrive at Norros that afternoon. The cold, gray winter sky looked rather ominous as the wind was kicking up, promising a rare dusting of snow in the Nashville area.

As they entered the diner, they received what was always present — a sense of warmth and welcoming from Stephanie and a counter covered with goodies that the girls would partake in as they chatted before they began their actual prayer time. The fare Stephanie had prepared ranged from fruit and sugar-free Jell-o for those who happened to be on a diet cycle to muffins, doughnuts, chess pie, and an array of baked goodies for the others.

Ever since Eleanor had had her surgery, she wasn't in the mood for dieting, and like a little girl, she giggled with glee seeing the spread before her.

"Oh my," she trumpeted as she hugged Stephanie and then headed toward the dessert tray. "My favorites . . . *all of them.*"

Stephanie teased her, "Yes, Ms. Eleanor, the chess pie will land on your knee caps, the doughnut will end up on your upper arms, and the double chocolate ice cream pie will sit nicely on your hips."

Not to be dissuaded, Eleanor simply whipped around with her plate filled to the brim. "How delightful. Thank you so much for thinkin' of every part of me. I was actually hopin' they'd all gather force and end up on my chest!"

Stephanie and Tonya froze, fearful that Eleanor had been offended by Stephanie's joke. But when a luminous smile broke across her face, the girls realized she was just being the ol', wonderful Eleanor they hadn't seen in a while.

"Ha ha, gotcha!" She wagged her finger at her friends. "Now I'm goin' to be tellin' you and the other ladies today that I want this nonsense to stop about not talkin' about anythin' that has anythin' to do with anybody's body, fashion, figures, or sex."

On the word *sex,* Lauren and Pam entered. "Whoo, sex! Did I hear sex?" Lauren yelped. Pam, on the other hand, was a bit more conservative in her response, offering an embarrassed grin.

Eleanor was in a wild mood. "It was me. I said it! *Sex, sex, sex!* It's not a dirty word. Today we're going to break that curse of fear off me."

Lauren and Pam gathered around the goody bar as Eleanor continued with glowing enthusiasm. "I just happened to lay eyes on my handsome husband over at practice, and I've decided that I need to get over myself. There are little demons of fear, self-consciousness and self-pity in me, and we're going to send them all back to the pit of hell where they came from in the name of Jesus, today!"

"Go girl!" Now Pam was excited.

"I like your words, Ms. Eleanor, and we haven't even sat down yet. . . . Praise God!" Tonya proclaimed, holding up her piece of chess pie in triumph.

"Ms. Eleanor's likely on a sugar high, Lord, but keep it coming!" Stephanie clapped her hands.

Oh, yes, Eleanor was on a Holy Spirit roll. "We're going to come together in agreement and put on the armor of God, . . . and we're going to call forth mighty angels . . . because we're the head and not the tail, girls, in Jesus' name. Yes, Lord, we're going to claim victory over the enemy! I am through with his blanket of pain and insecurity I've been wrapped up in! I am a child of God. . . . We are sisters in the Lord. We have a blood covenant with the one and only God of the universe! And we are going to prevail. Oh,

Lord! What a day! This is the day the Lord has made and in it . . ."

And they all chimed in, ". . . We will be glad!" All five women whooped and hollered shamelessly, laughing and filling their plates with treats. A glorious moment was enjoyed by all as they headed to the back booth to graze on their mountains of food.

Lauren was barely discernable through all the treats stuffed in her mouth. "Eleanor, I think you're fit to be tried."

"You mean 'tied,' don't you?" Eleanor looked confused until Lauren blew some of her doughnut's powdered sugar in her face. Then she looked silly.

"Whatever floats your tugboat," Lauren beamed.

Before Eleanor could unravel Lauren's tangled phrases, Stephanie gave her a bear hug, almost flipping her plate over in the process. "Do you know how long we've waited for you to say those words?!"

"Amen and amen. Happy days are here again, Ms. Eleanor," Pam confirmed.

Tonya fell behind to the back of the ranks. "Boy, if I knew all it took to set Ms. Eleanor back on track was to see her husband in shorts, I would have brought basketball practice to her hospital room."

Eleanor rolled her eyes. "Oh, girlie, it's

not his saggy knees that get me. It's that man's heart and soul."

"Hey, Ham doesn't have 'saggy knees,'" Tonya was quick to point out.

Feigning an angry expression, Eleanor threw one back at the girl. "Are you lookin' at my husband's legs, little one?"

Tonya froze. "No, ma'am, I was just . . ."

". . . Got you again. Ha!" Eleanor roared, having way too much fun for her own good. "No, Ham doesn't have saggy knees, but I just like to say he does because it makes me feel better about *my* saggy knees. Remember, misery loves company. And also remember, don't ever tell a lady that her stockin's are wrinkled because . . ."

Everyone chimed in again, ". . . She might not be wearing any!"

Lauren fell into the big booth, barely balancing her pile of calories on her plate. "Oh, Eleanor, you're more fun than a barrel of money."

Eleanor slid in next to Lauren. "Well, you know what they say, . . . 'When the cat's away, the mice will multiply,' so I better be getting back to my husband."

"Oooh," Lauren was fascinated with the new turn of phrase. "I like that one, . . . but isn't it, 'When the cat's away, the mice will play'?"

Pam couldn't believe what she was hearing. Everyone in their group had become accustomed to Lauren's nutty sayings. "Are you serious? Talk about calling the kettle maroon. *You're* the one who gets everything mixed up."

"Ooooh, I like that 'maroon' one too. Hey, . . . I've got another one for y'all. . . ." Everyone hooted at Lauren's newfound Southern accent. "Shush now, sugar pies, and listen up. I came to this incredible conclusion driving over here today that God does not have perspiration on his upper lip about me." Lauren raised her hands in praise. "Hallelujah! Just think, girls, today's mighty oak is just yesterday's nut that fell on the ground."

Eleanor jabbed Lauren with her elbow. "You are insane."

"Oh goody, I was worried I was becoming too serious."

Stephanie teased, "Lauren, please put your mind at rest. I don't know about the 'mighty oak' part, but you are definitely the 'nut!' " By that time all five women had stuffed themselves into the booth and lined their food chain up in reach of the others. And then the sharing frenzy began.

Within just a matter of moments, the food on all five plates was devoured. Stephanie cleaned the table in a flash, then brought over some small glasses of grape juice and a bowl of crackers, placing them gingerly in the center of the table. And with that, the ladies settled down, and the mood shifted to one of reverence.

Clearing her throat, Eleanor began as the others bowed their heads. "Dear Lord, we come to you today with contrite hearts. As Paul says in your Word, we search ourselves before we receive Communion. Father God, we thank you for your Son Jesus who tells us to partake in these elements whenever we think of him. It says in your Word that the disciples took Communion daily in remembrance of Jesus' sacrifice on the cross and the shedding of his blood to cover all of our sins. What a privilege it is to sit at your table, Lord. To be your children. To have this fellowship in your name. We love you and give you all the praise and glory for every breath we take. In Jesus' name."

And as their glasses were emptied, and the meal taken in remembrance of their Lord and Savior, there was not a dry eye or a hardened heart in the room, which was now filled with the sweet and compelling presence of the Holy Spirit.

CHAPTER 8
-CONNECTING THE DOTS-

Lauren sat in her truck staring through the windshield, mesmerized by the falling snow before her.

She recalled the amazement she had felt in grade school when she learned that no two snowflakes were the same, each is as individual as one's fingerprints. How could that be, Lauren pondered. Thirty years later her friend Suz was able to put such an incomprehensible fact in perspective while leading her to the Lord; the two would sit on hay bales in Lauren's little barn for hours talking about God and reading his Word, the Bible.

Suz always shared her knowledge with the enthusiasm, patience, and humility of a loving friend. "Did you know that we can multiply the population of the world from the beginning of time on through the ages, add our most advanced technology into the mix, and still mankind cannot create a single grain of sand. Lauren, I had to stop trying to understand God. But I did finally figure out that I'll receive from God as much as I offer him in terms of my capacity, so I decided to be bold about my potential. . . . He loves that in his kids."

Lauren enjoyed Suz's take on God. She was also thankful he had sent her such an inspiring friend, mentor, and sister in Christ. And then she'd push her buddy off her hay bale for being such a smarty-pants.

Suz was used to Lauren's unruly behavior. "Go on, be a brat. . . . But you can't give what you don't have, so you better listen up. . . ."

". . . I know, I know. Because 'the Great Commission is a commandment, not a request.' "

"Very good. Now teach me how to make your secret pot roast, and we'll call it a day."

"When pigs fly airplanes! You may know the mysteries of the gospel, but my power is in my pot roast. . . ." Lauren broke into song, ". . . And you can't take that away from me. . . . Noooo, you can't take that away from me!"

For grown women these two had it going in the silly department.

Backlit from the streetlight, the glimmering

snow continued to fall while Lauren cherished a few more moments of silence. She thought about how excited she was with the new shelter and all the details in her life that were to be retooled in the near future.

Suddenly the honking of a horn brought her back to reality. She flipped on her windshield wipers to reveal Pam exiting her car while motioning Lauren to let her in the truck. She hoisted herself into the passenger's seat, her hair sprinkled with snow. Lauren thought she looked like the leading lady in a fairy tale.

"Thanks, I'm so glad I didn't miss you. I wanted to talk to you privately. Do you have a minute?"

"Sure. I'm just on my way to get Tucker, but . . ." Lauren checked her watch. ". . . I'm fine. What's up?"

"I want to ask your advice, and frankly, . . . I didn't want to bring this up in front of everyone, especially Stephanie. . . ."

Lauren had never heard Pam so disjointed and agitated. "What's wrong?"

"It's about Chelsea. I'm going to need to speak to Irene."

Lauren became alarmed, but Pam immediately soothed her. "No, please don't worry. It's nothing drastic. . . . It's just that I feel frustrated because I don't think I'm making any significant headway with her."

"How come?"

"Well, without divulging the privacy of her sessions, I believe Chelsea is only coming to counseling to keep peace at home. She's shown little real interest in the healing from her past experiences."

Lauren was confused. "But Chelsea's been acting so much better lately."

"*Acting* is the correct word for her behavior." Pam paused, internally redefining her ethical and professional limitations. "Lauren, I know you're aware of the abuse Chelsea suffered. And frankly, I'm so protective of the counselor/client privilege, I'm struggling with my boundaries here. But I must do what I think is best for Chelsea."

"Of course. I'm all ears. . . ." Lauren turned silly as she was prone to do whenever she was nervous. " 'All ears.' . . . I always thought that was such a ridiculous sentiment. I immediately imagine myself covered with ears . . . like measles or something. Wouldn't it be better just to say, 'I'm listening'? I think so. That way I wouldn't be sidetracked by stupid images and . . ." Lauren caught herself babbling. "Sorry, sorry . . . go on."

Pam cleared her voice. "Chelsea hasn't divulged anything to me that she hasn't told half the world, which is the only reason I'm talking to you at all. What concerns me is her behavior. That's why I have to confer with Irene. Chelsea is still a minor, and her mother must be kept up to speed. Mind you, we're not dealing with a girl who is in a depressed state. I don't believe there's an emergency here such as suicidal behavior or anything of that nature. . . . But Chelsea's dysfunction is evident, and the transference of her emotional needs must be my point of focus. Lauren, I don't believe I'm stepping out of line to say that we all know that she and Trace are very close, and that relation-ship is what concerns me."

"Oh, . . . oh wow. What can I do? How can I help?"

"This is such a sticky problem because all I can really ask you to do is to get me together with Irene. Set the stage. . . . If her mom wants you to be there when we talk, that's her prerogative. I have to let her know that I can't keep . . . I'm really . . . well . . . I don't . . ."

"What? What are you saying? Are you say-ing that you can't keep seeing Chelsea for therapy?"

"There's a problem I can't fix, Lauren. And I really need your prayers here. . . . Chelsea is not a believer. The girl is adamant about that fact; and from all that I can gather, Irene is not either. Not that it's for me to say that. . . ."

". . . Pam," Lauren grabbed her hand in a comforting gesture. ". . . It's OK. No, they're not. I wish they were, but no, you're right, neither is a believer."

Pam exhaled. "Alright then. . . . That's the problem I'm having. You know as well as I do that true reconciliation and forgiveness in areas of deep woundedness come from God's grace. I don't know how to proceed in such matters of the heart without God's Word as the foundation for emotional freedom. I've tried to tell Chelsea that if you have a Volkswagen and it breaks down, you take it to the Volkswagen dealer to fix it because they are best qualified to do the job. God designed us, and only he knows how to repair us if we'll allow him."

"What a great analogy, especially since Trace has a Volkswagen!" Pam stared at Lauren, unsure of her point. ". . . Of course," Lauren continued, "you're not trying to fix Trace or his car. . . . See, I was just pointing out the Volkswagen connection. . . . Never mind. Did Chelsea get your point?"

"No. She just said she wasn't broken, and if she were, she'd be a Porsche."

Lauren shook her head. "Oh, . . . well, I thought you made a great point even if Chelsea didn't get it. Besides, God says when we speak in the spirit to those not in the spirit, it's gibberish to them. Pam, it's not your shortcoming. I'm living in a household of nonbelievers, . . . other than Tuck, and he's just a wee one. You can imagine why I'm hooked on our prayer meetings. I feel like I need a B^{12} shot of God coming from a background of Draino. And God has given me such cool sisters in Christ. Golly, even Mrs. Strickland has such a profound faith. But at home, it's often so filled with tension. It's like I'm all dressed up with no place to play."

Suddenly and uncharacteristically, Pam's eyes welled with tears. Surprised, Lauren sat back. "Oh, . . . I'm so sorry. This is not about me. You're so frustrated. Sorry, I can see that. . . . Don't cry."

But Pam was already past the point of no return, and the floodgates opened wide. She sputtered, "I'm just as tenderhearted as any of you, you know. I just haven't cried much since I lost my brother to suicide. . . . I couldn't stop it. I couldn't help him because I didn't know how! So I tried to learn. I asked Jesus to heal me so I could help others. . . . And he did. And he has. But not

185

this time. I'm supposed to be strong, be a rock . . . but I'm having my own struggles. I'm feeling so useless. I can't seem to help Chelsea, and I can't get the Hope School off the ground. I just don't understand. It's God's school. He told me to put it together, so why are all the doors closed? And why doesn't the Holy Spirit soften Chelsea's heart so I can tell her how much God loves her? If God doesn't want to lose her, he has to do something. If he wants reconciliation in this town, he has to do something. I can't do it myself. . . . I can't do anything by myself!"

Lauren knew exactly where her friend was, and her heart ached for Pam in all her frustration. Lauren chose her words carefully. "Pam, I have to tell myself 'I can't do anything by myself' on a daily basis. And when it comes to Rene, Chelsea, and my mom and dad, I can't save them. . . . I can't save an anthill. I get so frustrated. I think I must be doing something wrong or saying something wrong, or else my whole family would see the truth. But that's just my pride. You and I both know that we're supposed to plant the seed, but only God changes hearts. . . . Listen, the time that you've spent with Chelsea has made an enormous difference because there hasn't been the whiplash of depression as there usually is in cases like hers, right? That's a giant blessing."

Pam pulled some paper napkins out of the side pocket of the truck and blew her nose until her face turned purple. Lauren thought it best to give her a moment of silence since she seemed almost disoriented from the aftermath of her emotional catharsis.

Finally Pam came up for air, speaking in a small voice. "Thanks for your support . . . really. I've never felt so useless. See, I really believe Chelsea is about to make some classic mistakes most sexually abused girls make. . . . And she's going to make them with Trace. And I'm not sure what to say to Stephanie, or if I should say anything at all. Steph is spiritually sharp as a tack, and as a mother I'm sure she already knows what's going on with her son."

"I'm sure you're right."

Pam sat up in a panic. "Right about what? Stephanie or Chelsea? You have no idea what an awful time I'm having in our prayer circle . . . knowing what I know and feeling that I can't say what I need to say. I've got to remove myself from this. I feel like a lawyer with a conflict of interest, bound by ethical rules that disallow me to act on my instincts. I'm the one who needs counsel and prayer. I'm floundering, and my biggest problem is, I can't even think of where to advise Irene to send Chelsea. I don't believe she needs to be on medication. No, absolutely not. She's not acting out that kind of behavior, and there are so many teens who become suicidal from taking antidepressants. It scares the socks off of me. I have to explain all this to Irene. And when I do, I'm going to have one furious teenage girl on my hands. . . . So that's what I wanted to ask you before I lost it."

Pam paused again, embarrassed by her vulnerability. Still, she knew she could trust Lauren. "How do you think Irene will react to all of this?"

Lauren took her time before answering. "My sister is at the end of her tether. I'm just praying that her bogus court thing gets underway and is cleared up soon because she needs to go on with her life. She's torn in twenty different directions, and she's worried sick about Chelsea. It's just a horrible time for Rene." Lauren let her words settle. "And I think I'm going to have to ask you just to hang in there a little longer, Pam. At least for the next couple of days to see what happens with the court situation. Then I'll put you together with Irene, and she'll hear what you have to say. I'm sure she'll listen, . . . or I'll punch her."

Pam was grateful for the small reprieve of Lauren's humor and the big bear hug her friend surrounded her with. "When are you supposed to see Chelsea again?"

"Not until Monday."

"OK, then we have a little time. We can pray about it, talk about it. I can meet with you, gosh, over the weekend."

"Lauren, you've got the shelter to open and . . ."

". . . And I don't have anything more important to do than this. You've been there for me, . . . for everyone. So it's your turn."

Pam finally nodded.

"Just give me a call, and we'll set some time." Lauren checked her watch again. "Oops. I have to go get Tuck. . . . I can't let Brian win the 'late game.' And don't worry, Pam, you've been spectacular. You didn't let anybody down. . . . So, are you OK?" Pam just sat there for a moment. "Come on, honestly."

"Yes, I'm alright, honest."

"Good. Oh, and aren't you just out of your skin about Eleanor's breakthrough today?" Flailing her arms about, Lauren looked like a cheerleader.

Pam was visibly relaxing. "Yes, awesome.

And Mrs. Strickland with the shelter, praise God!"

"Now that lady is double awesome on a stick!" Lauren squealed.

Lauren's enthusiasm was contagious. "You really are a nut, you know that?" Pam yelled above her friend's yelps.

"I know. Isn't God cool?"

Buttoning her coat, Pam stepped out of the truck. "Yup, and so are you. Thanks for your help. . . . Oh, what time is court tomorrow?"

"Eight-thirty."

"Got it. And we're circling the building?"

"Absolutely. Do you know that Irene called Jeremiah from the Bible a bullfrog?"

Snowflakes were piling up on top of Pam's hair. "She called Jeremiah a what?"

"Oh, never mind. It's just a thing my sister and I . . . Never mind. OK, so see you tomorrow at the courthouse. By the way, you look like a caramel sundae with whipped cream on top."

"What?"

"Never mind." Lauren gave her a thumbs-up, then waited until Pam got into her station wagon before she put her truck in gear and headed off to get her son.

Grabbing her cell to check for messages,

Lauren put the phone on speed dial. The name "Suz" came up on the screen. Lauren listened as the phone rang, her mind buzzing from her conversation with Pam. To her disappointment, she only reached an answering machine.

"Hey Suz, it's me, the 'wandering gnome.' Sorry I missed your call the other day. I've just been running like a loon, . . . a 'loony gnome.' Ha! Everything's moving along here. The shelter got passed today. We're going to be opening on Monday! Can you see me smiling through the phone? . . . And Irene has another shot at court tomorrow, so pray, pray, pray. You're not going to believe this one. Brian's actually attending an Episcopal church in Nashville. Say, I'm happy about that. I need to talk to you. All kinds of weird emotions are floating about, and I'm craving a Suz fix. Well, I won't leave you a nine-hour message. We need prayer all around, and I hope everything is fabulous with you. . . . By the way, I just came back from our prayer meeting, which was awesome as usual, and I'm going to pick up Tuck at 'Father Brian's.' I'll give our boy a knucklehead for you and talk to you soon, Sweetie. Love you. Oh, it's 'Lauren the loon' in case you haven't guessed."

Lauren waited impatiently at a stoplight

at the end of a big line of traffic heading to the left toward the high school where the basketball game was about to start. The balance of traffic was heading toward the Kroger grocery store on the right. Lauren noted that Tennesseans did not travel well in inclement weather. If there is even a hint of a fleck of snow, everyone rushes to their local food chain and cleans the place out as if all were about to hole up for the entire winter.

The welcome sign at the front of Greystone High School read:

God is in the business of restoring stolen property.
Ham

Past the school at the back of the parking lot, there stood a huge evergreen tree with branches that bowed majestically to the ground. This natural refuge had become Trace and Chelsea's favorite place to park since the tree shielded the car from the outside world. There the kids listened to music, talked for hours, and shared their dreams and schemes.

Over the months since they'd met, the temperature outside had dropped so significantly, the couple was relegated to a running engine for heat; the smoke from the car's exhaust had blown their cover on several occasions.

The snow had all but stopped, and the parking lot was jammed with basketball enthusiasts streaming into the high school to watch the game. Chelsea and Trace procrastinated until the last second before starting to follow suit.

"We have to go. Ham's got his eye out for me. He didn't like me leaving early to pick you up, and he told me I better be there tonight."

Chelsea displayed her classic pout that instantly appeared whenever she didn't get her way. Staring out of the window, she responded, "I was thinking that we could go to the mall and grab a burger, . . . you know, bring it back to the car to eat. For once my mom's not on my case."

She leaned over to kiss Trace, a move that always worked to diffuse whatever ideas he had that didn't go along with her plans. But this time, after enjoying her pleasures for a moment, Trace reluctantly pushed away. "Really Chels, I gotta go. If I don't show up, I think Ham will have me for dinner."

"What's the big deal? He's not your

father. . . . He can't make you go to the game. You're not even playing 'til tomorrow night. You're just going to be watching, right?"

"Yeah, but we're supposed to be there to support our second team. I don't know, he just wants me there, and I gotta go, Chels."

"Fine." She pouted again as she buttoned up her coat. "I just thought that we could have a good time. We're always studying at school, or your mom's spying on us. . . . Or my mom is *following* us. . . . We never get time alone."

"Yeah, and I'm not so sure my mom won't be there tonight either. I got grilled this morning about our spending too much time alone."

"Well, I guess it's all just going to go down, isn't it?"

"Down what?"

"You're eighteen at Christmas break, right?"

"Yeah."

"So after that, your mom can't say anything, right?"

"She's always going to say something. She's my mom. Besides, this morning she was talking about college and all."

"That's not her decision. She doesn't own you. She can't tell you what to do!"

"What are you so upset about, Chelsea? I mean, she's right. I haven't been concentrating on my game. The scouts are coming tomorrow, and I got to get some sleep tonight. So I can't go to the mall and hang out later. You just need to chill a little bit."

That was definitely the wrong thing to say to this girl. Chelsea stormed out of the car and headed toward the high school.

"Hey, wait a minute! Hold up!" Trace yelled after her, but she stayed her course. He locked his doors and chased after her, grabbing her arm. She pulled away. "What's the matter with you?"

"Nothing, I just had a hard time in counseling. It's all . . . stupid and doesn't mean anything. The only thing that means anything is the time I can spend with you, and then I have to deal with your mother and stupid basketball."

Now that was something she shouldn't have said to him. Trace stepped back. "Basketball isn't stupid. It's my future."

"I thought your future was with me. Isn't that what you said that night?"

"Chelsea, look . . ."

". . . Or didn't you mean what you said?"

"Yeah, I meant what I said, but that doesn't mean I don't have stuff I have to take care of."

"But you said you'd take care of me."

"I will take care of you. This is getting . . ."

". . . Getting what? Hey, if you don't want me around, just say so."

"No, Chelsea, I just want to go in and watch the game, OK? I don't know what's wrong with you, and I'm sorry you're upset, but I'm going in to see the game. Do you want to come with me?"

The girl exploded. "No, don't touch me! I don't want to go with you! I don't want to go with anybody! I don't care!" She reeled around and ran toward the street, disappearing into the throngs of kids.

Trace yelled after her until everybody started staring at him, so he decided to wait there and see if she'd come back. She didn't.

A few minutes later Tonya and Eleanor passed Trace in the parking lot. They couldn't help but notice that he was on edge, scanning the crowds as he shifted his weight back and forth in nervous tension. Eleanor slowed Tonya down to let her know that she was going back to chat with Trace for a moment and she'd meet her inside. Then Tonya was off, anxious to hook up with Shooter, who was bringing their son Bobbie to the game.

Shooter had already made up his mind

that no matter how far he got in the pros, his son was going to surpass him as an athlete. Yes, he was determined to teach his boy how to play ball better than anyone had ever played before in the history of the game. Tonya teased Shooter that with that kind of pressure their son would probably end up a ballet dancer. Shooter was not amused.

Eleanor approached Trace from behind. When she called out his name, he jumped a foot in the air and whirled around, obviously expecting to see someone else. Disappointment was written on his face.

"Yes, ma'am."

"How are you?"

"Just fine, ma'am."

"Are you going into the game? I know Ham is hopin' you'd be there this evenin'."

"Yes, ma'am. I'll be there."

"Well, do you want to walk in together?"

"No, ma'am, I'm just waiting for someone."

Eleanor gave him a look. "Chelsea?"

"Yes, ma'am. She'll be right along, and then we'll go in."

Eleanor tried to give him an encouraging smile, but his behavior was so strange, she was cautious. "Are you sure you're OK?"

"Yes, ma'am, I'm just waiting. I'll be there."

"Alright." Eleanor hesitated another moment, then headed toward the gymnasium.

Ten minutes later Chelsea still was nowhere to be found. As the crowds thinned, Trace could hear from the parking lot that the game had begun. He checked his cell phone one more time; he must have called her ten times already and left messages, but she hadn't called back. By now he was red-hot mad and decided he'd go to the game by himself.

When Eleanor entered the gym, Tonya was already settled on the bleachers with Shooter and her son. The boy was talking a mile a minute, barely giving his parents a chance to say hello. Nothing new there, Eleanor noted. And as she watched them, she thought what a sweet picture it was to see the three together. Shooter put his massive arm around Tonya, and Eleanor said a little prayer for the boy. Then she asked God to have the scouts attending tomorrow's game notice both top players of the Greystone team — Shooter and Trace — because so much of the boys' futures relied on the scouts' opinions of their athletic prowess.

Then she wondered what it would be like

to have so much of her life dependent on someone else's opinion of her. Actually, she shuddered at the thought.

Ham was on the sideline when Eleanor approached. As she moved through the crowd, she thought about the decision she'd made that afternoon concerning her husband and how excited she was. She felt like a girl, all wiggly inside — she was actually shaking in anticipation. And once again she became profoundly thankful for the grace of God in her life and for the wonderful man she now stood before.

She jabbed him in the stomach playfully. "Hey, Ham-man."

He looked at her strangely. "Ham-man?"

Eleanor blushed. "I'm just bein' silly. Listen, I'm goin' to go home. . . . I'm a little tired, and I want to relax. That alright?"

Ham was concerned. This was not like his Eleanor; she always made the games. In fact, over the years Eleanor had only missed three to his recollection, and that was when she was in the hospital recovering from her operation.

"Sweetheart, what's wrong?"

"I'm fine. I told you. I'm just a little tired. We had an intense prayer meetin', and I'm . . . I'll just see you at home. Don't worry."

"But we were going to go out after the game for dinner."

"Ham, I'll pull somethin' together. Just come on home after the game, OK? I'm fine, really."

He looked at her, squinting his eyes as if he had X-ray vision. "Eleanor Grace, what's going on? I'm not letting you leave here until I'm sure only good is running around that mind of yours."

A little frustrated, she pulled her husband to the side so no one could overhear. "You are such a stubborn man! Why don't you just let your woman get ready for you?"

Her eyes had that "gleam" back, that look that he hadn't seen in months. He just took her in for a moment, making sure he was reading her correctly. "You mean, 'get ready' as in *ready?* Oh my. Yes, so . . . I'm so sorry to have kept you, my love. Off you go." Ham seemed visibly to stand several inches taller at the mere thought of his impending good fortune. "Would you like me to pick anything up before I get home?"

Eleanor simply smiled at him. "Just bring yourself. I'll have your bath drawn, dinner on the table, . . . and I'll be waitin'."

All Ham could do was grin, a smile that was so wide his cheeks started to ache. Eleanor ran her hand softly along his face, giving him a peck on the mouth.

"Hamilton, stop grinnin'," she whispered. "Everyone will start starin'."

With that she turned and sashayed away, giving him one last glance over her shoulder. And he thought, *Oh my, what a blessed man I am.*

Stephanie was scanning the hometown bleachers for her son when she noticed Trace finally walk in the gym's side door. She made a beeline to join him, curious about the expression on his face. He had a look of worry that she had hoped he would sidestep for many years to come. But despite her wishes, there it was, plain as day; and she knew it had to have something to do with Chelsea.

"Hey, Son."

Trace greeted his mother with a quick kiss on the cheek. She was thrilled her boy had never given up that show of respect once he hit his teens. Yes, Trace had always been uncomplicated about his affection for his mother, even in the presence of his peers. Conversely, she had noticed that all the other boys his age hemmed and hawed around their fathers and mothers, unsure of whether the simplest sign of emotion might dispel the idea that they were soon to be independent.

"How come you're late?"

"I was just waiting for Chelsea, but I guess she can't make it."

"Oh, that's too bad. Were you supposed to meet her here?"

"Yeah, . . . but we didn't really set a time. She'll probably show up in a while." There was an awkward pause. "You want to sit down, Mom? Let's grab a seat before they're all gone." He pointed toward a couple of places that were still open near Shooter, Tonya, and Bobbie.

"Lead on."

Stephanie had never seen her son so fidgety but decided to let the issue ride for the moment. As they made their way over to the bleachers, Stephanie caught Ham's attention with a quick wave, sure to make him aware that her son was present at the game.

Her overseeing that situation was birthed on the heels of a brief conversation she and Ham had earlier that evening about Trace's lack of concentration on the game. They agreed that Chelsea was the source of the boy's split focus. They also agreed on the game plan to tread carefully as parent and couch so as not to push Trace away instead of toward his former goals. After all, it was his life. They could advise him, but if he only had heart for the girl and not for the game anymore, nagging him would not make a difference.

Chelsea had managed to corner one of the few girlfriends she'd made in Centennial since she'd arrived and beg her for a ride home. Finally the girl gave in, announcing that Chelsea owed her a pizza with extra cheese for her trouble. And after making one quick stop on the way, she took Chelsea home.

Irene had already gone to her room when Chelsea arrived, so the girl quickly checked in with her grandparents and then knocked on her mom's door to tell her she was home. Irene was in the midst of frantically going through her closet looking for her next appropriate outfit to wear to court in the morning, so Chelsea was off the hook, happily making her way to her own bedroom.

When her door was securely locked and the window shades drawn shut, Chelsea paced her room for a while, then headed into the bathroom with her school backpack. Within minutes she returned to the bedroom where she paced some more before heading back into the bathroom.

The girl stood frozen over the sink, her hands covering her eyes. Then, ever so slowly, she peeked through her fingers at the EPT test balanced precariously on the counter's edge. When she saw the results of the test, her hands dropped; Chelsea met her own eyes in the mirror. Yes, she was pregnant. She didn't believe it could really be true at first, but now she knew. She knew for sure. Panic mixed with excitement flooded her mind, but eventually a smile crossed her lips, an expression with a meaning that was hard for even her to read. She finally stepped away from her image in the bathroom mirror, picked up her cell phone, and exited the room.

Trace jumped up at the sound of the ring. Practically falling over his own feet, he announced to his mother that he'd be right back. When he got to a relatively quiet corner of the gym, he answered the persistent caller.

"Chelsea, where are you?"

"I'm home. I caught a ride with Andrea. Look, . . . I'm sorry I got mad."

"Chels, you've been gone for over an hour. You didn't answer my phone calls. . . . Don't ever do that to me again!"

Another smile crept across her face. "I'm

sorry. . . . Did I worry you?"

"Yes, you worried me! You can't just go running off like that. . . . You're acting really weird, you know."

"I told you, I was upset about counseling. It won't happen again, promise. I just wanted to let you know that I'm alright. I checked in with my mom, and she's cool, so enjoy your game. You're going to pick me up in the morning, right?"

"Yeah, . . . of course."

"OK. Well then, I'll see you in the morning. And Trace . . ."

"Yeah?"

"I'm really sorry. I didn't mean to make you worry."

It was the first time since their argument began that his shoulders relaxed slightly. "That's OK. So I'll see you in the morning."

"Yeah, . . . night."

He pressed his phone to off, then looked around to make sure no one had overheard him. And as he walked back to the bleachers, it finally computed how seriously worried he had been about his girl.

CHAPTER 9
-REQUEST SLIPS-

Irene calculated that she had slept exactly nineteen minutes and twenty-six seconds during the entire eight hours she had laid in bed, and now she was so revved up, she resented the mere idea that her alarm was about to go off heralding six a.m. on a Friday in November.

She slammed the buzzer down on the clock with a vengeance before it had a chance to infringe on her private time, lying there for another moment to review the events of her up-and-coming day one more time. She tried to soothe her weary mind about her sleepless night, telling herself it was better than participating in the mish-mash of nightmares she always had prior to the tension of her potential court date.

One of the most annoying facts of her never-ending legal process was that every time she went in to green-light her trial, she had to review everything she would say, how she would say it, how she thought the trial would go in general, and worst of all, what would be the possible outcome. If guilty, would there be jail time, fines, a police record? If she was exonerated, would that fact get covered in the national news as relentlessly as her arrest and pretrial news had been? And what would the press say? Would they report an honest account, or would they slander and slaughter the truth for juicy headlines as they had since her entire fiasco had begun?

A modicum of solace was to be found in the fact that once all the buzz about Irene's husband's death had blown over, and the details of his affair had been kept under wraps for the most part, Ford Williams's estate hearings were sealed and closed to the public. Irene never imagined her trips to New York City to fight for her fair share of Ford's estate would actually feel like a vacation next to the frustration of Centennial's small-town politics. But it did. Frankly, the term "get out of town" had become her favorite saying over the last several months.

A pristine outfit was carefully laid out on the chaise lounge. Every button was fastened, and all accessories were in place as if

Irene were actually wearing the suit —
minus her body.

She stood over her empty clothes, considering what a fantastic book cover they
would make. She actually thought of pulling out her camera and taking a snapshot of
her outfit, pearls and all, then art-directing
it onto the front page of the imaginary
autobiography of Irene Patterson Williams
appropriately titled, *The Disappearing
Woman.*

"Uh, no, . . ." Irene considered. ". . . I'm
beginning to think like my sister."

Lauren was on her knees in the middle of
her porch now enclosed for protection
against the winter elements. Her prayers
never failed to be powerful and focused, but
this morning they were pleading on behalf
of Irene.

The porch was her prayer place where
every morning she could watch the perim-
eter of her yard change seasons. She felt at
home surrounded by the woods, by nature,
by God's glory. And that was something
Lauren never failed to note — the magnifi-
cence of God's creations. The birds that
moved through trees, the squirrels, the rab-
bits, and of course, her two wonderful pets,
Bingo kitty and William the dog, who both

had learned long ago that when Lauren was praying, they need not be playing.

She had arisen especially early this day for her communion with her Lord. Still, before she knew it, it was time to get Tucker up for his morning rituals, ready him for school, and smother him with her daily dose of hugs and kisses.

The plan was for everyone to meet in Lauren's kitchen and all have breakfast together before heading off for Irene's court date. Lauren was thrilled that her parents had been so supportive of her sister, and she thought, *Oh, they must be close to coming to you, Father God, because Mom and Dad are truly changing their behavior before our very eyes.*

As she stood from her kneeling position, Lauren couldn't ignore the fact that it took a couple of steps before the stiffness left her knees and back. That reality prompted her to ask in a small voice, "God, not now, but whenever you see fit, maybe I could ride again. I'm turning into a rusty old maid. You can keep the 'old maid' part; but oh, I do so miss my horse." Then she was quick to add, "But I don't want to be greedy here, so let's get Irene straightened out first."

Suddenly she could audibly hear her friend Suz's voice ringing in her ears. "Lauren. God says, 'Knock and seek.' It gives him pleasure beyond our comprehension to give his children the desires of their hearts. You know how much you want Tuck to have everything in the whole world. Well, just multiply that by infinity, and that's how much God wants for you. Ask away!"

And so Lauren did as she headed down the hall to her son's room. "OK, here goes, Lord. You say you want to bless me, and you know since I was a little girl my passion for horses. So may I have another one please? I miss Gracie so much. But I think I'd rather not have a mare this time. They're a little cranky like all of us girls. I'd rather have a bay gelding, please. I think dark bays are so spectacular, don't you? And my boy horse has got to be at least sixteen three or seventeen hands with a deep barrel so he takes up my leg. God, you gave me these long legs, and I went through a lot of pain growing them, so let's just wrap them around the most gorgeous animal you've ever created. And you know how much I love to show. . . . I want to be the best. Oh, and maybe he'll be a horse that also loves to go out on the trails. But please, please, please, make sure you protect him so he doesn't go lame because you know that geldings don't have much use if they can't be ridden . . . other than becoming expensive lawn ornaments, that is. So, yes, . . . a wonderful, spectacular gentleman of a horse would suit me perfectly. And if you're so inclined, he can be youngish but not too difficult to handle. I don't bounce very well these days, Lord. Oh, and a little white snip on his nose and a star on his forehead would be really cool. And don't forget his four white socks so when he moves like a gazelle the judges will melt in their seats and have to give him first place in the under-saddle classes, like they did with *Amazing Grace.* First place, *Amazing Grace* — remember how cool that was, God?"

Lauren puffed up like a pelican at her sweet memory. "I'll name my new horse something biblical and strong, not that you need the PR. . . . Just out of respect, of course. Thank you, God. Oh, and you can fill this request slip out whenever you're in a fanciful mood because I know Christmas is every day for you, God. After all, you gave us your Son on that day. I love you so much."

By this time Lauren had reached Tucker's door, shadowed by Bingo and William. They all couldn't wait for their morning romp with the kid.

■ ■ ■ ■

Lauren's kitchen was particularly rowdy that morning. Everyone was on their own mission to have a good breakfast, clear the table, clean everything up, get Tucker to the bus stop, and be on their way well before eight o'clock for Irene's court date.

As usual, Tucker was at the kitchen table picking the raisins out of his cereal for first nibbles when Chelsea made a brief appearance through the kitchen before exiting out the back. She had learned over the months that there was no escaping through the front of the house without letting everyone know that she was heading off to school.

Yes, Chelsea had finally recognized that it was far easier to adhere to the simple rules than argue over the little things. Ever since Lauren had suggested to her niece to pick her battles, in a moment of camaraderie, Chelsea had taken her advice to heart.

This morning Chelsea had her overcoat on before she even entered the kitchen. Her behavior was noted by her mother, yet Irene was so engaged in reviewing her notes for court and checking her makeup that she decided not to comment on Chelsea's unusual garb. Busy or not, Irene should have because her daughter had something to hide — an inappropriately short skirt and plunging neckline to be precise.

Not one to take any chances, Chelsea had stuffed a sweater and jeans in her book bag just in case her teachers censored her outfit. OK, she'd play their game, she told herself, but she wasn't dressing for them. It was all about Trace. Chelsea had an important date with her boyfriend after the basketball game that night, and everything had to be "just so" since she had decided to tell Trace she was pregnant.

As Chelsea made her way down the driveway, her thoughts whirled. If everything was so cool, why was she shaking and sick to her stomach? Chelsea figured the sick part was normal with her pregnancy, but she was hating the nervousness she was feeling. No matter how many times she told herself that having a baby was what she wanted, she wasn't sure that Trace would agree, and she was scared to death he might reject her.

"No!" she rationalized. "I'm pregnant, so it must be right. It's supposed to be," she told herself before Trace picked her up for school. "And he'll love me forever now. He'll always be all mine."

Chelsea hopped into Trace's Volkswagen, waiting until the car disappeared around the corner before moving in for a kiss.

Reaching for more cereal, Tucker stretched over William who was lying on the floor with his paws protectively around his bowl of food. Having scarfed down her meal, the cat was eyeing William's still-to-be-finished canned goodies.

Tucker observed that Bingo was about to pounce and warned, "Cat, touch the dog's food and you die."

The boy's statement put skid marks on Lauren's morning routine. "Tuck, where did you pick up that kind of saying? It sounds like a bad Western."

"From you," the boy said matter-of-factly.

"Oh, well, . . ." Lauren floundered. "That was just a silly joke . . . whenever I said that. When did I say such a thing?" But before Tucker could answer, Lauren thought better of her question. ". . . Never mind. Let's just not say that, OK, Tuck? Because it could be misconstrued."

Tuck looked at his mother. "Why, is it 'rude'?"

"Yes, . . . that's what I meant. Even if you're just kidding, it sounds a bit rude to say that anyone should die over a food fight. So let's just erase it from our memory banks. . . . Poof!" She waved her hands across an imaginary blackboard. "There, all gone."

Tucker had learned to take his mother's rather unique behavior in stride.

"OK, Mom."

The boy had almost snagged his cereal box when Lauren intervened. "I'll get that for you."

"No, I can get it." The five-year-old was ever insistent about being as independent as he could. "Dad lets me climb up the ladder to clean the windows with him."

Lauren tried to hide her concern. "Good, Tuck. Exactly how big is the ladder?"

"I don't know. Bigger than Daddy."

"Oh, is Daddy on the ladder with you?"

"No, then it wouldn't be like I was doing it myself."

"Well, is he *near* the ladder?"

"Yeah, he's standing right next to it, and he always has his hand on my ankle . . . like I'm going to fall or something."

"Well, better safe than sorry, Son."

"Yeah, Mom, but he doesn't understand that I have my Superman cape on, so I can't fall."

"Oh, OK. I'll make sure he understands. But ladders can be dangerous."

Suddenly Irene let out a wail from the other side of the kitchen. "So can roll-on mascara! I just practically poked my eye out. Lauren, do you have some drops? I'm going to look like Bozo the clown with one eye running down my face."

Irene had been leaning against the counter taking in the morning light to fix her makeup before her mishap. She now sat next to Tucker who was refilling his bowl to overflowing with cereal. Lauren grabbed eyedrops out of her purse and handed them to Irene as she whirled back to the stove to rescue some boiling eggs she'd been cooking for her dad.

The toast had popped and was buttered, the eggs were on the table, and Margaret and Sam were enjoying their early morning breakfast when Tuck announced, "Seven-O-two. Bing, we're late. Hey, Mom, can I walk myself down to the bus stop?"

"Well, . . . your grandfather would just hate missing his stroll with you. Wouldn't you, Daddy?"

Sam stuffed the last piece of yoke from his egg into his mouth, then jabbed the remaining slice of Canadian ham and packed it in to round out his taste fest. Lauren was always amused at how much her father enjoyed his breakfast, sectioning off each food group on his plate so he could mix and match the morsels into perfect proportions.

Lauren was careful to tell Tuck that Granddaddy's eating style was not really polite — rather, it was an eccentricity of his.

That's when Tuck asked, "Why does Granddaddy have electricity in him?"

By the time Tucker had been taken to the bus stop, Bingo and William had been walked and ensconced on the back porch, Irene's eye had stopped flooding, and Lauren escorted Margaret out to Irene's car, the Patterson caravan was on its way to the lawyers' office by seven forty-eight sharp.

It was a glorious morning, one that held promise, Lauren hoped, as they drove through the already crowded downtown streets of the village of Centennial.

She thought of her sister in the car behind her with her mother and father and how Irene's heart must be in her throat by this time as they approached the town square where the courthouse was located. As usual, there was no place to park, which was beyond Lauren's comprehension since she always considered Centennial a one-horse town. Still, whenever they had to go to court, it seemed like the rest of Tennessee had moved in and taken up residence at every available parking spot as they lurked on every available corner to make record of Irene's court case.

Stephanie was particularly pleased with her son that Friday morning. He was pumped about the varsity game that night, and she hadn't seen that level of enthusiasm in Trace since Chelsea had entered the scene. Yes, he was a bundle of energy as he ate a double order of eggs at breakfast.

When Stephanie came home from the diner the night before, she had noticed Trace was already asleep. He hadn't beat her to bed in months, and at first she was concerned. But looking at her boy in the light of day, his enthusiasm to make the grade with the scouts dispelled any concerns she might have had.

Stephanie gingerly placed a sign on the diner door stating they would be late opening that morning, then drove over to the courthouse area where she and the rest of her friends were going to commence their march on Irene's behalf. She had arrived at town square a bit early, as was Stephanie's bent, so she decided to stop in Irene's lawyers' office building to see if she could give the family a hug before they went in to wait to be called to court.

Stephanie made a beeline to her space at the back of her church's parking lot adjacent to the center of town. She had already checked with Pam to make sure it would be alright if she parked in front of the day care door. That way she could make a quick return to open the diner so Norro wouldn't dock her pay.

Chastising herself for not thinking of allotting her space for Lauren's family, her eyes scanned the area hoping to spot either Lauren's truck or Irene's car, but they were nowhere in sight.

As it so happened, grace shone down not only on Lauren but also on Irene that crisp morning. Finding two side-by-side metered spots on the street just in front of the lawyers' office was heavenly intervention, Lauren concluded.

She stepped out of her truck with a look of satisfaction, pointing at their parking spaces as Sam, Margaret, and Irene piled out of the BMW. Irene was more concerned about making it into the building before the paparazzi spotted her or her sister reveling over their parking spaces. Too late.

"See, see, Rene. Everything is going to be just fine. God is already smiling at us. Look at that, two places right outside the office. Couldn't be better. . . . Mom doesn't have to walk far. See!"

Irene twirled around, adopting her all-too-frequent look of frustration while pointing at Lauren to be aware of the photographers. "See, see . . . *see* the paparazzi on the corner? Let's hold your commentary for inside if you don't mind."

Irene scrambled into the doorway first, then Lauren gathered up her parents and followed close behind. But Irene knew in the pit of her stomach that the photographers had already caught their exchange on film. *Perfect stills,* she thought, to make them all look like blithering idiots on the front page of the newspapers.

When Stephanie entered the back hallway of the office building, she caught a glimpse of the Patterson tribe disappearing through the lawyers' doorway. She also noticed a flash coming from down the hall. Curious, she made an immediate left and headed out to investigate.

Knowing the building like the back of her hand since she'd worked there when she first moved to town, she dashed down the side hall to see which photographers had invaded the building. But when she came around the back corridor, she saw Norro changing a roll of film as he crouched like a rat behind one of the water coolers in the hall.

Stephanie stepped back to avoid being seen, taking a moment to decide her next move. She had a hard time digesting the fact that her boss was there lurking about taking pictures. And then, all of a sudden it made sense — all those times recently she'd discovered Norro in the back room of the diner. She realized he was probably trying to overhear her friends' prayers or conversations. Or worse, had he recorded them? She could actually feel her face flush with anger.

Stephanie paced as she pieced together in her mind some of the pictures that had appeared in the newspaper. Eventually she recognized that they must have been taken by Norro because the backgrounds of the photos were in close proximity to the diner. In fact, she remembered thinking it rather odd that there was one particular close-up shot of Irene in the newspaper taken at a table that she now knew had been cropped to protect the identity of the location — Norros! It must have been taken during one of the rare times Irene had come with her sister to chat with Pam about Chelsea's counseling *in the privacy* of the back booth at the diner. Stephanie was horrified, and although she had had no idea of her boss's complicity, she somehow felt responsible for not protecting her friends better.

Stephanie peeked around the corner again, waiting for just the right moment to expose her employer to an onslaught of verbiage he'd never forget. But as quickly as that thought crossed her mind, she stepped further back into the hall, deciding that it would be better to take counsel with the other girls to see how best to handle the shocking situation. Not only that, but this country girl needed to simmer down before she did something she'd really regret.

Inside the lawyers' office Irene, Lauren, Margaret, and Sam gathered in the waiting room. Within moments they were shuffled into another private conference room to down their nineteen millionth cup of coffee since six a.m. as they waited for Irene's courtroom drama to unfold.

After about ten minutes the lawyers' personal secretary popped her head in, ever the positive one. Lauren liked this woman. "Good morning, y'all. May I get you something else to drink? Water?" All four shook their heads in unison. "Well then, we'll just be waiting to hear. You've been through the drill before."

Irene concurred under her breath. "Ad nauseam."

The secretary simply sloughed off Irene's remark with another sweet smile. "I'll be back in a little while to keep you posted."

As she closed the office door, Irene pulled her compact out again. Drawn by the available light, she moved over to the window to touch up her makeup. Meanwhile, Lauren proceeded to chatter, holding court with her family, an opportunity she relished since she knew no one could leave the room.

"I was just thinking this morning that real loss is feeling like there's nothing to lose. . . . So we're going to win, right? No matter when this trial gets going, it will be the perfect timing for victory. Rene, just think of all the people who are committed to pray for you and are standing behind you. Oh yes, . . . how true the difference between 'involvement and commitment' . . . like an egg and ham breakfast. The chicken is involved, but the ham is *committed.*"

"I don't get it." Sam and Margaret looked at their daughter as if she were an alien.

"Dad, it's simple. . . . The chicken can have more eggs, but the pig has no more ham to give because he *is* the ham. . . ." Her explanation fell on deaf ears. ". . . Never mind. I just wanted to make the point that we're all committed to see this through, Rene. We're with you, and you'll make them all eat their words. . . ."

". . . And the pig, I suspect," Irene countered. "At this point, Lauren, victory has become a relative issue since I've already lost my reputation and my mind, and I haven't even gotten to court yet."

"I think 'Everything is relative' should be put on our bathroom mirrors, don't you, Rene?"

Irene's voice dropped an octave. "Why?"

"Because we're so hard on ourselves. Like you, standing there trying to fix perfection. Why don't you just sit down and relax?"

"I'm just keeping busy, alright? Now please, let's just be quiet for a minute."

Lauren indulged herself in another slurp of coffee. "OK, that's fine. I'll just be here praying . . . silently . . . although it's more powerful to agree in prayer. God says in his Word that . . ."

Margaret put a firm hand on Lauren's shoulder indicating silence. Her daughter reluctantly complied for the moment.

Stephanie arrived on the corner of the

courthouse steps where Tonya and Pam had already gathered. Both ladies were hopping about in an effort to stave off the cold.

"Hey there, girls, where's Eleanor?"

Tonya rubbed her hands together, blowing on them before stuffing them back into her pockets. "I stopped by the school, and Ms. Eleanor told me that she and Ham were going to be just a few minutes late. They needed to check in with the principal."

"Ham's coming?"

"Yup. He wants to pray, and then he's going to take off, and we'll do the marching."

Tonya looked around to see who was gathering at the courthouse steps. Pam shook her head in amazement. "I can't believe how many people are standing around here with Nikons hanging from their necks. It looks like we're at a convention."

"Or a hanging," Stephanie offered with a somber expression.

A sudden wind came up. Pam pushed her long blonde hair out of her eyes for a better look as she pulled a knitted cap out of her overcoat pocket. Within moments the three women were showing signs of frozen toes and noses when Eleanor and Ham arrived. They all embraced, and immediately Eleanor recognized that Stephanie had an odd expression on her face.

"What's up, girl? You look like you saw a ghost."

Stephanie gave a deep sigh. "We'll talk about it later."

Concerned, the women moved in closer when Ham rerouted their attention. "Ladies, let's pray. . . . I've got to get back to school."

He stepped up, putting his arms as far around the women's shoulders as he could. They all bowed their heads.

"Father God, we are here in agreement to stand for righteousness and justice for Irene on this day. There is no task too difficult for you, so we ask that you take control of this situation as these sisters march around the courthouse. I ask you, Father God, to give wisdom to everyone from the clerks all the way up to the judge to bring this situation to a close with the correct conclusion for Irene. If it is your will, and the proceedings start today, will you oversee the choosing of the jury and the righteousness of every ear and every heart that will be involved in hearing this case? We ask that Irene and her family will be released from all their pressures, . . . that Irene will be exonerated, and that everyone will recognize that you intervened as protector and overseer, loving Irene and her family as unconditionally as you do all of us. But most importantly, Lord, bring Lauren's family to your saving eternal grace. Soften their hearts to know your truth. And I ask all that in Jesus' mighty name."

As the women raised their eyes and agreed with their "Amens," they looked at one another in confidence.

Eleanor gave Ham a quick kiss before he took off, then addressed her friends. "OK, ladies, remember as we start our march what God has given us by example in the book of Jeremiah:

"Prepare your shields, both large and small, and march out for battle! Harness the horses, mount the steeds! Take your positions with helmets on! Polish your spears, put on your armor! What do I see? They are terrified, they are retreating, their warriors are defeated. They flee in haste without looking back, and there is terror on every side, declares the Lord. (Jeremiah 46:3–5)

"Father God, you tell us that our battles are spiritual warfare, so we put on the armor of God:

"Stand firm then, with the belt of truth

buckled around your waist, with the breastplate of righteousness in place, and with your feet fitted with the readiness that comes from the gospel of peace. In addition to all this, take up the shield of faith, with which you can extinguish all the flaming arrows of the evil one. Take the helmet of salvation and the sword of the Spirit, which is the word of God. (Ephesians 6:14–17)

"And now that we are protected, we'll march around the courthouse in obedience while we praise God in Jesus' name." And with amens from all, they started off.

Her compact was now closed and laid on the windowsill. Irene stared out into the bright winter morning, numbly watching the press gather in throngs in front of the courthouse. She had mixed emotions about going out into the fray. Frankly, she felt like she couldn't face the circus one more time; but on the other hand she so wanted this situation to be resolved. And as her mind once again raced through all the possibilities that lay ahead, the secretary reentered.

As Irene turned to hear the update, she noted details about this plump, rosy-cheeked middle-aged woman with whom she had shared some of the most excruciating hours of her life. And she realized in that moment that she couldn't even remember the secretary's name.

But now, before the secretary's words formed on her lips in slow motion, Irene took in every detail — the print of her blouse, the flare of her skirt, the color of her shoes, the brooch she wore at her neck a little askew. Oh, and her hair, Irene noted, needed a color touch-up. Her observations weren't critical in nature, just simply taking in what had previously gone unnoticed. And then the woman's name popped into Irene's head: "Rose Beth." She remembered now that it sounded like a bath oil to her.

Now Irene refocused when Rose Beth cleared her voice, visibly uncomfortable with the news she was about to bear. "I am so sorry, Mrs. Williams, but both your attorneys, Mr. Blankenship and Mr. Hudson, will be calling you later. They are being detained in court on your behalf, but your proceedings have been postponed again. They asked me to let you know that so you and your family don't have to continue to wait here. As we speak, they are trying to get your case on the docket once more."

"Postponed? . . . Why this time?" Irene said weakly.

"Oh, Mrs. Williams, I believe Mr. Blankenship said something about the officer having the flu and being unable to make the hearing."

Irene repeated Rose Beth's words with great precision. "He . . . has . . . the . . . flu? Is he in the hospital with pneumonia on his deathbed? Short of that . . ." And now the volume of her voice escalated. ". . . Why isn't he here with his redneck, round-faced lies?"

Lauren was up and by her sister in a flash. "Rene, it's OK. It's probably just a ploy to get you upset, and they're not going to be successful, right?"

"Wrong. I *am* upset, and I'm going to strangle them!"

"No, no." Lauren threw Rose Beth her most compliant smile. "My sister is just a little overwrought. Rightfully so, wouldn't you say?" Rose Beth nodded with fervor. "Mrs. Williams is just kidding, of course. Thank you so much. We will trot right out of here and wait to hear from the lawyers. Thank you again for the coffee; it was very good."

Irene yanked her arm away from Lauren, turning toward the window to hide the tears forming in her eyes. A rage was rising from the pit of her stomach, and Irene felt like she was about to lose it completely.

By this time Margaret and Sam were hovering around their elder daughter while Lauren made sure Rose Beth exited the room.

Irene slowly addressed her family. "I am going to be getting the first plane to New York. Would you all please keep an eye on Chelsea? I need to get out of here. I'm going to New York to see my *other* lawyers. . . . Then I'm going to have a massage, get my hair and nails done, go shopping . . ." Now the tears started streaming down her face, yet her expression remained stoic. ". . . I don't have any money, but I'm going to buy everything on account, send it to Ford's suite at the Carlisle Hotel, break into his wine cellar, smoke a carton of cigarettes, try everything on with the latest in-house movies blaring, order room service for four, and roll out of there Sunday morning so the front desk can have everything packed up and returned to the stores by Monday morning."

Margaret couldn't stand her daughter's teary deluge anymore and began blotting Irene's streaked face with a mound of Kleenex from her purse. But after a beat Irene batted her away like a pesky fly as she addressed her sister.

"Lauren, I will be back for your opening."

"Oh no, Rene. You don't need to do that. If you want to stay in New York, it's not a problem. We have everything covered."

Irene put her hand up again, this time actually making slight contact with Lauren's nose. "I will be back, but I need to go now."

Lauren understood there was no more to say, so she stepped back to allow Irene to pass. Then Sam uncharacteristically intervened, quickly moving to open the door for Irene. But before he let the seal crack, he looked up and then away for a moment as his eyes too became pools of emotion. "Irene, I was always hard on you because you were the oldest. . . . And, well, . . . your mother used to point out to me that I was expecting to have a boy first, so I treated you like one without realizing it."

Although Sam was having trouble letting his true feelings show, he was determined not to have Irene misinterpret his words. "Hey, of course I was happy to have you. But I still expected you to be tough and strong, to take care of your little sister. And you did that, but along the way I think I forgot that you were a little girl too."

Sam looked away again, choking back his tears as he cleared his voice. Then he took a big breath and regarded his daughters again who stood before him speechless (as did his wife). And as uncomfortable as he was, it was as if he had waited years for this moment and he wasn't going to let it slip by out of embarrassment. Then he laughed slightly from being so open in front of the women of his family.

"But you girls spoiled me, didn't you?" Now he looked at Lauren. "You were more the tomboy type, and I got to throw some baseballs with you." He grinned slightly at his younger daughter. "And a little touch football, huh? Except when I got too rough and your mother would yell out the window, 'Don't forget she's a girl, Sam!' " He adopted a falsetto voice for effect as he quoted Margaret. "But I never really forgot that, even when I broke your arm. . . . You know I didn't mean to do that. That was about the slippery grass, right?"

Lauren nodded, stunned at her father's words. "Right, Dad."

"And I never told you this, Irene, but I wanted to punch that first husband of yours in the face more than once. He never treated you right. But your Mother and I decided to stay out of it because, . . . who knew, you might work it out in the long run with the clown and then he'd hate my guts. And then where would we be? Spending Christmas apart or watching football games at Thanksgiving at opposite ends of the couch. Stupid guy things. But I swear, I regret that I didn't nail him for hurting you so badly, and if I ever see him again, he's going to have to answer to me because no one treats my little girl like that."

There wasn't a dry eye in the room while Sam paused briefly to gather his thoughts. "And Lauren, same thing goes for you and that pip-squeak of a first husband, as your mother called him. Bottom line, what I'm trying to say is that you probably think I was never there for you because . . ." And now Sam really choked on his words. ". . . Because I wasn't in a lot of ways. Now I'm not sorry for the rights and wrongs I taught you both. I think it was a good thing I scared you because your mother was such a softy. But I never told you I loved you, or that I was proud of you both. I never took my girls to the movies, or the circus, or even out for a hamburger alone. And now your mother and I are trying to make up for that with Chelsea and Tucker. . . . So maybe you'll forgive . . ."

Sam was interrupted by a light knock on the door. His demeanor instantly changed as everyone stood at attention.

"Just a minute, OK?" He responded gruffly. "We'll be right out." He looked back at his daughters. "I'm just saying that I'd give my right arm to go in that courtroom and make this alright for you, Irene. I'd do anything in my power to make that happen . . . to protect you, you know?"

And with that Sam opened the door without waiting for a response from anyone. "So let's go. We're going to win this thing, whenever it gets to trial, you hear me?"

The man couldn't even let the moment settle, and yet he had said what had been on his heart for a number of years. But instead of making a quick exit, he surprised everyone again by standing back and holding the door open for his wife and two girls. And that felt really good to this man.

As Irene passed her father, she whispered, "Thanks, Dad."

Lauren merely touched his hand in gratitude. And when Margaret passed, she looked up at her husband with renewed respect. And Sam thought, if he didn't live another moment in his life, he had just lived the best one.

CHAPTER 10
-THE WINNER IS . . . -

"Been there, done that, didn't get the T-shirt for it," was how Tonya had begun teaching every one of her abstinence classes for the last two school years.

Pam had asked her friend to sit in on the program as a senior at Greystone, and before she knew it, Tonya had been recruited as leader. She kidded with Pam that she was the last person who should be standing before young girls speaking a moral message. Those "gossiping, primping, dating time bombs of potential mistakes and early motherhood," as Tonya affectionately called them, were exactly who Tonya was when she fell in love with Shooter at the tender age of fifteen. And out of that love arrived her bundle of "Bobbie-joy."

No, Tonya was never sorry for having her child, but she recognized she could have chosen better timing for becoming a mother. And that's exactly why Pam insisted that

Tonya was the perfect person to teach the abstinence class. Still, the young mother wasn't easily convinced.

It was true, Tonya admitted, that most people thought she was beautiful and concluded she must have the world by the tail. But in reality, she had low self-esteem and jumped the gun when it came to being intimate as a young girl.

Her family life was nonexistent, and she just wanted the attention and love that came with having a serious boyfriend. All she could think about was not losing Shooter. She never even considered the consequences of being sexually active with no real commitment aside from meeting in the backseat of a friend's car and the branding of the discount store "friendship ring" Shooter gave her.

No, Tonya had never contracted any kind of venereal disease or physical downside to unprotected sex because she and Shooter were first-time lovers. And now that she was older and wiser, Tonya knew she was fortunate in that regard. It was also one of the reasons she had stayed with Shooter all these years.

Soon after she gave birth to Bobbie, she had confided in Eleanor that she was committed to abstinence until she and Shooter were finally married, and then she could walk down the aisle on Ham's arm with Bobbie by her side and she would feel "white as snow." Eleanor had taught the girl over the years since she was under her tutelage at church and home that they all served a God of "starting over", and that Tonya, Shooter, and Bobbie would thrive as a family if they did it God's way from there on out. And that was exactly the message Tonya passed on to the young girls she so graciously taught in her abstinence class.

The teenagers gathered in the back of the small room barely big enough to accommodate the seven to ten girls who attended Tonya's class Fridays right after school. Some were put in the program at the insistence of their parents after displaying "bad behavior." Others were there because either the school counselor or their private therapists/counselors required them to go through the course. And that's where Chelsea fit in; Pam had sent the girl to attend as part of her counseling for her sexual abuse healing since statistics proved that girls, and boys for that matter, who have been sexually molested typically move into a promiscuous lifestyle following their abuse.

There were also one or two girls attending

who were looking for a support system to make it through their changing hormones and the peer pressures of being a teenager. These girls attended a church nearby and were part of its youth group. Tonya was particularly happy to have them in class because their purpose was not only personal, but they were desirous of extra counseling from her so they could form an abstinence group of their own as one of their church activities. Needless to say, Chelsea considered these girls "dorks" and wasted no time telling Pam so.

Pam knocked lightly on the back door and entered as Tonya was nearing the end of her session. Her purpose in showing up that day was to touch base with Chelsea since their last session had ended so abruptly, but she immediately noted that Chelsea was not present. Disappointed, she decided to wait and talk with Tonya to see if she knew where the girl was.

"My mother used to tell me this little ditty. . . ." Tonya gave her class a little wink. ". . . There was a girl with a curl right in the middle of her forehead; and when she was good, she was very, very good; but when she was bad, she was horrid."

The girls in the room scrunched their

noses and giggled, which in turn amused Tonya. "Although I'm not that much older than you guys, things have kind of changed since my mom was a little girl. My point is, there was this stigma of 'good girl'/'bad girl' my mother laid on me when I was growing up. But none of that really mattered to me; I just wanted to be a 'grown-up girl.' I didn't have the benefit, as I've told you before, of my faith in Jesus until Ms. Eleanor took me under her wing. So, as she taught me and we've learned this semester, our esteem comes from how God sees us, not what other people think of us. Still, that's a hard thing to remember when you all are dealing with competition every time you step on the school grounds or go out to the mall. Forget your wacko hormones. Forget all your insecurities about when you develop, when you get breasts, when you finally get your period. . . ."

The girls shifted in their seats, still a bit shy about Tonya's direct approach. ". . . All those signs that are supposed to tell you you're a woman are coming at you like a freight train. And forget about whether you think you're pretty or not."

Tonya squared off in front of the group. "Listen, the only thing that has ever been consistent in my life and has sustained me since I went down the wrong road is God and God alone. And again, I want to make sure you know there are consequences to 'going too far.' . . . And I love mine, even if he came into my life a little bit too early."

Everybody looked over to the corner of the room where Tonya's son happily played in his own world at a little table and chair set up especially for him. Although Bobbie was surely a blessing, at the same time the girls understood the boy was also a *consequence* of Tonya's hasty actions, and she had been forthright about that fact since the course began.

Tonya had decided that it was OK to use her circumstances to vividly point out the enormous responsibilities that come with having a baby, especially as a teenager. Most of the girls confessed that they were in no way ready or desirous of becoming a mother yet. And that certainly was not any kind of insult to Bobbie. All the girls adored this chunk of a little boy, and Bobbie felt like he had a roomful of aunties who spoiled him at every turn. Still, the point was well taken by the girls concerning the realities of stepping through a doorway if they were not willing to walk into the room, as Tonya put it.

"There have been people for a good long

time now who say I can model, so you'd think I'd get up in the morning feeling like a million bucks, but I don't. Yes, I know I'm tall. I could fit in the clothes, but sometimes I don't feel very alluring or pretty because I still don't have that ring on my finger, do I?"

Tonya was willing to peel like an onion emotionally to make her point to her class, and she paid a price every time she laid herself bare. But if she hesitated, she would hear Eleanor's resounding reminder that God says, "The truth will set us free," and with that comfort, she'd always forge ahead in her inevitable style. "Shoot 'em straight" was her teaching motto.

Now that she had the girls' full attention, Tonya continued. "So, whenever I feel that way, and I forget what the real barometer is to my esteem and value . . . and why my behavior needs to reflect that value, I go to another one of God's love letters."

Tonya passed a sheet of paper to each girl as well as to Pam. "I have a new one for you girls today; and, as always, it's all Scripture. So put your love letter from God on your refrigerator instead of 'I'm too fat' or 'I'm too skinny' and remind yourself how much God loves *you* just the way you are!"

And then Tonya and the others read the

following Scriptures aloud:

God's Love Letter

Please accept this extravagant gift of life that I'm offering you (Romans 5:17–21). Come to me and you will find that I am gentle and humble (Matthew 11:29). I am merciful, slow to anger, and full of grace (Psalm 145:8). My heart beats wildly every time you look my direction (Solomon 4:9). Follow me and I will give you the desires of your heart (Psalm 37:4) because I am passionately in love with you (Psalm 45:11). Nothing, absolutely nothing can change My love for you (Romans 8:38–39). Trust in me and I will help you (Romans 10:11). I'll welcome you with open arms (Mark 10:16), and I will meet all of your needs (Philippians 4:9). I will love you all day and sing songs to you at night (Psalm 42:8). You mean the world to me and my love for you knows no limits (John 3:16).

Let me live in your heart, and I'll breathe new life into you (Romans 8:11). Just invite me in, and all of heaven will celebrate (Luke 15:7). I'll be with you every day (Romans 15:13) because you belong to me. You are mine (Exodus 19:5). I gave up what I loved most to win your love

(Romans), and I've waited an eternity for you (Ephesians 1:11). If you believe in me, I will save you (Romans 1:16). I will come to you riding on a white horse (Revelation 19:11), and I will be your champion (Jeremiah 20:11). I am Jesus, the lover of your soul.

Pam could not believe how bold her friend had become, how honest, down-to-earth, and effective Tonya was as a young woman and leader. Then again, she had a powerful teacher in Eleanor, who encouraged not only Tonya but all of her circle of friends every step of the way to be the "real deal" and not pass along the hand-me-down heartaches of generational sin.

Yes, Eleanor would trumpet on a regular basis, "Use your hard-won lessons to benefit others and encourage them not to step on the same land mines we've frequented. Remember, we never change the things we accept."

Then a little "come-hither" expression would cross her face like a kid about to share an ice cream sundae with his best buddy.

As Pam approached Tonya after the class was dismissed, she wondered how Chelsea could possibly not grasp the incredible message of God's love that was being shared with her not only by Pam but by Tonya and Lauren as well. But then again, Pam knew that it wasn't up to her or anyone else to soften Chelsea's heart. That was God's business.

"Hey, what's up wee-one?" Tonya tugged on Pam's long blonde curls. "You spying on me again?"

Pam gave Bobbie a hug as he handed his mom his crayons and coloring book. "Tonya, you rock! It always takes my breath away how powerful those love letters are."

"Amen," Tonya agreed. "Truth is, I have to read 'em myself on a regular basis."

"And why exactly are you suffering from low self-esteem, oh gorgeous one?"

"You know, . . ." suddenly Tonya was almost quivering, "maybe it's nothing, but just maybe tonight's the night! It's the big game, and I know Shooter's going to blow everyone away. He's got to make his move for us. I can't *stand* this anymore. . . . This not knowing. 'Yes or no,' but this not knowing . . ."

Pam gave her a quick hug. ". . . It'll all fall into place in God's timing."

"Good one, squirt. And I'll say exactly the same thing to you about your school funding. You know how hard it is when it seems like *nothing's* moving along."

"Oh, you know it," Pam commiserated. "And on that note, where's Ms. Chelsea?"

"Don't know. I waited a little bit to start the class, but she didn't show. I wouldn't get too worried. You know, she's done this a couple of times before. Once it was all about getting a nail appointment."

"Yeah, well we had a pretty lousy session yesterday, and I just wanted to see how she was doing." Pam couldn't hide her concern. "Alright, well, . . . she'll be at the game tonight for sure, so I'll see her then."

"Right, . . . and I'm going home to get gorgeous for my man. Not that he'll even notice me or what I'm wearing while the game's happening."

"At least you can't complain that he's not focused."

"True, but I'd rather have him a little more focused on me." She started to put Bobbie's coat on. "By the time this evening is over, mark my words little-one, Shooter will be offered a college scholarship, and I'll be engaged. How's that for positive thinking?"

Pam gave her another quick hug. "Rockin'. Go girl!"

■ ■ ■ ■

As always, Stephanie was serving the Friday night crowd at Norros single-handedly, teetering trays upon trays of food with expertise that should be patented.

In addition to her balancing act, she had her cell phone precariously perched on her shoulder on top of a kitchen towel that was folded over three times to bring it up to ear level. Securing the creation with her head, which rested at an uncomfortable right angle, she strained over the boisterous crowd to hear Eleanor on the other end of the phone giving her a blow-by-blow account of the varsity basketball game in progress at the high school.

Earlier that afternoon when Norro announced to Stephanie that there was absolutely no way he was shutting down the diner for Friday night business so she could go watch Trace play basketball, if the waitress had had a cleaver in her hand, she probably would have used it on his thick head. And although she tried her best to bite her tongue, Stephanie found herself muttering her true feelings behind Norro's back. "You're so ugly, you must have been locked up in a closet by your mother as you grew up just for breathing the air."

Stephanie now turned to her boss. "What's the matter with you? Can't you understand how important tonight is to me? *My son is playing for the scouts!*"

"I don't care if he's playing for the president. You shut down Thursday morning for your court parade, and I'm not losing any more business. So, unless you want to get to the back of the unemployment line, you'll be here on time with a smile on your face."

It took every ounce of Stephanie's control, plus a quick prayer, to sidestep the comments she really wanted to make, but she could tell by the look in his eyes that he was serious as a heart attack about his threat, and she simply could not afford to lose her job. Besides, she was going to come up with a plan with the girls, one that would not be labeled vengeance but rather action based on righteous indignation, to take care of this man's bad attitude and bad behavior once and for all.

As Stephanie moved about the diner that night, she couldn't help but recognize that she was going to spend a pretty penny on the local chiropractor to get her neck realigned after spending an hour fifty-six minutes and counting with Eleanor on her propped-up cell phone.

■ ■ ■ ■

Greystone High School gymnasium was packed to the rafters. This wasn't just another scrimmage; this was the night scouts from all over the country would be watching. And they had arrived — not one, not two, but four.

Eleanor had observed her husband following his players up and down the court, but she'd never seen him glance over his shoulder so many times to check out other people's reactions as he did during that evening's game.

She and Ham had stayed up late the night before for a little lovin' and a lot of talkin'. Her husband was wound up like his namesake, "hamstring." His tension was not born of concern about his reputation as a coach but rather for his team, especially Shooter and Trace. He was painfully aware of the pressures they were under because he had been in their exact position many years ago when he had played for Greystone High. Ham wasn't a star team member like Shooter or Trace; he was one of the starting five and had a clear shot at a scholarship and the recognition his boys were now vying for. But during Ham's warm-up before the game, he suffered an injury — a fluke twist of his knee and *bam!* Having torn his ligament, he hit the floor and never got to play one minute of the game.

It was an excruciating injury to have to deal with both physically and emotionally, leaving a four-inch incision scar on his right knee from the operation and a longer one on his heart. What was really frustrating was his career was over in basketball, but his injury didn't keep him out of the Marines and Vietnam. "Timing is everything" was written across the door of his Chevy.

Eleanor always called Ham her old war-horse, but in hindsight he had to admit that coaching was the part of the game he did best. Not only that, he got to play out his talents where he most loved to be — in his hometown. And yes, he knew all about the trap of living vicariously through anyone else's talents, but twenty-five years later he took enormous pride in presenting to the scouts the two finest athletes he'd seen come down the pike in his entire career. And tonight his boys were making him particularly proud.

The tension was out of control since the score was closer than identical twins and there was so much riding on the perfor-mances of the athletes that night. To top it

off, Greystone High was playing its tough-
est rival, and whichever team prevailed
would win the bragging rights of being the
best in the area.

It seemed the entire town was there to
cheer on their team. The bleachers were
packed, and all available standing room was
taken. Ham had confided in Eleanor that he
was thankful they were playing the game on
their home turf. There was always an advantage of having such strong local support.
Yes, it was an evening of legendary perfor-
mances and on-the-edge-of-your-seat competition with both teams putting forth their
very best.

Chelsea was in the first row behind the
player's bench next to Tonya and Bobbie,
and by now everyone's voices were practically hoarse from screaming accolades and
directions.

Trace was shooting better than he deserved, having not practiced much in the
last several months; but despite the boy's
stunning performance, the star of the
evening was Shooter, hands down.

The game was in double overtime, and both
teams had stepped up their defense. With
ten seconds left on the clock, the score was
86–84, leaving Greystone High down by

two. During a layup attempt, Trace was ruthlessly fouled by the other team's center, causing him to hit the floor hard. The impact of the fall left a ringing in his ears and his right hand throbbing. Nonetheless, he got up to take his two free throws.

If Trace sank both shots, the game would go into triple overtime, giving his team a chance to win it all; but if he missed, he'd be letting down the whole town of Centennial.

The pressure was crushing. As the crowd hushed, the boy stepped behind the free-throw line. Trace took a deep breath, finally nodding to the referee. Then he bounced the basketball, one . . . two . . . three, and prepared to shoot. His first attempt swished through the hoop — nothing but net. There was an immediate explosion of cheers from the stands; and as quickly as it had appeared, the noise dissipated as Trace prepared for his second shot. It all came down to this — the game, his future, and his chance to be a hero in front of the entire town, the town that had called him "white trash" when he moved there from Alabama. And then there was his girl, Chelsea. It all rode on this one little shot.

Trace went through his free-throw ritual again and prepared to shoot once more.

After taking another deep breath, he let the ball soar. It all happened like he was watching a movie in slow motion, the ball spinning ever so slowly as it headed for the hoop. After circling the rim for what seemed an eternity, the ball fell. He had missed! But then out of nowhere Trace saw Shooter in the air going for the rebound. After grabbing the ball, he dunked it seconds before the final buzzer blew, resulting in a final score of 87–86, Greystone. Shooter had saved the game!

Ham always insisted on good sportsmanship, calling his players to shake hands with the other team whether they won or lost. But tonight it was particularly difficult for him to maintain discipline over his boys since the taste of victory was so sweet and everyone in the gymnasium was going absolutely wild.

After pats on bottoms and all of the other odd things young men do in celebration of victory, the team went to their respective families and girlfriends for hugs, kisses, and congratulations. Shooter hoisted Bobbie up on his shoulders and pranced around like the Lion King. Tonya watched him, taken by the athletic excellence Shooter had displayed through the evening as well as the obvious adoration he felt for his son. She couldn't have been more proud.

Rightfully so, the attention was split equally between Greystone's star players while all eagerly awaited the response of the scouts. There was one guy in particular who Shooter and Ham couldn't take their eyes off of, and in fact, no one could quite believe he was actually present. He was the topflight scout for the Chicago Bulls, and even a nod from him was beyond the dreams of most any high school boy, no matter how talented. But there he had been all evening, watching Shooter.

Chelsea smothered Trace with kisses, unconcerned about her display of affection in front of the crowd. She was more aware of "marking her territory" for the reams of girls standing around looking at Trace with admiration and desire.

And then, after the team hoisted Ham up on their collective shoulders and marched him around the court, his players finally headed off to shower.

Eleanor couldn't have been more excited for her husband's win than if he had personally dribbled the ball every inch of the court and made every rebound and basket. She wondered what the end of the season's tournament might bring after such a night of jubilation.

Stephanie practically threw her trays of food on some of the customers when she heard from Eleanor about the team's victory and Trace's performance. Then the two ladies decided on the phone that Eleanor and Ham would rustle everybody up and all would celebrate at Norros as fast as the troops could get there. Oh my, what a night!

As the crowd began to thin slightly, Eleanor whispered into Ham's ear, "Do you know, sir, that you are no less than seven foot three to me?"

Ham beamed, wiping the perspiration off his face so he could give her a kiss. The only thing that could have broken their private moment of joy was the sight of two scouts heading their way. A veteran of sports etiquette, Eleanor immediately took her cue to step aside and let Ham have this sweet moment of success and conversations with the guys.

And as she was about to depart, she told her husband, "Later, my love. . . ."

And as if it were even possible, Ham's grin widened as he considered all the possibilities before him. "My, my, . . . what a night. Thank you, Lord!"

Eleanor ran her finger lightly along his

face, engraving his jubilant expression in her memory. "I'll wait for you at Norros." He nodded as she joined Lauren and Pam, who were standing by the door sidestepping the crowd as they piled out of the gym.

How sweet it is when life's highlights are choreographed together by God's fanciful design to bless so many of his loved ones at the same time.

CHAPTER 11
-CROSSROADS-

"What's the matter with you, girl? Why can't you be happy for me? I made it big time. . . . What are you, stupid? *Big time,* don't you get it?!" Shooter's harsh words froze in the winter's night air, backlit by the school's overhead parking lights.

Bobbie had never heard his father yell so loud and quickly retreated back inside the double doors of the gymnasium at his mother's prompting.

"Don't yell like that in front of Bobbie, and please listen to me!" Tonya tried to de-escalate their level of conversation, which was getting out of control at an alarming speed. "I *am* happy for you, and I'm not stupid." She paused for emphasis. "But you've got choices to make . . . options. What about college?" Tonya clutched Shooter's hand hard. She felt if she let go, he'd simply vanish.

"The NBA wants me, girl! I'm going

directly to the NBA from high school, and that practically never happens. The Bulls are one of the best teams in the world, and they want me! You should be screaming happy over this."

"I'm happy, I am . . . I just, I don't know . . . I'm just surprised." She fumbled for words while Shooter stared at her in disbelief.

"Tonya, it's what I've worked for all my life, and it's here faster than I thought. There's nothing bad about this."

"I know, but what about your education?"

"Man, you sound like the father I never had." The young man tried to control himself, taking a breath to settle. "Now I'm gonna go by to tell Ma the good news, and then we're all gonna go out and celebrate. Are you comin' or not?"

Tonya glanced at four cars behind him packed with his high school friends and cheerleaders with their pom-poms tied to the car antennas. Cigarette smoke billowed from the windows, and exhaust from the cars' pipes created a surrealistic background behind Shooter's head.

"That's good, go talk to your mom, but then let's go to Norros to celebrate. Bobbie can come with us there, and he can be part of the excitement."

"I ain't going to Norros to sit and have no cheeseburger with all those uptight . . ."

". . . Don't. Come on, Ham and Eleanor are going to be there."

"I'm goin' over to Billy's."

Again Tonya looked around Shooter at the cars, noting that Billy and Robert Jack were waving Shooter over. "Hey man, let's hit it. It's freezing, man," they yelled.

Then Billy stepped out of the car and opened the back door for his teammate. "I gotta get things cranked up at the crib. Come on!" Everyone was hooting and hollering as if they had already been on a bender. Clearly Tonya was worried about how the night would unfold.

Shooter waved his friends off for the moment and addressed his girl again. "Look, like I said, I'm goin' to get my ma and go to Billy's. If you don't want to come, I'll drop you and Bobbie off at Norros. . . . Whatever you want."

Tonya couldn't believe what she was hearing. She felt like she was looking at somebody she didn't even know. "Shooter, what's going on? We've talked for years about getting a college education. I know how important basketball is to you, but what if something happens? What if you get hurt? You've got nothing to lean on. Our future . . ."

Shooter pulled his hand away from hers hard. "I don't want to hear this stuff right now. You talk to me like I'm a kid, and I'm not. Last year I got recruited by Columbia, and you didn't want to go to New York City. So I said OK, I'll wait. . . . Take a chance and get something nearer to here to make you comfortable and all."

Now Tonya's voice escalated. "It wasn't about me; it was about raising Bobbie in New York City. A lot of great colleges are in towns that would be better places for us to get started in our marriage."

"I'm takin' the best place for me to play ball . . . period! If you want me to cover the family, then get out of my way. Especially seeing that one of the best in the world just picked me up! I'm going, and I want you to come with me. Get this sweet deal signed, and we'll get married, OK?"

Tonya took his hand again. "I just need you to tell me you'll think about it. You could get lost there. Chicago's so big, so fast. People get hooked up . . . killed even. Tupac Shakur just got shot and died. It's dangerous!"

By now Shooter was seething. "Tonya, that guy was a rapper. He got shot in Vegas, not Chicago. I play ball, and I'm gonna stay clean!"

Fed up, he started to walk but stopped a few feet away and turned slowly to face her. His voice was low and even, and he looked like he had aged years within moments. "Girl, you got to believe in me or forget it. I'm going in the fall as soon as I graduate to play for the Bulls, and if you ain't by my side . . ." He just shook his head.

"No! You're going to get your mama so you can go with your friends and go drinking. I'm not interested in that kind of celebrating. You can't go out and buy beer legally, so you're going to be sitting in Billy's house doing stuff you're not supposed to do, and your mama's going to be right there doing it with you. And that's what I'm afraid of . . . that you're going to end up like her."

It was the first time since Tonya met Shooter that he'd ever stared at her with pure hatred. "Don't you *never* talk about my ma like that! At least I have a mama standing by me. . . . You got no one but your stupid little sewing circle. Go on with yourself, grow old with them in this stinkin' town. I'm gone."

She could tell by his expression he had a lot more to say, but he walked away instead, and for that she was thankful because she already had been served up more than she could digest.

Tonya stood frozen in disbelief. What just happened? How could he drive off without her and Bobbie? She started to choke back her emotions, at first wanting to scream after him to stop, but she didn't. Was it her pride? Or was it her pain? It didn't matter. All that mattered was that the love of her life had walked away, and she knew if she were really honest with herself, this was the moment she had feared for some time now.

Everything flashed through her mind, the six years she and Shooter had known each other. All their dreams and aspirations, and all that waiting — waiting on the "right time." Yes, she always believed Shooter had been faithful to her. So what was wrong? Was it a check in her spirit or her own insecurities? Was she reading the script right? Was Shooter wrong to be drawn to fame and fortune? She really couldn't blame him for wanting more out of life.

The problem was, in the end his priorities weren't the same as hers, simple as that. Everything he was doing was based on his own power, and that scared Tonya.

She told herself she wasn't a small thinker, just a more careful dreamer than Shooter. Besides, she always believed that fact was what gave them a good balance as a couple. But suddenly she had seen his frustrations turn to anger. No, he didn't want to hear logical or practical thinking; he wanted to fly unencumbered. He wanted to glide above it all on the ride of his life. So why couldn't she go with him? Oh, she knew any of those girls waiting in the car to go party with him would pounce on Shooter the second they smelled a breakup coming, so why wasn't she going with him? Was she just scared?

Bobbie stuck his sweet face out of the double doors, tired of waiting for his parents. "Hey, Mom?" His little voice brought her back to reality.

"Yeah, Bobbie. I'll be right there." She dried her tears, which were partly frozen on her cheeks, and stepped inside the building. Pulling herself together, she noticed a few people straggling behind in the gym while the janitor started picking up around the bleachers.

And much to her relief, she saw Pam standing in the corner waiting to make sure her friend was OK.

Norros was a cacophony of sound as the basketball crowd jammed through the doors ordering everything from coffees to pork chops and apple pies with mounds of ice cream on top.

Over the din Stephanie heard Eleanor and Lauren singing as they entered the packed establishment. Stephanie screeched at the top of her lungs, running over to hug her friends. She was deliriously happy as she jumped up and down like a jack-in-the-box. "Kentucky! Oh, praise the Lord, the University of Kentucky wants my boy! Did Ham say anything else?"

Now Eleanor started bouncing up and down in time with Stephanie. "What more is there to say? *He's in!* Ham said he'd go over all the details with you when he got here. And the scout's comin' back next week to talk to you and Trace personally."

"But it's a done deal, right? It's real . . . It's a real done deal?"

"Yes, yes, and yes! Ham's just cleanin' up, and then he'll fill you in. But yes, you have a college boy on your hands, missy!"

In Stephanie's delight her mind traveled over the four years of her son's college in an instant. "I can't believe I wasn't at the game! Thanks for staying on the phone with me, Elly-Belly."

"Excuse me?" Eleanor feigned a look of shock.

"No insult intended," Stephanie chortled.

"Actually, I always wanted to call you Elly-Belly, but I wasn't sure you'd care for it."

"I don't, but you're allowed anything tonight." Eleanor stopped jumping, then dramatically grabbed her chest. "I think I just bounced my 'full-figured foam form' clear out of my bra." Lauren and Stephanie instantly stood at attention to cover Eleanor as she discretely rearranged her top.

"Thank you, ladies, and if I start jumpin' up and down again like a fool, just slap me silly."

The crowd was starting to get raucous, calling out for Stephanie to attend to their ravenous appetites. "Girls, help me take care of these crazy people, will you? My heart's beating so fast I feel like I'm gong to pass out."

"I'm in." Lauren headed toward the kitchen. "And if anyone gets rude, I'll serve them up a dog tranquilizer."

"No, let's save 'em for Norro." By now, Stephanie was downright giddy.

"Oooh, good idea!" Lauren vanished into the crowd.

Before Eleanor could join Lauren, Stephanie grabbed her arm, unintentionally dislodging Eleanor's chest placement. Without skipping a beat, Eleanor performed a quick shimmy and righted herself once again.

"Sorry. . . . Where's Trace?" Stephanie looked worried.

"He'll be right along. I saw him gettin' in his car with Chelsea."

"Oh, now *that's* comforting."

"Don't worry. . . ." Eleanor patted Stephanie on the top of her head. ". . . He promised he was comin' right over."

"He better be. He's not too big to have me cross him over my knee."

"Now *that* would be some picture for the newspaper." Eleanor rolled her eyes as they headed into the clamoring crowd toward Lauren, who was already standing on a counter stool taking orders like a pro.

Steam totally fogged Trace's Volkswagen windows.

Parked under the giant evergreen tree, as usual, the kids' hiding place was easily scouted by the telltale exhaust smoke making a steady curl through the majestic branches of the natural forest tent. Trace and Chelsea were in a lip-lock that seemed to last an eternity when Trace finally pulled away.

"Hey Chels, we have to go. My mom's waiting. I promised everybody we'd see them at the diner."

Instantly Chelsea's infamous pout appeared. She had other plans for the evening and wasn't going to give up easily. "Oh, come on. We can get there later, in a while. This is so exciting! The University of Kentucky wants you!"

"Yeah. I can't believe it finally happened." Trace looked dazed.

"What's so cool is that it's not far, and I can keep working on my singing and music and you'll be a college star."

Trace leaned back in his seat, taking in the reality of the moment for the first time. "You know, . . . I was scared I was going to miss out, Chels. No one scouted me as a junior, and I haven't been playing very good lately. This is an amazing break. Kind of like what my mom says. Maybe God *is* watching over me."

"Like that you have a little fairy godmother?" Chelsea asked with a hint of sarcasm.

"Actually, she calls it 'God's favor.' She says, no matter what *I* do, she's praying enough for the two of us. Then she says she can't do that forever; I have to do my own praying. That's when she pokes me with a fork and says, 'Just kidding.' "

"She pokes you with a fork?"

"Yeah, she's just kidding. She's done that

since I was a kid. She says she's just checking to see if I'm well-done, like a roast or something."

"How weird." Chelsea looked out the window. "I've got an idea — why don't we stop by Norros quick, then we can take off and go get something to eat alone. We can celebrate by ourselves, OK?"

"That's not going to be cool with my mom. No way she's going to let me out of her sight — not tonight, anyway. Come on Chels, she's been waiting as long as I have. We'll have a good time."

He started the car, but she turned the key back off before he got it in gear. "Trace, I have some stuff I want to talk to you about. It's private."

The boy looked at her for a minute, then turned the ignition back on. "We can talk later. Right now I gotta get where I said I was going to be so I don't worry everybody."

"Since when are you such a mama's boy?" The girl gave him one of her flirtatious smiles, but her question boomeranged.

Trace slammed the car in gear. "There's nothing wrong with wanting to share this with my mom. She's worked as hard as I have to make this happen."

Chelsea knew she'd pushed the issue as far as she could for the moment, but that did not stop her from reclaiming her pouty expression. "Whatever."

They drove in silence for a few minutes before she countered with another question. "So, where do I fit into all of this?"

Trace tensed. "It's not even 'til next fall, almost a year from now. We've got lots of time to talk about that. What matters is, I don't have to worry about getting picked up by the scouts. I just have to keep my grades up and play good because there're lots of rules and regulations to this scholarship thing, and I've got to get it all straight and make sure I don't mess up."

"Right. . . . You've got to keep your grades up. You know I help you with that."

Softening a bit, he looked at his girl. "Yeah, thanks. . . ."

She nodded, trying to show more enthusiasm. "Hey, it's great. I'm really proud of you."

Affirmed, he put his arm around Chelsea, satisfied that for the time being all things were right in his life. And he smiled as they headed to Norros.

Tonya, Bobbie, and Pam made their way to Pam's car, both women holding the young boy's hands and intermittently swinging him high in the air. As cheery as Tonya was trying to be for the sake of her son, she was clearly devastated about what had just transpired between Shooter and her.

Pam watched her friend for several strides before speaking. "You know, you can do something in an instant that gives you heartache for a lifetime. I'm sure he'll come around. Maybe part of it is that you have to hear what he's really thinking too. Hey, can you imagine how excited he must be? I'm not even a big basketball nut, but as far I know, going straight to the NBA out of high school is just about unheard of."

Tonya picked Bobbie up, rubbing him in her arms to warm him up before putting him in the car. "I know, I know that. I probably sound like a downer to him, but you know the problems with his mother. . . . And you know that stuff gets passed along. Sure she had a hard time with his father, but all she does is sit at home since her back problem, drink beer, and watch soap operas. And he thinks that's OK! Well, I don't. There's nothing wrong with her mind. She could work. What kind of example is she for Shooter . . . or Bobbie?"

Tonya was derailing fast, and Pam had to get her back on track. "None of that is new, Tonya. She's been like that since you've known her."

Tonya snapped at her friend; she was hurt and defensive. "Whose side are you on, anyway? I happen to know that Shooter and his mom sit around when she wants company and play checkers, and she gives him beer! She says it doesn't matter in the privacy of her house. How can that be good? What's going to happen to him when he's in Chicago in the middle of that lifestyle? Pam, you know what it took to talk him out of going to New York City. He'd never get along at Columbia. He may be big and fast, but he'd be a laughingstock at that swank school. 'Big city' is just not Shooter."

Before Pam could respond, Tonya was off on another tear. "OK, maybe I'm underestimating him. I even thought about doing my modeling thing there in New York while he was going to school. Everybody said that it would be perfect. But what would happen to Bobbie if we're both off in this fast-lane world? I don't know. Maybe *I'm* just scared. I've spent so long trying to be responsible. . . . Truth is, sometimes part of me just wants to fly off and be free. I can't imagine that's not what Shooter thinks about too. All I remind him of is responsibility. . . . 'Make good grades. . . .' 'Get your rest. . . .' 'Take Bobbie to the park. . . .' 'Babysit while I study.' "

Tonya paused for a moment, staring into the distance with vacant eyes. Then she exploded. "I don't want to be his mother! Or his teacher! I want to be his wife! And I don't want to ask any man to marry me. I want to be swept off my feet. I want a knight in shining armor. And I don't want to believe, at twenty years old, that it's too late for me."

Pam automatically handed Tonya a Kleenex like she would any of her children at her day care or patients in counseling. "You're just beginning, girlfriend. Trust me." Then she opened both car doors and helped Tonya strap Bobbie in a car seat she'd permanently set up in the back for him.

Before Tonya got into the front seat, she regarded Pam. "Eleanor's always said, 'It takes years to build up trust and only seconds to destroy it.' I feel like I just got stabbed in the heart."

"Just try to give him some time. I know what he said to you stinks, but he's all excited right now. And about Norros, he's never been comfortable around our crowd. I don't know, maybe his mom made him feel that way. Ever since his daddy left her, she's not been interested much in other people. She probably assumes everybody's talking about her. Hey, she didn't even come to the game tonight."

Tonya held her forehead. "I know, . . . and that kills me! But I also know that I can't make Shooter love me."

"Tonya, the boy loves you. Come on."

"I'm just saying that he's going to make his own decisions about his future, and either Bobbie and I are going to be at the top of his list or not."

"How about I give you a counselor's response to that? You can't make someone love you, but you can make sure you're lovable. And you are, don't forget that. Remember, you've got lots of time before anyone has to make any hard, fast decisions."

Tonya looked at Pam with baleful eyes. "I don't think I want much more time like this. I need Shooter to step up . . . or step away."

Dressed to the nines, Ham strutted down the street headed for Norros. Sporting a fedora at a rakish angle, his cashmere overcoat covered his Sunday black suit accented by a gray shirt, white tie, and black-and-white wing-tipped shoes.

Eleanor paused at the diner's window to search the street when she spotted her husband approaching. Oh, she just loved the fact that her stomach did a little flip at the mere vision of her love. And when he saw her, he blew her a kiss in anticipation.

CHAPTER 12
-THE AFTERMATH-

With her teddy bear in tow, Stephanie shuffled down the hall in her big pink furry slippers, her chenille bathrobe tied askew, and her hair up in rollers, looking more like an alien with antennas than a middle-aged mom with a beauty parlor arrangement crowning her head.

Shafts of light cut across the small kitchen into the adjacent living room marking Stephanie's direct path to her refrigerator. Once she settled in front of her personal feast-fest, she stubbornly held onto her teddy bear while grabbing a glass of lemonade, two ice cream bars, and a handful of popcorn from the big yellow bowl on the counter.

And as she turned back toward her bedroom, she let out a blood-curdling scream, throwing all the contents in her arms about the kitchen in abject fear. Her terror instantly turned to defensive anger toward the shadowy figure before her, but when Trace stepped up into the light, she visibly relaxed.

"I hate that! You're lucky I didn't shoot you."

"With what? Your popcorn?" Trace teased, gallantly pulling out a seat at the kitchen table for his mother.

"I'm serious, you scared me silly."

"Mom, come on, sit. I'm trying to be polite. You always taught me to stand for a lady."

"Only after you clean up her kitchen."

Stephanie reviewed her treats trashed all over the floor with dismay. Without further discussion they both proceeded to pick up, far too happy about the evening's events to be irritated by the mess before them.

"What on earth are you doing sitting in the kitchen at 3:03 in the morning?"

"Probably the same reason you're raiding the icebox at 3:02 in the morning. . . . I couldn't sleep." His expression turned to pain. "Mom, how can you stuff one more thing in your stomach? I ate more tonight at Norros than at our last three Thanksgivings combined."

"And that's saying something for a bottomless pit."

Stephanie gingerly shook her teddy bear off in the sink and placed it on one of the empty chairs as if he were a third member to their after-hours party. Trace grabbed the bowl of popcorn off the counter and placed it in the middle of the kitchen table while Stephanie poured another couple of glasses of lemonade.

Rubbing her stomach, she noted the presence of a miniscule belly bulge and decided to return her unopened ice creams to the freezer. "Mark my words, Son. I will be 'lean and mean' by your commencement day, even if I have to get up and run with you in the mornings."

"When I get to college, the guys are going to want to date you. You're hot, Mom."

Stephanie switched on the kitchen light and stepped in front of her son, pointing to her rosy cheeks. "Look at that boy, you're making me blush. . . . And please note my rows of crows feet while you're handing out the sugar."

"I'm telling you the truth. . . . Let your hair grow a little longer and get some cool jeans, and you could run for Spring Queen."

Stephanie joined her son at the table, loving every second of his compliments. "All this sweet talk and you're not even in trouble, . . . are you?"

He gazed at her, dreamy eyed. "I'm happy."

"So am I, Son. The University of Kentucky! I always knew it would happen, but now that it actually has come true. . . . Now that it's the real deal, I had to pinch myself all night to make sure I wasn't dreaming."

"Me too. Not the pinch part . . . but, yeah, I'm going to have to work harder before I graduate, that's for sure."

"You better. Remember what Ham told us. . . . There are strict stipulations to this scholarship thing. You've got to keep your grades up, and . . ."

". . . I know, I know, Mom. I'm on it."

The two allowed themselves a sweet moment of silence to revel in the realization that all their lofty plans were actually coming true.

Then Stephanie looked at her son square in the eye. "Don't you just love it when God shows up with a cap and gown and a college degree in one hand and a ticket to your future in the other? It's because he loves you so much. Now that's . . ." And they finished the sentence in unison, ". . . favor!"

Trace gave his mother one of his drop-dead smiles. "You probably won't believe it, but I told Chelsea that tonight."

Stephanie leaned back in her chair. "You're kidding!"

"Nope, I did. You've been pounding that

'favor' gig into my head since I can remember . . . and that God loves me. It sure felt like it tonight. I really didn't play that great, you know, and they still took me."

"Let me say this, Son. At times I've played better than you did . . . tonight."

Trace laughed, blowing his lemonade clear out of his nose. Stephanie was on a roll. "Now boy, I raised you better than to spray me with lemonade."

Trace buried himself in a napkin and begged for a truce.

"OK, time out. . . . You're just going to show them how good you really are."

They relaxed for a moment as Trace regained his composure. Stephanie studied her son once more. "So is Chelsea OK? She didn't seem too festive this evening."

"Yeah, I know, but she said that she didn't feel good. That's why I took her home early. She felt nauseous. Probably the flu or something. But hey, Mom, she's really helping me a lot with my homework and stuff."

"I know. It's not that I don't like Chelsea. It's just that I don't want you to get side-tracked."

"I'm not."

Stephanie paused to gather her thoughts. "I'm just not accustomed to you being so serious about a girl. Remember, I've never seen you hang around with one for more than the length of a movie or a dance. So you'll have to bear with me. As much as you're seeing Chelsea, it gives me . . ." Stephanie searched for the right word.

"Nightmares?" Trace was half kidding.

"No, not *nightmares*. . . . Caution, maybe? Just keep your priorities straight and take your time. You know what I'm talking about. Lust is always in a hurry, but true love can always wait for the right time."

By the time she finished her last sentence, Trace was blushing as he struggled with a guilty conscience.

Stephanie was acutely aware that she was broaching a subject that he preferred to sidestep. Little did she know that despite all her warnings over the years, her son had already gone over the line with Chelsea, and he wasn't proud of his behavior. He looked extremely uncomfortable.

For the sake of some breathing room, Stephanie got up and started to brew some coffee. "I might as well not go back to bed. I can't sleep anyway. I'm so excited about your scholarship."

"Thanks, Mom."

And with that her boy fell deep into thought. These were the moments Stephanie waited for — the little slivers of openings her son would give her when she could inject a seed of wisdom or lessons hard won that she could share so Trace wouldn't have to go through the same hurtful scenarios she had. And on a rare occasion he actually listened and learned.

Stephanie ventured, "I can remember before I lost my mama and daddy, times around the kitchen table where they had my brothers, sisters, and me reading Scripture. I've told you, my daddy was a farmer's philosopher in his way. And mama had these methods of teaching us kids that put his words of wisdom in our minds to stay." Now Stephanie looked over her shoulder at Trace. "You want some coffee?"

"Nah, I think I'd jump clear out of my shirt." Trace grabbed a banana from the fruit bowl, hunkering down for one of his mom's "sessions." But for some reason that morning he didn't mind because as excited as he was about his future, he was just as confused about his relationship with Chelsea, and just maybe his mother would have some advice for him.

Nonetheless, he was guarded about sharing his personal thoughts with Stephanie, concerned that expressing his real feelings and fears would cause her to try to control his relationship with rules and regulations he didn't want to hear about. So he opted to sit there silently, eat his banana, and listen to what she had to say.

Trace had labeled the times such as he was about to share with his mom as their "speaking in code" conversations. They both knew what they were talking about, but neither would ever hit the subject matter at hand square on the head. For instance, when he was eight and he stole a pack of gum from the drugstore, he knew, as sure as he was breathing, that the pharmacist, Mr. Keller, had spoken to his mom about his wrongdoing. But instead of coming right out with a confrontation and punishment, Stephanie decided to handle the situation by telling Trace a story about when she was a little girl and how she'd learned that being honest, not envious, was an imperative virtue in life.

Stephanie had been playing dolls with one of her school friends one day and inadvertently took home the little girl's gown for her Barbie doll in her overnight bag. When young Stephanie got home and found the gown, she hid it with no intention of giving it back to her friend. Born of her adolescent thinking, she conveniently decided that "finder's keepers" was her motto since she was sure she'd never be able to buy such a pretty dress for her own doll.

When her mother found the doll dress, she didn't confront Stephanie directly, but rather, she sat her down and talked to her about something *she* had done as a kid, and how she had learned her lessons about stealing and coveting. And while Stephanie's mother was making her point to her daughter, she was also designing and sewing a doll dress for the offended child's birthday, a dress no one had because it wasn't store-bought.

Through the entire lesson Stephanie couldn't believe her mother was going to give her friend the special doll dress; but by the time her mother finished the design, not only did young Stephanie help her wrap the doll's gown with care for the girl's party, but Stephanie also included the original dress inside the box with a written apology: "This got mixed up with my doll's dresses. Then I wanted to just keep it . . . I should have returned it sooner. Sorry."

As an adult, Stephanie was thankful for the way her mother had taught her lessons of life. They were always based on the Word of God, and somehow she made the verses apply to everyday life without humiliating her daughter concerning youthful indiscretions.

Stephanie built a solid foundation to pass along to her own children. As it turned out, she mothered only one son; and Stephanie was determined, even as a single parent, to pass along those life lessons with the same grace and wisdom her parents had shown her.

And now she was having one of those rare opportunities with Trace. "When we kids used to go to the grocery store, my mama would sit in the truck and give us the list of things to pick up. It would have been a lot easier and faster for her just to go in and get the milk, eggs, flour, and everything we needed; but she took the opportunity to teach us how to be diligent and responsible. She used to make us count how many things were on the list and then count what was on the check-out counter so we'd know if we'd missed anything."

Stephanie joined her son at the kitchen table. "We never had a lot of money growing up, so we had to be careful how we spent it. Your granddaddy always used to say, 'Money is a lousy way of keeping score of life, especially with people you love.' That's why your college education and scholarship are so important, Trace."

He rolled the banana peel up into a ball and shot it into the garbage can. Swish. Perfect shot.

"Being in debt stinks. I know, Mom."

"That's why we live within our means. And I know you've always hated this trailer. It was hard for you when we moved here and the kids saw you living in a place like this. But it's neat and it's clean, and we can afford it. So to me, it's my palace."

Trace shifted in his seat. "You won't have to pay a cent for college with the full-ride scholarship. You'll be able to open up your own place if you want to. And as soon as I graduate and they let me make money, you'll have everything you need."

"I'm fine, Son." She melted at her son's sweet words. "You have a great heart. You're generous, and that's good. But it's not your responsibility to take care of me . . . at least not yet. But wait 'til I'm all bent over and have a bunch of long hairs growing out of my chin. . . . Then I'll be on your doorstep."

"That's gross, Mom."

Stephanie was enjoying herself. "Gross but true. Anyway, my point is, I'm not your focus now, and that's the way it should be. How you're going to shape your life is. Where you go, who your friends are, who you hang out with. Some people kick you when you're down; some people help you get up. I remember when I was little and it was a big deal when those huge spaceships would launch out of Cape Canaveral to search the heavens."

Now Trace laughed. "You're such a romantic, Mom. They launched satellites so we can watch better TV."

"Fine, but I had a reason for talking about those little rockets that are attached to the sides of the big missiles. They're called 'booster rockets,' and they are there to get the journey off the ground. After launch they fall away, and the missile keeps going. That's what it's like with some people. They're only there for a season while others are there for a lifetime. It's figuring out 'who's who in the zoo' that makes such a difference. Remember, the success of your journey is not only your destination. It's also how you go through, not just where you're going that matters."

"And, 'We're all responsible for everything we think, say, and do.' I remember when you made me write that down, when I was ten, at least twenty thousand times."

Stephanie laughed at the memory. "It was twenty times . . . but good, it stuck. Remember this one? 'If you stand for nothing, you'll fall for anything.' "

She leaned over and touched her son's arm for emphasis; her eyes were gleaming. "I already have my restaurant, and you already have your diploma in God's plan. We just have to claim them. Hey, remember the story about the great cathedrals in Europe? How none of the artists ever lived long enough to see their artistry fully evolve because just one building took close to a hundred years to complete. But it was enough for them to be a part of the process for the glory of God. Their job was in the doing."

Trace thought back. "Yeah, you told me about that roof going up over some cathedral, and the artist that still carved a little bird on a rafter that they were going to cover anyway. And when they asked him 'Why'd you even bother? No one will see it,' he said, 'God sees it.'"

"Oh yes, another good one! We've got to have grand dreams because God has bigger ones waiting for us than we could ever think up. Hey, maybe you can tell this one to your Chelsea. I know she dreams of being a big country star, and maybe she'll make it. But when she's on the red carpet, ask her who she'll be wearing."

"What do you mean?"

"Who's her designer? Is it someone who

made her dress or her jewelry, or is it God, who gave her her voice and her talent so she could be a star?"

Trace pulled back in his chair. "You don't like her, do you?"

"I don't dislike her, Trace. Yes, I want the best for you, . . . and the best for you is all about who you can really share your life with. Look, I know you've been angry at God since your dad died. But you're about to go off on your own, and you'll be making decisions by yourself. Hopefully you're going to choose the right ones. Not the right ones because of any rules and regulations but the right ones because you know right from wrong. And I'm not going to be there for most of your future decisions, but God is always there, and he'll always steer you in the right direction if you'll listen to him."

Stephanie sat back, sure that she had probably said more than her son would digest at one clip. Still, she was satisfied that they had had what she considered a 'God appointment' in the wee hours of the morning. She called them "cherished times," when the business of life didn't claim the sweet moments of true communication and loving exchanges.

She smiled at Trace, who now had an expression on his face of "let me out of here." Nonetheless, she knew that some of what she'd talked about with him that winter morning at their little kitchen table would seep in.

"Ding!" She slapped her hand down like a court mallet. "You're dismissed."

Trace laughed, his shoulders relaxing slightly. "Yeah, . . . well I'm going to grab a few more Zs." Standing, he gave his mom a perfunctory hug.

He started down the hall but then turned back to her with a mischievous grin. "Hey, I got one for you. . . . What's the alternative to Alzheimer's?"

"Are you trying to tell me something?"

"Nope, listen. . . . The alternative to Alzheimer's is remembering things that never happened."

"Ha! Good one!" She pointed at Trace as she got up to join him.

"Yeah, Ham wrote that on the school board yesterday. But here's one from me . . ."

"Shoot."

"Is God a single parent?"

Now that stopped Stephanie in her tracks, unsure of how to answer.

Trace smiled, "Ha! Stumped you! Remember, there will be a test."

"Yes, well, . . . I'll get back to you on that

one." Stephanie nodded, knowing that would be the first thing she'd bring up at the next meeting of her circle of friends.

CHAPTER 13
-BEST INTENTIONS-

Ford Williams's penthouse apartment at the Carlisle Hotel looked like someone had hosted the ultimate all-night sorority party. Clothes by an array of designers were strewn about pulled from shopping bags and boxes. Chanels, Manolo Blahniks, Christian Diors, and Dolce and Gabbanas hung from the tops of lamp shades, flung over the furniture and spilled across the floors. Food carts of delicacies from room service were overflowing, partially eaten plates balanced on coffee tables and desktops along with a collection of opened white and red wine bottles merely tasted and then abandoned for another year and winery.

The trail of excess made a path into the master bedroom where Irene lay splayed across the satin sheets and triple-down comforter atop the California king-size bed. Her hair looked like a bird's nest, and her eye makeup was smeared down her face and onto the sheets from a night of crying.

It took the persistence of the telephone endlessly ringing to jar Irene from her semiconscious sleep. And with obvious resentment she grabbed it to silence the intrusion.

"What?" She answered gruffly, her voice hoarse and raspy. She pulled the phone away from her ear as Lauren's ever vivacious morning salutation echoed in her ear.

"Hi, Rene. Rise and shine! I've got good news!"

Irene painfully rolled over, staring straight into the morning sun that reflected across the glistening snow-capped trees lining the street below. Despite her discomfort at being awakened, Irene couldn't help but note how magnificent Manhattan was, especially in the ritzy neighborhoods of the Upper East Side.

"Please, I'm resting," she half whispered into the phone. "Can we talk a little later?"

Lauren was seated with her parents in their apartment at the kitchen table with the Centennial Saturday newspaper spread out before them. The front page headlines and photo were of Shooter rebounding the winning shot of last night's game.

Local Basketball Star More Than Just a "Shooter"

As was his habit, Sam dissected his eggs and bacon while Margaret partook in a bowl of fresh fruit and whipped cream. Bingo was sprawled across the floor while William sat politely at attention exactly three and a half feet from the table where both animals had been put on a "sit, lie down, and stay" by Lauren. Obviously, she had resolved the "William rude noises and smells" situation by changing his diet, resulting in the pets being allowed to attend the goings on in the Patterson apartment.

"I can call back, Rene, but I figured it was an hour later in New York, and I just wanted to give you the good news that we *are not* on the front page of the paper, or *any* page of the 'rag' for that matter. The only 'court' proceeding found to be newsworthy by the local reporters was the action that happened on the basketball court last night. And that's a good thing because airing any more of our dirty laundry stinks."

Irene hoisted herself onto an elbow, placing one of the fluffy pillows over her head to shut out the light and at least part of Lauren's bellowing voice.

"This is a good sign, Rene. Maybe the

press is getting bored with the story. I was just about to find that editor guy, Brandon whatever-his-name-is, and give him a piece of my mind. But I guess I don't have to now. Thank God for small favors . . . literally. Yeah team!"

Irene struggled to clear her head. "Can you please keep the cheerleading at a minimum? I'm recovering from life."

Concerned, Lauren tried to eke out some more information about how her sister was doing. "Sounds like you did some serious unwinding."

"Yes, . . . I did *a little* unwinding, *a lot* of damage at the stores, even *more* damage to Ford's wine cellar, as promised."

Irene tried to push her hair away from her face, but her fingers got stuck in her tangled mass of bangs. "I am also pleased to announce that I was successful in making an appointment with my hairdresser today. Otherwise I would have to pull out the clippers and adopt a Gandhi look. I think I still have half of a crème brûlée stuck in my 'forelock,' as you would call it."

"Oooh, I'm jealous. Exactly how many desserts did you order?"

"Only three," Irene groaned. "But I didn't just taste them; I ate every last morsel. If I put one more piece of food in my mouth in the next ten days, shoot me and put me out of my misery."

"Rene, if you stuffed yourself for the next ten days, you still wouldn't make a shadow at sunset. Oh, Mom wants to speak to you."

Irene began to protest; but before she knew it, Margaret was on the line.

"Darling, are you having a glorious time?"

"Absolutely, Mom. Actually, it's a beautiful day here, . . . I think." Irene stared out the window. "At least it *looks* nice, but I'm not really up yet."

"Well, we just wanted to give you the grand news about the newspaper and check to see if you were fine. Oh, and don't worry, Chelsea came home rather early last night and has been in her room ever since. I checked." Margaret looked at Lauren, proud of her maternal performance on Irene's behalf.

"It seems your daughter is a little under the weather, though. But at least she didn't have us tracking her like a bunch of baffled bloodhounds wandering about in the cold of night without a clue."

Irene pulled herself out of bed; she was fully dressed in a rumpled yet still stunning Chanel outfit. Looking down, she realized she should have put the clothes back in the box to be returned *before* she fell asleep.

"Oh well, . . ." was as much concern as she could muster at the moment. More importantly, she didn't like the sound of Chelsea's early bed report.

"Mom, Chelsea came home because she didn't feel well? Now *that's* something to worry about. Remember she had a 102 temperature about a month ago and insisted on going to the movies with Trace."

"Oh, darling, don't worry. She's here, and I'll check on her again in a little while. You just enjoy yourself. Did you see your lawyer yet?"

"No, he didn't have time for me yesterday. But I'm going to meet with him for a late lunch after I get my hair done and try to pull myself together. You know, you've got to look the part, especially here in New York."

Irene started to walk toward the bathroom, catching her image in one of the floor-length, pearl-inlaid mirrors. She was a scary sight. "On the other hand, I think we'll just lunch in the penthouse."

"Good. He can come to you, especially considering how much you'll be paying him."

"Whenever I get some money."

"Yes, that's what I meant."

"Right. So, how's Dad?"

"He's fine."

"Good. Let me talk to Lauren again, OK?"

"OK, love you. . . ."

". . . Me too, Mom. And I'll be back tomorrow afternoon."

"Good. Bye, dear."

Margaret handed the phone back to Lauren, who was midway through a piece of toast; she blew crumbs everywhere as she spoke. "Hey there. . . . I'm going to be on my cell if you need me today."

"Thanks. My plane gets in tomorrow at five-thirty. Can you pick me up?"

"Oh, that's perfect. My troops over at the shelter have been unbelievable. They've just about gotten everything done, and the girls have called some special meeting at Norros after church, so five-thirty will be perfect. . . . Hey, did I hear Mom say you're going to meet with your lawyer?"

"Yes."

"Well, don't let him know that you're walking on thin times. Otherwise he'll just take advantage of you."

"It's thin *ice,* Lauren, and ice is just what I need for my forehead right now. I've got to run. I'm supposed to be over at Pierre's by eleven."

"OK, bye Sweetie. I'll see you tomorrow, and maybe Chelsea will come with me to pick you up. I'll ask her."

"In my grave." Irene moved into the bathroom as she undressed.

"Now don't say such a thing, Rene!"

"Fine. I'm too fat to die anyway, . . ." Irene exhaled. "Got to run, really. Love you."

"Double." Lauren blew a kiss into the phone and hung up.

And with that she was up and away, gathering the newspapers in a wad and throwing them in the garbage. Then she scurried around and gave her parents a kiss as she headed out the door with William and Bingo.

"Rene sounded good, huh?" she remarked over her shoulder.

Sam pulled himself away from his breakfast long enough to shoot Lauren a furrowed brow. "I didn't even talk to her, and it sounds like she's gone off the deep end."

"She'll be OK, Dad. She just needed to get out of here for a break. . . . I don't blame her. Anyway, she promised she's coming back tomorrow."

Her father grunted. "I heard that too. Five-thirty."

"Yup. . . . See you guys later."

"I'll make an early dinner. You'll be tired after working at the shelter."

"Super. Thanks, Mom."

"Is Tucker going to be home?"

"Nope, Brian has him for the weekend. OK, as Rene would say, 'Got to go.' "

Shopping on Saturday at PetSmart in the local mall was like trying to take a stroll through Grand Central Station at rush hour.

Lauren had finally finished her rounds and was paying for the odds and ends she needed for the shelter. The young boy checking her out was oblivious to Lauren's incessant one-sided conversation, which hadn't stopped since she'd piled her merchandise before him.

". . . So tell all your friends. . . . We'll be bringing some flyers over later announcing that the shelter is opening on Monday. It's a full veterinary facility with free spay and neutering. Anyone who has an unwanted pet knows where to go now! I'm sure you're aware of the animal chutes that used to be around here. . . . Or maybe you're not. But they're history, thank God . . . literally."

She looked down at the piles of dog bowls and bones before her. "I can't believe I didn't get these through a catalog. You guys are pretty expensive, by the way. Do you give any discounts for buying more than one?" The boy didn't realize he was actually being asked a question, having tuned Lauren's dialogue out as soon as she'd arrived at his counter.

Lauren was waiting for the boy's response to her question when she noticed Tucker heading across the way into the movie theatre from the mall's escalator. Instinctively, she threw her hands up in the air and yelled, "Hey, Tucker!"

At her outburst, the salesboy dropped several of the aluminum bowls that clattered across the floor causing everyone in the immediate area to grimace.

"Oops, sorry, sorry. That was my son. . . . OK, sorry."

She looked up again and saw that Bobbie was running behind Tucker into the theatre.

What a coincidence, Lauren thought while she looked around for Brian. Within moments she spied him from behind the escalator wall with Tonya by his side. Lauren froze, watching the four enter the movie theatre together. But it was when Brian and Tonya stopped at the ticket counter and he put his arm around Tonya's shoulder briefly that Lauren's jaw actually dropped. She stared in disbelief, only returning to reality at the insistent whine of the salesboy's voice.

"Ma'am, debit or credit?"

Lauren whirled around to find that her purchases were bagged and ready to go, and everyone in line was impatiently waiting for her to conclude her transaction.

"Credit, . . . sorry." She complied mechanically, unable to stop her eyes from roaming over to the movie theatre. She quickly signed the slip, then grabbed the oversized plastic bag full of bones and bowls that virtually covered her from the waist up.

Instead of veering off to the right to head out of the mall, Lauren was drawn like a magnet to the movie theatre. Once she reached the entrance, she hid behind her purchase bag as she observed Tonya, Bobbie, Tucker, and Brian at the snack counter ordering popcorn and sodas. She couldn't help but note that they looked extremely relaxed and happy with one another, almost like a family. Her mind raced as she fought back spikes of jealous emotions, telling herself, *Oh, you're being ridiculous, Lauren. Tonya's your friend. The little boys are friends. They're all just going to the movies together.*

But then that little nasty negative tape started playing games with her mind. *So why did Brian have his arm around Tonya? Oh, and if they're just friends, why did he pay for the tickets? Obviously this was not the first time they've all been together. Why are they laughing so much? Look at Tucker and Bobbie; they're having so much fun.*

Thankfully, her spirit-voice reprimanded her jealous thoughts. *The boys have known each other for a while now; of course they're having fun. And there's no reason that Tonya would have felt compelled to mention their going to the movies because there's nothing wrong with it; they're just having a playdate.* Lauren's thoughts scrambled again, attacking the meaning of playdate. *Date . . . Tonya, Brian. What on earth is going on?*

But before Lauren could finish debating with her own thoughts, the four vanished into the bowels of the multiplex theatre, leaving her in the mall wondering if she had dreamed the entire scenario.

Eleanor sat tall in her chair across the large oak desk of her friend and physician, Dr. Ned Logan. As always, she had her Bible clutched to her chest, but her expression was not tense. Rather, it was one of peace and resolve.

"First off, Ned, thanks for seein' me on Saturday."

"No, no, it's not a problem. I've told you, *anytime,* Eleanor."

"Yes, you have. Thank you. Well, I've made a decision and . . . Actually I want to confirm it with you . . ." A slight smile crossed her face, ". . . before I change my

mind, which of course is a woman's prerogative."

The doctor smiled. "Of course."

"I've been strugglin', as you know, with
this reconstruction thing. And bein' a nurse
I'm pleased with how everythin' went
technically in regard to gettin' all the cancer."

The doctor quietly cautioned her. "And
as you well know being a nurse, the ultimate
results remain to be seen over the next
several years. But as the surgeons and I told
you and Hamilton, it couldn't have gone
better, even though the surgery was radical."

Eleanor put her hand up. "We don't need
to rehash, Ned. My point is, the reconstruction part is strictly optional in terms of my
physical well-being, and I know that my
husband has been to see you more than
once out of concern for my emotional . . ."
Now she struggled with her words, ". . .
female sides. And I have to admit, I had a
little bit of realignin' to do with my Lord
and Savior because part of me was miffed,
to say the least, about havin' such an ugly
thing come upon me. But God told me
straight out that I was going to be fine and
that going through this was goin' to leave
me in a better place than when I started.

And as hard as that felt for a long time, I'm ready to move on with my life and my relationship with my husband."

"That's wonderful, Eleanor. Believe me, you won't regret it."

She was sure to make this point clear. "My husband doesn't care one lick whether I get this reconstruction thing done or not. Now that I've gotten over myself a bit . . . You know, feelin' sorry for myself and all, and Ham and I are back to our old selves or . . ." She looked down a little bit embarrassed, ". . . or even better than our old selves, truth be known. . . . I thought, what's the point of more surgery? But frankly, I'm tired of holdin' my Bible to my chest and not feelin' it, or walkin' down the street thinkin' if I bump into somebody they'll just bounce off of me like runnin' into an inner tube at Water Works."

The doctor couldn't help but be amused by his old friend's sense of humor and visual descriptions.

"I've even considered writin' a comic strip about a woman in my position and how it feels to have the better half of herself not really hers." She sighed for a moment. "So, with all that said, . . . bring 'em on! I'm ready to give Halle Berry a run for her money."

The doctor was pleased at her decision, jotting some instructions down on his prescription pad. "Marvelous, Eleanor. I want you to get some blood tests and go in for another checkup with your surgeon and your oncologist. Once they give you the thumbs-up, which I'm sure will be soon as far as your initial healing goes, we'll schedule the surgery."

Once again Eleanor looked down out of embarrassment, then back at her doctor. "I know we'll go over all the details, but however best they can put me back together just the way I was is what I'm lookin' to have done. I don't want to be pumped up, twirled around, and reinvented like some calendar girl."

Now the doctor laughed outright. "Never fear. A lot of women have made a good thing out of a bad and rather enjoyed ordering up exactly how they would like to look."

"Well, I leave that up to my husband, and he's always seemed to be mighty pleased. So unless he has a new request — which of course if he does, he can just get a new woman — what I was, the way God made me, would suit both of us just fine."

The doctor walked around his desk to give his friend an affectionate hug. "Then that's just how it will be, Ms. Eleanor. You've been a trooper through every moment of this ordeal, and you deserve to get back to being you . . . because this is the best time of your and Ham's life."

Eleanor grinned, looking not much older than an exuberant teenager. "That's just about what I was thinkin'."

Miraculously, Lauren was able to ascend the shelter stairs, balancing her cumbersome bag of bowls and bones without breaking her neck.

As she approached the front glass door, she turned around so she could back into the lobby while holding back the double swinging doors. But before she made the second set of obstacles, Carla was at her side to assist her.

Lauren quickly plunked her load on the ground and looked around in total amazement at the half dozen extra bodies who were zipping around the shelter painting, trimming out, attaching chairs to the floor, and sanding the front desk where hand-hewed wooden planks were being placed artistically around the main reception area.

Carla squealed in delight as she pointed out her station. "Look! Look what they're doing. That totally rocks! It looks like they took part of my grandmother's dining room set and put it on my desk."

Lauren just shook her head. "Who are all these people? Where did they come from?"

Mrs. Strickland's voice reverberated from down the corridor. "Little worker bees, my dear. A few helping hands to finish up so everyone can have their rest on Sunday and not have to worry about the opening Monday morning."

At the grand dame's entrance, everyone from Lauren's staff — Clive, Savannah, Brenda, Carla, and the other six workers — stood at attention while Mrs. Strickland strutted through the room introducing Lauren to each new crew member.

"What you have here is your own personal creative team, Ms. Lauren. All the craftsmen happen to love animals and support what we're doing here. Every single lovely finishing touch is donated, just so you know . . . they won't siphon your 'care' budget. Isn't that lovely?"

Lauren was overwhelmed. "Thank you, . . . everyone. I know in my heart that we do not serve a $1.98 God; and yet, when it comes to caring for his creatures, it seems we're always running short of funds." She squealed in delight. "Oh, this is a fairy tale! People will walk in here and see excellence at every turn. Thank you, thank you, thank you!"

An impromptu applause filled the room. After hugs and handshakes by all, Carla took the pile of bowls and bones and headed down the hall to put them in place while Mrs. Strickland escorted Lauren into her office.

Closing the door behind them, Lauren pulled out a chair for Mrs. Strickland, then took a seat behind her desk. Her furniture was smart yet simple, with only her veterinary license and graduation diploma hanging on the wall.

"I wouldn't be so bold as to venture a guess at how you would like your office decorated, . . ." Mrs. Strickland chimed, ". . . but there's a little check in the right-hand drawer from me personally, not the foundation, for you to dress it up anyway you see fit."

Lauren started to object, "No, Mrs. Strickland, you've . . ."

". . . Yes, Ms. Lauren. There's no arguing with me. We must get that clear right off. You're going to be spending a lot of time here, probably more than you even imagine, and I want you to feel at home. That said, we've turned the utility room next door into a sitting room area for your private use. That way Tucker can come and do his homework after school, or he can have a friend over. I'm sure, if I know the fiber you're made of, you'll be having that boy of yours here most of the time teaching him how to be of service, playing with the puppies and kittens. . . . So he needs to have a place he can relax too. I've installed a little kitchenette. . . ."

Lauren couldn't believe what she was hearing. ". . . A *kitchenette?* We have the staff kitchen."

Mrs. Strickland waved her cane in Lauren's direction. "Now don't interrupt. As I was saying, you're going to need your privacy, believe me. The only thing I wanted to review with you before our opening on Monday is what we had touched upon at our last luncheon but really didn't clarify. I've prayed about the door-to-door services you suggested, and I think it's a marvelous idea. So I just wanted you to know that it is my desire to move in that direction, . . . to use veterinary students and qualified individuals to take our services to those who otherwise wouldn't come to us."

Lauren was flabbergasted. "You mean, what I was talking about . . . Not the animal protective services. A whole other program? We could see the animals in their home environments and . . ."

". . . Yes, yes, all that. We'll go over everything in detail once we have the shelter up at full steam. Also, I've already put my office on collecting applications for your animal behaviorist position as well as re-training an assistant for that program so we can evaluate our rescues properly."

"Oh, Mrs. Strickland, punch me, please. . . . I think I'm imagining all this!" Lauren was having a hard time holding her joy down to a low roar. In fact, she looked like she was about to become flat-out hysterical. Perhaps she had had too hard a run of it lately — concerns about Irene's state of mind, Chelsea's counseling difficulties, and of course, all the work at the shelter. And now, the lunacy of running into Brian and Tonya was just too much. Yes, her Pandora's box of old emotions had been cracked open, and a flood of uncontrolled behavior was beginning to rise up.

"Oh, my," Mrs. Strickland murmured in response to Lauren's obvious overload. "Are you alright, dear?"

Lauren got up and paced behind her desk in an effort to harness her tears and stave off a bout with her frazzled nerves. "I'm fine. Fine, fine, just fine!" Lauren waved her finger in the air as if she were speaking to some invisible visitor. "I know that few people are fast enough to keep up with their best intentions. Yes, but that's not a reason to stop trying, of course. When everything you've ever hoped for is sitting right in front of you . . . Oh, I'm feeling very surreal."

Mrs. Strickland watched Lauren unravel but remained calm, recognizing that she was merely witnessing a glitch in performance, not a full-fledged breakdown. She had become so fond of the woman over the last several months.

"Lauren, even God put things in order before he did any miracles. Now don't get overwhelmed; just take one step at a time. Everything is exactly how it should be, so give yourself a break and a big pat on your back. You're doing a superb job."

Mrs. Strickland's soothing words did the trick, and Lauren began to calm.

"Thank you. You're right. . . . Everything's OK. God does not have to perform triage. . . . He can take care of everything we throw at him all at the same time. . . ." She took a long life-affirming breath. ". . . Oh, I feel so much better!"

"Of course you do, dear. Everyone is allowed to lose her mind at least once a year, I say." And with that the woman was right back to business. "Now we're going to have press here Monday, so that's why I was reviewing all the programs with you."

"Press?" Lauren instantly tensed again. "I thought all you were going to do was take some photos so we can have the opening memorialized."

Mrs. Strickland raised her cane again, steadying it in front of Lauren's face in a mesmerizing circular motion. "How are people supposed to know about the shelter without coverage in the press? There will be newspapers, radio, the five o'clock TV news channels; and hopefully the Associated Press will pick up the story that our shelter is one of the most advanced in the country. Of course, we're not 'up and running' as yet, as far as the long-term capacities of this establishment; but I want the cameras to get the overflow of animals arriving from the five neighboring towns, especially the critters the other shelters don't feel they can place. That way we'll have ongoing humane stories of rescues, the placement and physical care of these animals to keep playing in the news. We must make clear from day one what our goals are. You've already reviewed all of our flyers and bulletins. Thank goodness we don't have to deal with any board members other than my own, so we can make swift decisions as they come up to cover whatever needs arise."

Mrs. Strickland finally dropped her cane back down to her side, satisfied she had Lauren's full attention. "Now all we need to do is seal our mission here in prayer, and as your staff so eloquently puts it, 'We're good to go.' "

"Amen."

And then Lauren and Mrs. Strickland knelt at the side of the desk and prayed.

CHAPTER 14
-Is Less More?-

Pam was waiting outside the doctor's office for Eleanor, who emerged from the building with a special spring in her step. Pam was amazed and thrilled at how quickly things had turned around for her friend.

While Eleanor danced between a few ice patches on the street, Pam took the opportunity to remind herself that any given day could feel like the world was crashing down, but then the very next day could just as easily bring a little Fred Astaire out in even the most reluctant positive thinker.

She gave herself a miniature talking-to as she now watched Eleanor dodge an oncoming car with the ease of a matador. Pam simply needed to stop taking herself so seriously. She actually could be responsible without being maudlin. And right then and there, she decided that over Christmas she was going to take some time off. Maybe she'd even allow herself to be a wild and crazy girl and go skiing. Yes, she was going to leave the details of life behind for at least a week; and when the next crisis cropped up, she'd be out of range, challenged only by the advanced ski slopes she would conquer with ease — or, hopefully, without breaking any of her appendages.

Pam considered all the resolves she'd made over the years at the slightest prompting. For her, every day was New Year's Day, with new horizons to be mulled over. And that was OK with her, because she figured if she kept even a small percentage of her bids for a better life, she'd be further along than most undisciplined wishful thinkers.

When Eleanor slid into the front seat, she flung open her coat in an expression of freedom. Pam looked at her for a moment before she put the car in gear. "Hot flash?"

"Don't jump the gun, I'm only forty-seven." Eleanor rubbed her hands together gleefully, then pulled her gloves off and flipped them into the backseat.

Taken with her odd behavior, Pam stared at her as if she were a specimen in a jar. "My, my, you look terribly pleased with yourself."

"Let's just say, I'm goin' to have a lot of fun playin' God for a time."

Pam was stumped. "OK, I give. What on

earth are you talking about?"

"I get to choose my bust size, shape, . . . the whole shebang. Well actually, I believe Ham and I do."

Pam was still confused. "Please, Ms. Eleanor, I'm happy about your re-up of your nuptials, . . . but I just find details a little embarrassing."

"Shame on you, sweet pie. Our details have always stayed in our bedroom. . . . I'm talkin' about my reconstructive surgery. We get to choose, if you know what I'm sayin'."

"Oh, sorry." Pam reconsidered Eleanor's situation. "Actually, that sounds kind of cool."

"Well, you know what they say, . . . 'The grass is always greener.'" Eleanor fluffed up Pam's long, blonde hair. "For instance, I've always wanted hair like yours."

"I think the color would be a little trashy on you." Pam smirked.

"I didn't mean your color, silly girl. I meant your straight and thick mop."

"What an attractive description. Remind me not to have you write my eulogy."

"Are you planning on leaving us?"

"Only for a short vacation, but that's another conversation. Let's get back to coveting. . . . I've always wanted a husband like yours and . . ."

Eleanor was on it before Pam could finish her sentence. ". . . Well, you can't have him."

"I said, '*Like* your husband'! But fine, if you won't share, you can't have my hair."

"Fine, . . . then you can't have my bust line!" Eleanor whistled. "I think we just wrote a country lyric."

"OK, you've totally lost it. Let's get back to the doctor thing."

"Oh yes, . . . the doctor says I can have any kind of bustline I want. So, if I could just lose twenty pounds before I have the surgery," Eleanor turned to Pam, "that might change the shape of things, . . . jelly bean. My, my, . . . I'm a poet, and I know it!"

"And I'm serious. Quit the rhyme thing please. You're scaring me."

They bantered on like schoolgirls as they approached the town circle. Pam looked at Eleanor. "The shelter?"

Eleanor broke into a wailing rendition of the Stones' hit song, "Give Me Shelter." Pam didn't even attempt to curb her silliness, joining in on the chorus as they made their way across town.

The progress in the lobby at the shelter continued to be miraculous. Everyone had worked nonstop through lunch as evidenced by the half-dozen bags of fast food and piles of soda cans.

Lauren was surprised to see Pam and Eleanor make their way through the front doors, singing at the top of their lungs. "Whoa, time out. You must have the wrong building. The concert hall is two blocks to your right. What are you guys doing here?" They all hugged as the interlopers settled down and the workers went back to their duties after their miniature entertainment break.

"The cheap labor has arrived. We're here to sign up, but it looks like there's not even an inch of room to stand in here that isn't being remodeled into . . ." Pam looked around in amazement. ". . . Oh my gosh, what a beautiful place!"

Eleanor concurred as Pam took a quick stroll around the waiting room and then on down the remodeled halls. But first, she just *had* to get her hands all over the carved wood on the reception desk.

"Amazing, isn't it?" Lauren beamed. "Mrs. Strickland sent all these incredible artists over to make everything special."

"Well, she can send them right on over to my hut when they're done." Eleanor whistled again in admiration.

"Sorry, I've got first dibs."

The two took in all the activity as Lauren pointed out various details to Eleanor.

"Where's your doggy? By now, he'd have licked me clean and silly."

"Oh, I had to leave him at home today. Bingo's nose was getting out of joint. The cat is incorrigible. Yesterday I brought William over here by himself, and she left me a little 'treasure' on my bed pillow in protest."

Eleanor made a face. "What *kind* of treasure?"

"A dead bug."

"Eeeew." Eleanor jumped up and down shaking her hands. "How disgusting!"

"Most of the time when cats leave you little presents, they're signs of affection. But I suspect that Bingo was trying more to annoy me than please me. She does not like to be left behind when I take William out alone."

"Either bring her or put a muzzle on her little face."

"I'll bring her, but she can't come here yet. . . . With everybody going in and out of the doors, I'm afraid she'll get lost. . . . But once we get settled, they both can come to work with me."

Pam had taken a quick tour of the back kennels before rejoining Lauren and Eleanor. "It looks like a pet hotel. . . . Can I

319

move in? Some of those dog runs are bigger than my apartment."

"It is beautiful, isn't it?" Lauren puffed up like a bantam rooster. "Mrs. Strickland spared no expense. By the way, she's got about a million press people coming on Monday for the opening, so I'm glad you think it looks impressive."

Pam quickly scanned the lobby. "Everything looks fabulous."

"Yup. All we need now is the patter of furry little paws, and we'll be in business."

"So how can we help?"

"Actually, there's nothing much left. Thanks anyway, guys, for coming down."

Eleanor piped in. "We were all coming over, but Steph's slave laborin' it at the diner as usual, and Tonya's out with Bobbie somewhere. But she said she could come over anytime after three if you need her. She asked if she could bring Bobbie with her."

Lauren stiffened. "Sure, . . . after the movies."

"Oh." Eleanor noticed Lauren's sudden shift of mood.

"Tonya's at the movies . . . with Bobbie, . . ." Lauren explained.

"Alright. . . . Is there something wrong with that?"

"No, nothing's wrong. No, absolutely not. Actually it's all helpful because Brian took Tucker this weekend so I could work and . . . they were all at the movies together having fun. Tonya and Brian and . . . the boys know each other, of course. I've had Bobbie to the house myself to play with Tuck. It's kind of curious though, if you were all coming to help. . . . Maybe Brian could have taken Bobbie and Tonya could have come over here with you guys. But I don't need the help anyway, as you can see, so that's fine. . . . Everything's fine."

It was obvious to both Pam and Eleanor that Lauren was upset, but they decided not to pursue the issue as Lauren promptly changed the subject.

"Hey, let me show you my office. It's not done, mind you. Later on I'll need your help with that, girls. Mrs. Strickland made the adjacent room a place for Tucker, or you guys, or any one of my millions of fans and friends." Lauren laughed nervously. "It's for my personal use with a kitchenette. Boy, when I think that three months ago I didn't even have a job, and now, . . . look at all this!" She put her arms around her friends and started to usher them into her office.

"I was just thinking about that in the car," Pam added, trying to pull the conversation in a less confusing direction. "We all need to make a pact that whenever we feel like everything's a total mess, we'll remember that it can turn around in a split second. God loves to do that."

"Yes, he does, sister," Eleanor concurred.

And then they all said, "Amen," in unison.

Lauren was on her cell phone as she wove through the Saturday afternoon shopping traffic in Centennial heading home.

"Right, Mom. But she's there now? Uh-huh. . . . OK. Well, do you think I need to bring her something? Does she need some aspirin or something for the nausea? . . . OK, well, she's never been great at being sick. The only one who rivals her in that area is Dad. But then again, if a man has a little pimple on the end of his nose, his life simply ceases. Right. . . . Just hang in there, and I'll be home in five minutes, and I'll handle Chelsea. Besides, she can't be going out if she's that sick, even if Irene was home. OK, Mom, bye."

Lauren considered how much she was not looking forward to another confrontation with her niece. She was sure that telling her she couldn't go out that night with her boyfriend was going to go over like World War III. She then speed-dialed Suz in

California, muttering under her breath, "Be there, be there, *please* be there. Hey, Suz! How art thou?"

Suz was making some curtains at her sewing machine in the utility room of her home. As she cradled the phone against her ear, she continued her masterful stitching. "Hanging like a bat. . . . You? Are you ready for the big day?"

"Better than that. Mrs. Strickland did it again. She brought in a ton of extra people, and everything looks fantastic. On top of that, she's called in a lot of press for Monday. I'll get copies of everything and keep you posted. I'm *so* excited!"

"Well, you deserve it, my friend. How's my boy, Tuck?"

" 'Splendid,' as you would say. He's still doing great in school and can't wait for Christmas vacation. Speaking of that, what are the odds of my getting you out here then? How's Fred feeling?"

"Medium."

"Oh. . . . You know I'd bring Tuck to visit you, but with the shelter and all just opening, I don't think I can leave."

Suz sighed, looking at her husband through the crack in her door. He sat at the table in the next room, vacantly staring at the newspaper held askew in his slightly shaking hand.

"I'm not so sure I'm going to be any more mobile than you are. Fred's doing better with his physical therapy every day though. And I do honestly believe some of his motor skills and memory are returning. Of course, I'll be able to tell a little better when the kids come home for the holidays. They'll be a good barometer because they haven't seen him since he first had the stroke."

"Gotcha. . . . Hey, I've got a suggestion. When I used to get a horse, like a rescue horse, I would take pictures and videos of them once a week. That way I could track their improvements instead of guessing."

"Good one. . . . So, would you mind sending me your bridle, and I'll stick it on Fred's head, and we'll see if I can get him to take the correct lead at the canter."

Lauren's enthusiasm shriveled. "I can't see your face, but I really hope you're kidding."

Suz moved on to her next panel of curtains. "Of course I'm kidding. I've also had one too many coffees today, can't you tell?" She glanced over to at least seven cups lined up on the window sill.

"Coffee makes you talk funny; it doesn't make you mean. I was just trying to help. I didn't want you to misunderstand. . . ."

". . . Oh my goodness, Lauren. *I was kidding!* What's up with you? Are you hormonal or just exhausted?"

"Both, and you know I hate being teased."

"Get over it. If I can't be silly with you, I'll lose my mind. I have no one else to play in the sandbox with."

Lauren missed her nutty friend. "Sorry, sorry. I hate when I go off in a little huffette."

"So do I, but you're forgiven. You need to chill out. Did you know that women have more heart attacks than men? It's one of our biggest killers."

"Where'd that come from?"

"Looking at my half-empty coffee cups with globs of heavy whipping cream floating on the top staring back at me. . . . The killer concoction *you introduced me to,* by the way."

"Ah, I remember. But I also remember telling you that it tasted great but it would probably kill you. I am a doctor, after all."

"Yes, and if I contract rabies, you'll be the first one I'll call. By the way, do animals go through menopause?"

"Kind of, but I don't think they realize they're miserable. Remember when I had to give Gracie hormones? She turned into Godzilla every time she came into season.

Brian used to say that the only thing that put my PMS in perspective was my horse's raging moods and gnashing teeth." Lauren's manner changed with the mention of Brian. "Speaking of Brian . . . No, never mind. It's incredibly stupid."

Suz could tell by Lauren's tone that whatever was bothering her, she undoubtedly would have to pry out of her friend. Nonetheless, she also knew from experience not to let Lauren's 'never minds' go by because they'd just build up and later explode into bigger issues.

"OK, what's up with Brian? First you're concerned he's going to church, which, by the way, should be a good thing. And now what is he doing?"

"I know it's a good thing, Suz, . . . that he's going to church. I just don't get why he didn't go with me. And now he's out with Tucker and a friend of mine and her little boy going to the movies."

There was a long pause. ". . . And?" Suz urged her on.

". . . And I was just surprised, that's all."

"About what part? The movie, the other little boy, the friend? . . . Who's the friend? This isn't going to be an 'Irene best friend thing,' is it?"

"It can't be. Brian and I are divorced. . . ."

". . . Remember that point, Lauren. I was just about to remind you of that little fact."

"Alright, alright."

"So what else?"

"It's Tonya, one of the girls in our prayer group. I was just surprised that she didn't mention it to me."

"Well, maybe she didn't know she was going to the movies last time you saw her."

Lauren considered the possibility. "You're right, I'm being an idiot. . . . I'm sorry It was nothing. It's just me. . . . But the way he put his arm on her shoulder and paid for the tickets was . . . That's what bothered me. She didn't do anything. *He* did the arm thing, and *he* paid for the tickets, so even . . . oh, never mind."

Suz noticed some movement in the next room, realizing that her husband needed assistance. "Sweetie, I have to help Fred. He's not really good at maneuvering yet, and he's obviously trying to get up."

"No problem. I'll talk to you later. I'll try to call you after church . . . and if not, I'll call you after the opening Monday."

"Perfect. Sorry I have to run. I love you and miss you."

"Double." Lauren hung up again and started to dial once more but then stuffed her cell phone in her pocket, making a definitive decision to give herself a moment of silence so she could clear her head before tackling the demands of the teenage tyrant at home.

In a way she wished Pam hadn't confided in her about all the trouble she was having with Chelsea in counseling. Now she felt quadruply responsible when Irene wasn't around to oversee the girl. At least she did plan with Pam to meet a little early before all the girls gathered at Norros after church tomorrow to choreograph Pam's counsel with Irene. Hopefully a new plan would be forged.

The plot thickens, Lauren thought, hating that Irene was about to have even more problems hoisted upon her.

Tucker and Bobbie were tearing through Chuck E. Cheese while Brian and Tonya sat at one of the corner tables polishing off the remnants of two extra large pizzas. Their conversation was exchanged at heightened decibels to overcome the incessant videos and music playing throughout the restaurant.

Brian pointed to a weary mom at a table of five kids ranging from a toddler to a six-year-old. "I saw that woman over there with her kids the last time I was here with

Tucker."

Tonya laughed. "How can you remember anyone in this mad house? Everybody looks the same to me, especially the kids. They're all just a blur, running around like wild animals."

"I noticed her because all her kids look different. . . . So she's either babysitting, or she has weak genes." They both laughed. "Anyway, my point is, she must live at this place because I've only been here twice before, and she's been here both times."

Tonya leaned in so he could hear her better. "Well, maybe she's thinking the same thing about you."

"Nah, that's impossible. I'm a logical man. What would the odds be that she and I would both be here at the same time if I've only been here twice. She has to *live* here."

"Your point?"

Brian thought for a minute. "I had my reservations about moving to Tennessee, but now I have further concerns about turning into a Chuck E. Cheese permanent fixture as a father. There must be some more educational or inspiring places we could take the boys . . . like Cirque Du Soleil."

"I agree, but the circus only comes to town once a year. Other than that, our choices are relatively limited."

"Then let's get out of town. Do you ever take Bobbie on day trips or weekends to different places? I hear Gatlinburg's only three hours away, . . . or we could always fly down to Florida and go to Disney World."

"Oh sure, Brian, let's just hop on a plane. It fits right in with my school schedule and budget."

Brian gave her his most charming smile. "Well a guy can dream, huh? Seriously, I was going to ask you if that was something you might be interested in since I have extra frequent flyer miles and Tucker's never seen Disney World. Of course we went to Disneyland all the time when we were out on the West Coast, but my boy never gets tired of Mickey and Donald."

Tonya sat back, a little shocked. Speechless in fact.

Brian was stalled by her reaction. "I hope I haven't offended you. I just thought the boys get along so well, and your schedule seems about as hectic as mine. A little relaxation is good for everyone. Then again, if you think Bobbie would be OK with it, I could just take him along as a buddy for Tuck. I wasn't sure he was old enough to go without his mom."

"Oh." Now Tonya felt silly for reacting

with such surprise. "That's incredibly nice of you. . . ." She fumbled for a minute. "I could definitely ask Bobbie if he wanted to go alone. But first, I'll have to check it out with Shooter."

"Absolutely." Brian got her message loud and clear. "I was thinking about going over Christmas vacation, just for a long weekend. Let me know if that works for you and Shooter, . . . and Bobbie, of course."

They were spared an awkward moment when their boys careened into the table, almost knocking their sodas over.

"Hey, Dad, there's a really cool pinball game. Can we play?"

As soon as Brian pulled out some tokens for the boys, they were off again. Tonya and Brian watched them interact in silence for a while, occasionally glancing at each other and then away again.

"They sure get along great, don't they?" Tonya finally broke the ice.

"Yup, sure do."

Sam paced back and forth in front of his bay windows, the setting sun behind his head intermittently blinding Margaret who sat on their living room couch. They were in the middle of one of their heated arguments.

"What do you want me to do, sit on her? She says she's going out, and I can't lock her in her room. She's got the only key, and it only locks from the inside."

"Sam, I don't like this at all." Margaret was highly agitated. "It's such a huge responsibility. The girl doesn't listen to what either one of us say . . . But I'm *not* going to call Irene because they'll just get into it on the phone. Besides, there's nothing she can do long distance."

Frustrated, Sam peered out of the window. "Lauren's back."

As Lauren ascended the steps of the house, she saw her father standing in the front doorway with his arms crossed over his chest. The vision instantly brought back terrible memories for Lauren as a child about to get reamed by her father for some wrongdoing. She had to remind herself, as she took each step, that she was an adult and that her father was a guest in her house, and he couldn't spank her anymore.

"What's wrong, Dad?"

"It's *your niece!* Chelsea's been arguing with your mother all afternoon, and when I put my foot down, she basically told me where to go."

"You mean, *your granddaughter?*"

Sam glared at her.

"Sorry, sorry. . . . I was just trying to make a funny."

Lauren hurried in the door, patting her welcoming committee, William and Bingo, as she made her way over to her parents' apartment. Her father was on her heels.

"That girl needs to learn some respect."

"I know, Dad, but she's been really better for a while, don't you think? Never mind; what happened?"

"Ask your mother."

Lauren banged on the door as she walked in. "Hey, Mom, what's going on? You told me everything was in control on the phone."

"I lied. I didn't want you to drive off the road . . . Chelsea says that she's going out in a little while with Trace. It was more of an announcement than a request. And when I said that her mother wasn't home, she said, 'So what? I'm seventeen, and it's Saturday night, and I'm going to go out with my boyfriend.' "

"That's it? Dad looked like she had gone through the house with a hatchet."

Sam's face was getting redder by the minute. "That's enough. I believe your mother is putting their exchange in more respectful words than Chelsea did. Anyway, Margaret is going to get dinner ready, and we're going to let you deal with your niece."

"I made enough food for her too, of course. Your father just doesn't want to lose his temper with her. So it's best . . ."

". . . No, no, Mom, it's fine. I told Irene I would take care of her, and I will."

Lauren had shed her overcoat in the hallway and was at Chelsea's door in no time flat. She knocked three times lightly, not wanting to begin any kind of confrontation with an aggressive first round.

"Chelsea, it's Aunt Lauren. May I come in?" There was no answer, so Lauren checked the door, which, as usual, was locked. Now she stiffened her knuckle and hit the door with firmer action. "Chelsea, I need to talk to you now. Open the door." She waited a few seconds, then banged adamantly again. "I'm serious. Open the door now!"

With that the door flung open, and Lauren almost fell into the room. "I'm going out with Trace, that's all. It's Saturday night. I didn't do anything wrong. I came home early last night. We're just going to the mall to eat, and I don't see why Granddaddy's saying I can't go!"

Suddenly the girl looked green and ran

into the bathroom, closing the door behind her.

Lauren moved closer, speaking through the barrier. "Well, for one thing, Sweetie, you've been sick since yesterday. I called to see if you needed any medicine." Lauren paused when she heard Chelsea retching, deciding to take a seat on the girl's bed and wait for her to come out.

Within moments Chelsea was back in the bedroom, verbalizing her stream of logic. "So Trace is picking me up at seven, and I'll be back by ten, OK?"

Lauren walked over to her, holding her by the shoulders. She looked into the girl's eyes. "Are you alright? Do you need a doctor?"

"No, it's just some bug or something. A lot of kids have it at school. I was good all day, and I'm just upset, that's all. I don't want to argue with the grandparents, but there's no way I'm not going out tonight."

"Well, Chelsea, there is a way. Your mom's not here, and you know what her rule is: if she's not here, you need to stay in. But she and I discussed it when I took her to the airport, and she said it's fine if you'd like to have Trace over here. Mom's made dinner, and you guys can just hang out and watch TV. . . ."

". . . No! I don't want to hang out and watch TV with my grandparents, OK?"

Lauren noticed that Chelsea seemed extremely overwrought, but she assumed her intensity was due to the fact that she wasn't feeling well.

"I'm sorry, Chelsea, but that's the only option, especially if you're sick. Why don't you let me take your temperature. If it's up, no one's supposed to be around you anyway. You have to go to bed and get some liquids in you. When was the last time you ate?"

"I don't need to eat. I'm fat. I'm on a diet."

"OK, now you're really scaring me. You're not making yourself throw up, are you?"

"Oh, how incredibly gross is that? What's the matter with you?"

All of a sudden the girl looked green again and ran into the bathroom once more. And once again Lauren sat down to wait. She decided her niece couldn't fake looking green, so she probably was really sick. On the other hand, she hadn't heard about any flu going around. By that time Chelsea was back out of the bathroom with a wet wash-cloth in her hand.

"Sweetie, I'm worried about you. I'm going to get the thermometer and take your temperature. So just sit tight, and I'll be back. If you don't have a fever, Trace can come over. But that's it."

Lauren started out the door with Chelsea on her heels whining. "I've got to see him tonight! But not here. Come on, I know you understand. It's just dorky to sit at home and watch TV."

Lauren stopped short causing Chelsea to pile into the back of her. "Dorky or not, Chelsea, I'm getting the thermometer, and you're not going out."

When Lauren started up again, Chelsea exploded. "I hate you! I hate it here! I hate all of you!"

But Lauren was determined not to fold. "Back at you girl. I love you, but I don't like your behavior one lick. So sit down and relax, unless you want me to call Trace's mother about this."

"No, don't do that!"

"Then sit down and be quiet!" With that Lauren vanished down the hall feeling rather proud that she had been staunch.

Stephanie slammed through the front door of the trailer, moving a mile a minute with mountains of grocery bags piled in her arms. She threw the fresh food into the refrigerator in haste, leaving the rest on the counter.

Scurrying down the hall to change for her evening stint at Norros, she could hear Trace's voice coming from his room. She could also overhear some of his conversation.

"Chels, it's cool. You don't feel well. It's no big deal. I've got a bunch of homework to do anyway. I'll just hang here. . . . OK, but just calm down. . . . No, I don't. . . . No, don't sneak out! I don't want to do that. . . . Yeah, I want to see you, but I can see you tomorrow, when you feel better and your mom gets back. . . . Chelsea, don't . . . hang up."

As Stephanie passed his doorway, it was clear that the girl had in fact hung up on him. He looked at the phone for a minute and then put it in its cradle.

"Hey, Trace." The boy jumped, turning around to find his mother in the hall.

"Hey, what's happenin'?"

"I'm just changing for work."

Trace got up, looking a little frustrated.

"You OK?"

"Yeah, it's just that Chelsea's mom's in New York or something, and her aunt won't let her out tonight. She's still got that flu thing, so I told her to chill. Anyway, I have some stuff to finish for school."

Stephanie waited for more, but that was

338

all her son was going to give up. "Plus, there's a good game on tonight."

"Yeah, that too." Trace smiled, knowing he was caught.

"Well, do a little homework and enjoy the game. You don't have to go out every night. If Chelsea's not feeling well, it's a good thing she has to stay in. I'm late, so if you get hungry, stop by the diner. If not, you're here, right?"

"Yeah, Mom. I'm just going to stay in."

"I just picked up some groceries. . . . There're some TV dinners and salad from yesterday."

"I'm straight. Thanks, Mom."

"OK, see you later."

Trace picked up his guitar and sat on his bed to start to pick a little bit, deep in thought. Before he knew it, his mom was heading back down the hall to leave.

"Trace, are you going to church tomorrow?"

"Naw, I'm just going to hang out I think. . . . Get some stuff done."

Stephanie knew better than to push the issue. "Well, if you change your mind, let me know. I'm going to the ten o'clock service instead of eight."

"OK. Maybe I'll come."

She stuck her head back in. "Yeah? Leave

me a note, I'll wake you up."

"OK."

"Night, love you."

"Love you too."

Chapter 15
-The Plot-

Eleanor couldn't remember experiencing a more beautiful winter morning than she was with Ham at her side as they made their way to church. In fact, it was so glorious outside, they had decided to take the brisk walk instead of driving, something they hadn't done in quite some time.

Their November morning promenade was a little different from the summer strolls they'd shared over the years when they'd observe the Alans' recently planted rosebush or the Parkers' brand-new car in the driveway. Being winter, most everybody was inside. It was as if the town was built specifically for that morning to surround Eleanor and Ham with postcard beauty as they made their way to the second service to praise their Lord.

It seemed with each passing month their church had grown leaps and bounds. The allure of their anointed pastor and the diverse nature of the congregation were topics of conversation through all the outskirts of Nashville. In fact, the church recently had to add another service just to accommodate the influx of visitors and members. And today was the first time since Eleanor was diagnosed with cancer that she had accepted the pastor's standing request for her to sing a solo during the praise and worship time.

With his wife securely on his arm, Ham looked adoringly at Eleanor. "I'm not trying to sidle up to you, my love, but I never heard you sound better than you did in the first service."

Eleanor enjoyed his encouragement. "Oh, Ham, it was just the song. Stephanie picked it out especially for my range, and it was absolutely perfect, wasn't it?"

"Absolutely."

"To tell you the truth, I've missed goin' out with Steph to sing at other churches."

"Well, we'll just have to get you back in gear now, won't we?"

"Yes, we will." She was glowing with enthusiasm.

As they approached the front lawn of their place of worship, a crowd gathered, extending their greetings to one another, catching up on the latest news before they shuffled their children off to Sunday school and went in for the sermon.

Lauren was already chatting with Stephanie and Trace, who surprisingly had accompanied his mom that morning. ". . . Yes, she's still pretty sick, Trace, but she seems to be better than yesterday."

"That's good, Ms. Lauren."

"Yes, she wasn't up to coming to church this morning, but she said if you were here to tell you that she'll be seeing you tonight. I'm picking her mother up at five-thirty, and as long as Chelsea isn't running a temperature, I'm sure my sister will give her the go-ahead."

"Thank you, ma'am. I'll just take her for something to eat and have her back early."

Lauren couldn't help but be impressed with the boy's politeness, but she also wasn't so old that she couldn't remember back on how easy it was to snow adults. On the other hand, she did have a comfort zone in knowing that Trace was Stephanie's son and that his upbringing was, if not perfect, certainly well intended and biblically based.

Stephanie put her arm around her boy with pride. "You can take her to eat something as long as she can keep it down. We'll just see, Lauren."

"Sure."

"Oh, I'm still in la-la land about Trace's scholarship. I woke up this morning and had to reroute my prayers from requests to thanksgiving."

"I'm surprised my mom has any kneecaps; she's prayed so much over me."

"You're a lucky boy to have such a faithful mom. I've got a long way to wait before Tucker is up for such an important request, but I can only imagine how amazing you both must feel."

Trace's eyes shifted, putting his hand out to shake Ham's as he and Eleanor approached. "Good morning, sir."

Everyone said their appropriate hellos while Ham stood there, smiling at the boy. "Have you been to military school since Friday night?"

"No, sir, but where I'm going to be is at practice and any place else you can think of to help me with my game."

"Sounds to me you've realized God slipped you a pass card."

A little embarrassed, Trace looked at the others around him. "Yes, sir."

"Trace, you're one of the most gifted players I've run across. You and Shooter have different talents, but you're both superlative. He just happened to be working a little harder than you have lately. But you know that, so that's all that needs to be said."

"Yes, sir."

Lauren spotted Tonya, who waved to the group on her way to take Bobbie to his children's class. As she left, she mouthed, "I'll meet you inside."

Lauren chastised herself for her thoughts of jealousy that immediately sprung to action at the mere sight of Tonya, reminding herself that this young lady was her friend. Still, she decided then and there she was going to address the movie/Brian thing with her if for no other reason than she was tired of having a debate with herself over what was probably nothing to worry about.

The congregation was still buzzing from morning welcomes and handshakes up until the time Pastor Mark took the podium to read the weekly announcements. His youthful good looks belied the profound wisdom he carried in his spirit. This pastor was a masterful communicator with an extraordinary heart for the weary and downtrodden. If anyone could pull the community together with the power of spiritual reconciliation, it was he.

"We're still in need of help for our nursery

during the eight a.m. service, please. Also, group Bible study will be held on Monday nights at seven for men, and Tuesday nights at the same time for women."

He read several more updates before finally concluding. And when he did, a wide smile crossed his face. "We have a special treat for all who are in attendance today. Our solo this morning will be sung by someone who is certainly blessed by the great and mighty Lord we all serve. She's a living example of what God can do in all of our lives. Please help me in welcoming her back. . . . Ms. Eleanor, the congregation is yours."

As she stepped up to the microphone, Eleanor could feel the old familiar fluttering butterflies in her stomach. And as the band began her intro, she drifted away to the place she always went when she sang, a place where her soul was free from the concerns and troubles of the world.

Her performance of the classic hymn "How Great Thou Art" sent chills up and down the spines of everyone in listening range. Emotion poured from the verses, and each note rang true and clear, leaving the entire church in awe of the presence and power of the Holy Spirit expressed in Eleanor's extraordinary voice. Her rendition could only be described as a heavenly instrument from God.

When she finished her solo, Eleanor opened her eyes to see the entire congregation on their feet, many wiping away tears, others deliriously praising the Lord. The roar of applause, cheers, and hallelujahs was deafening — a glorious sound to Eleanor's ears.

Yes, it seemed that, as God had promised, through her trials and tribulations, Eleanor's heart and soul had actually grown. She had gone through the fire and had come out the other side better in so many ways. And all she could think of, as she pointed toward the heavens to give credit where credit was due, was how amazingly faithful her God was.

Pastor Mark reclaimed his position at the pulpit, and the entire congregation was rapt at attention waiting to hear this man of God's word for their edification.

"God never asks us to do anything he doesn't empower us to do. Last week we talked about forgiveness and how important it is to God that his children do not hold anyone in unforgiveness, *including ourselves*. And when we recognize how much we have been forgiven, through the blood of Jesus, it makes forgiving others a little easier, does it not?"

There were scattered amens and nods throughout the congregation.

"We discussed the fact that love is a verb and that Jesus loved people, but he didn't necessarily trust them. We must remind ourselves that people are fallible; and when they disappoint us, it mustn't throw us into surprise or depression. And we discussed the physical ramifications of unforgiveness and anger, which are responsible for three times the heart problems or ailments we suffer. We need either to control our anger or attitudes, or they will control us. It is wise to recognize that many of us use anger to control other people, and the moment I begin to hate someone, I become their slave.

"Today I want to talk to you good people about going *through* as Jesus did when he went into the wilderness to be tested by Satan for forty days. He didn't say on the third day, or the thirty-eighth day, 'I'm hungry, I'm exhausted, I don't want to do this anymore.' A designated period of time was required of him to go through so that he could emerge on the other side victorious.

"We've all worried during different seasons of our lives through trials and tests.

348

And I know that we all agree those times are not comfortable. But God never promised they would be. . . . There are no shortcuts in the process of 'going through.' You can't be looking for the results, for example, of a fast in order to bring something about in God's design until that designated fast is over. But God is so generous to us that he sometimes inspires us with blessings along the way. Still, his promising that he will never leave us nor forsake us and that he will never give us more than we can handle supports the fact that we are not going to be comfortable during those times of growth and revelation. So, even if you pray diligently, tithe and contribute extra, and desire nothing more than to have an intimate relationship with Jesus, the truth is, what is familiar doesn't necessarily mean it's good. In fact, it is often fatal.

"Just consider some of the bad habits we carry along with us through our lifetimes. Yet burying those familiar bad habits is a painful process. You'll learn that you can go through tests and refinement without becoming what you've survived in the process. Eventually, you'll come to know that, even if God never gives you the house or healing or breakthrough or release you've asked him for, he is still God. That is real faith. And faith and obedience are inseparable.

"Really knowing we are blessed is knowing that God has given us everything we need to do whatever we are supposed to achieve. Because, my friend, it is already done. We just have to step into the shoes God has left on the path with our names written in them, signed and sealed with Jesus' blood. So if you come to a crossroads in your life, and you will, ask God to show you which way he has already made for you to travel . . . and enjoy the journey because wherever he leads is the way to his will. Remember, God says in his Word that if we want to be in his will, we will worship and praise him in all things, no matter our circumstances. That way, our joy cannot be stolen."

And as the sermon unfolded, so did the revelations for those in attendance. And although that morning's sermon continued for another half hour, everyone agreed as they left the church that it seemed to be over in a flash.

After the service Ham volunteered to watch Bobbie while Eleanor grabbed a ride with Tonya for their emergency meeting at Norros. But before they left, the two women stood for a moment enjoying the vision of

Ham walking down the street holding Bobbie's hand as they made their way back home.

For Tonya, it was a picture of the grandfather her son didn't have on either side of his family; and for Eleanor, it was a flashback of when her son, Mark, was growing up and walked down that very street with his father holding his little hand. What a sweet moment, and both women adored Hamilton for stepping up to the plate as godfather and surrogate grandfather to little Bobbie.

Then, as the ladies made their way to the car, Eleanor paused to address something that had been on her mind. "Tonya, before we meet the other girls, can I ask you something?"

"Shoot."

"Yesterday Pam and I went over to the shelter. By the way, did you go there later?"

"No, I called, and Lauren said they were all finished working. . . . She said thanks but she didn't need my help. She told me you guys had been there."

"We were, and it looks fantastic."

"Oh, good."

"I told Lauren that you were goin' over in the afternoon, and she seemed to know that you were at the movies."

Tonya grimaced.

Eleanor observed, ". . . Yes, and her face did pretty much what your face is doin' right now. What's goin' on?"

"Nothing's going on. I just went to the movies with Tucker and Brian."

"OK, . . . so why are you both acting so strangely?"

"I don't know, Ms. Eleanor. Is she acting strangely? Maybe I should have said something to her."

"Yes, I think that would have been a good idea."

"OK. . . . No, I'm confused. . . . It just happened at the last minute. Should I call her up like I'm asking permission? She and Brian are divorced, aren't they?"

Eleanor took Tonya's face in her hands. "That's not the point. Obviously it still bothers her. She's your friend, first and foremost, so I think you need to straighten this out with her today. Just tell her that it's nothin', and if she prefers you don't do things with Brian and Tucker, then don't."

Tonya turned her face away. "I don't know, Ms. Eleanor, I'm confused."

"Well it's simple, girl. You just tell Lauren. . . ."

". . . No, I'm not confused about Lauren.

I'm confused in general. I'm really confused."

Although Tonya hemmed and hawed for a
moment more, she couldn't avoid Eleanor's
gaze. "OK, Brian's really nice, and I enjoy
my time with him. I never even thought
about spending time with anybody until
recently when it all went crazy with Shooter.
He hasn't even called me all weekend, and
I'll be hog-tied if I'm going to call him."

"Sounds like you're both bein' a little
stubborn."

"No, ma'am. I deserve an apology. I
deserve some answers."

"I can't disagree with you there, but what
docs that have to do with Brian?"

"Nothing . . . other than I do find him attractive. Eleanor, he's a grown-up. I don't
feel like I have to initiate everything with
him. In fact, he asked if I wanted to go with
Bobbie to Florida to Disney World with him
and Tucker."

Although it took a lot to shock Eleanor,
Tonya had just succeeded in doing so. "He
did what? Now I'm confused."

"No, it's not like that. . . . It's just that we
have so much fun with the boys, and the
boys have fun with each other. . . . And he
was going to go down for a long weekend
with Tucker to Florida and wanted to know

if we wanted to go . . . actually, if Bobbie wanted to go. But he thought Bobbie wouldn't go without me. I told him I'd check with Shooter, and I've made everything clear."

"Except with yourself, obviously."

Tonya sighed. "Yeah, obviously. I don't know what I'm doing, so I should just do nothing, right?"

"That's right. And if Bobbie does go with Brian, yes, ask Shooter first. It might even be a good thing to break the ice over what's between the two of you. And then ask Lauren."

Tonya looked frustrated. "OK, . . . but what am I supposed to ask Lauren? If my son can play with her son?"

"No, if you can play with her ex-husband!"

Embarrassed, Tonya threw her hands up in frustration. "I'm not playing with her husband!"

Eleanor studied her friend. "Then why are you so upset?"

Tonya shook her head. "I don't know."

"Well, I would advise stayin' far away from the whole situation. You're too emotionally confused to make any kind of right decisions about anythin'."

"OK, you're right . . . but I don't get this part. . . . If they're divorced, why's it wrong if I decide to see Brian?"

Eleanor took Tonya by her shoulders. "Sweet cakes, you are committed to Shooter, least 'til somethin' more definitive happens with you two. One fight doesn't mean you're over, even if it's a biggie. Just because two people argue doesn't mean they don't love each other, and just because two people *don't argue* doesn't mean they do love each other. You need to pray about all this, girl. It's too important. And about Brian . . . Put all other factors aside like Lauren and Bobbie. Brian's older . . . Brian's white . . . Shall I go on?"

"He's *white?* You have a problem with that?"

"Tonya, God doesn't have a problem with that, so I don't have a problem with that. But the society we live in has some problems with that. And even if Brian were purple, it's not time for you to entertain startin' another relationship right now. If you don't want my opinion, don't ask. But if you ask, I'm goin' to tell you the truth."

"I am asking, and I do want to hear. I'll talk to Lauren, OK?"

"OK. But just make sure you keep talkin' to me along the way. I'm not your mother or your keeper, but we are accountable to each other. That's why God put us together.

I'm talkin' about *lovin'* accountability, not criticism. I've just been around the block about twenty million times more than you have, so listen up."

"I will, promise. . . . Thanks."

"Good girl. I believe you just sidestepped a big ol' fatty mess."

Behind the diner's counters, Pam was pulling cakes and pies out of the refrigerator for their gathering while Stephanie brewed some coffee.

"Just because this is an emergency meeting doesn't mean we can't eat. My stomach was talking to me all through church." Pam swiped a mound of icing off the double-chocolate fudge cake.

"Hear, hear." Stephanie filled the creamer and grabbed a sugar bowl.

Eleanor placed some dishes on the counter, all the while her eyes were riveted on the chess pie before her. Then out of the blue she turned on Pam with a vengeance. "Put that back! You know that's my very favorite. Now how am I supposed to lose my twenty pounds with a chess pie in my face?"

"Whoa, OK." Pam instantly obeyed, sliding the pie under the counter out of view and reach.

"Don't get me wrong. I'm not sayin' everybody has to starve with me, but I only have just so much willpower."

"Is the key lime pie OK?" Pam asked sheepishly.

"If you don't talk about it, you can keep it at the other end of the table. But no chess pie!"

Stephanie was already confused. "What's with the twenty pounds?"

"Well, I was goin' to announce it at the meetin' . . . I've decided to have my reconstructive surgery, and I want to be in my best proportions when I transform my body."

"Go, girlfriend!" Stephanie cheered.

"Thank you. Now I'm goin' to need every bit of encouragement I can get, so hound me if you see me stuffin' my fat face."

"You know you'll hit us if we hound you." Pam cringed.

"You're such a wuss. I promise to be nice."

"OK, . . . but don't forget that when we pull the food out of your hands . . . as the whipped cream is just about to dribble onto your tongue." Stephanie moaned with expectancy.

"Shush, girl!" Eleanor glanced outside where Tonya and Lauren were in a rather intense conversation by the side fence of the diner. She dropped her eyes for a moment in prayer, hoping their exchange was going better than it appeared to be.

Pam set the cake and pie on the near side of the end booth's table. "What are Tonya and Lauren doing outside? They're going to be blocks of ice if they don't come in right quick."

"They'll be along. Patience is a virtue."

"Tell my stomach that. Besides, I can barely stand the suspense. This is only the second emergency meeting we've ever called." She looked at Stephanie. "What's up?"

"Just hold on. Wait 'til the other girls get in here." Stephanie glanced at Lauren and Tonya, who now were hugging.

Eleanor whispered, "Thank you, Lord."

In a matter of less than ten minutes, the women leaned back in the booth, stuffed to the gills. Disgruntled, Eleanor had turned her back on the others and diligently sipped on her Diet Coke while her buddies gorged themselves. She waited until all the plates were whisked away by Stephanie before calling the others to attention.

"Since you requested the meetin', Steph, why don't you open the prayer . . . before I eat the crumbs off the table."

"Sure." And everyone bowed their heads. "Father God, we come before you today for your covering in all that we say, do, and decide with your wisdom and grace. We know that you say in all things to forgive and leave all the retribution to you, but Father God . . ."

Stephanie looked up at the others who remained with their eyes down in fervent prayer. ". . . I ask you for a big favor. Let us know exactly where we end and you begin. Help us see the overview and around corners as you do, Father God. And let our hearts be still knowing you're our protector and that you love us. And I ask that all in Jesus' mighty name, Amen."

"Amen, in Jesus' name." They all agreed.

Then Lauren bellowed, "What's going on? I only have one more nail left to chew down to the quick in anticipation."

"OK, I'm sorry. I didn't mean to be so mysterious. I just didn't want to do anything without talking to all of you first. I want to address this situation prayerfully because, left to my own devices, I'd be in the hoosegow for assault with a blunt object — my tongue."

Eleanor pointed her fork at Stephanie. "I am hungry and short-tempered. Spill it!"

"OK! . . . Friday I went over to the

lawyers' office to see if I could catch Lauren and Irene and their parents for my quick hug before the march-around. . . ."

Impatient, everyone spurred her on. "Yes, yes."

"Alright. Well, when I got there, Lauren had just gone into the lawyers' office when I noticed a flash, so I went down the hall to investigate. Long story short, I found rattail Norro literally hiding behind a water cooler in the hall reloading his film."

Lauren shook Stephanie by the arm. "What do you mean 'reloading his film'? What film? What are you talking about?"

"Just think back. . . . I don't know whether it was last week or the month before. Whenever that close-up of you and Irene was on the front page of the paper . . . or maybe it was the month . . ."

". . . I'm going to sit on you if you don't spit it out." Eleanor flicked her wet straw at Stephanie.

"OK! When Lauren and Irene were on the front page of the newspaper, maybe for the third time, if you look at the background of the picture carefully, it was taken here in the diner. Remember the time Irene came here?" Stephanie focused on Lauren. "I've kept copies of all the stuff printed about Irene and you, and when I studied the shot, it had to be taken by someone *inside* the diner, not by any of the paparazzi outside."

Suddenly Stephanie raised her voice and pointed to each corner of the room like a mad person. ". . . If you're bugging us, Norro, I'm going to . . . Whatever! I'm going to do something. That's what we're here to decide."

"Norro's buggin' us?" Eleanor looked around, wide-eyed. "Why would he be buggin' us?"

Lauren gulped her coffee. "No . . . He . . . What . . ."

Tonya and Pam just sat there, stunned.

"I don't know. Maybe to sell information to the newspapers. We all know he's a slime."

Pam finally spoke up. "Yeah, but I didn't think he was a slimy snake."

"Hold it, girls," Eleanor reasoned. "Let's not get carried away here. Nothin' we've said in our meetin's has shown up in print anywhere. So I don't think we're bein' bugged. Think about it. The last thing Norro'd want to listen to is a bunch of women prayin'. Point is, we don't sit around here to gossip."

Everyone agreed.

"But," Stephanie was persistent, "listen, the regular press wasn't here for that first set of photos. Remember Irene and Lauren outside the school with the cigarette looking like crazy people, . . . stomping the cigarette out on the sidewalk and all?"

Embarrassed, Lauren held her hand up like a traffic cop. "OK, OK, . . . we get the picture. That was Chelsea's first day of school, and the court stuff hadn't happened. Matter of fact, Irene hadn't even been arrested yet!"

"That's my point."

"So somebody in town had to have taken that picture," Eleanor concluded, proud of her investigatory conclusion.

"I say it was Norro," Stephanie insisted.

Tonya remained baffled. "But why would he be taking their picture?"

"I don't know why he even breathes. . . ."

Lauren cut Stephanie off. ". . . Maybe he was just covering the new people in town. I don't know. . . . You know him. I don't know how his furry little mind works."

"I'm telling you! I think he sells his pictures to the paper." Stephanie was on a tear. "Norro would sell his mother to the milkman if he could make a buck. Who else would be doing it? Besides, it has to be him. He's the only one who could have taken that other shot from inside this diner."

"Still, there's nothing we can really do,"

Pam interjected. "It's not illegal to take someone's picture."

"Especially if they're a public person, . . ." Lauren reeled, ". . . like my sister."

Stephanie snapped her fingers for attention. "If we all agree it's Norro, what can we do to him? First, to make him stop, and second, . . . I confess, a little payback feels more sweet to me than it should right about now."

Eleanor finally emerged from a bout with some deep thinking. "Well, like Pam said, it's not illegal."

"Ooooh. . . ." All of a sudden Lauren tensed. "That creep Brandon Chase! He must be buying the pictures."

"Easy, you're goin' to pop a gut-string," Eleanor soothed. "All newspapers buy their pictures if their staff photographer doesn't get the best shots. Let's keep our focus . . . Norro's the culprit, and we've got to stop him. Now, think girls, . . . how can we pull the plug on him?"

They all sat there for a moment, scheming. Lauren was the first to talk. "OK, I thought of a million things we could do to that creep, but if we do any of them, we'd basically go to hell. . . . Not really of course, if we repented. . . ."

". . . Maybe we should all confront him

and say he was a 'bad boy,' " Pam said sarcastically.

Stephanie exploded. "I got it, . . . I got it, I got it, I got it! He plays poker, right?"

"Yes. . . ." Everybody waved her on.

"Well, I happen to know that on Sunday nights, when he thinks nobody knows it, he and a special group get together at that E-Z Motel of his for some big-buck hands. I overheard him on his cell one day calling his buddies."

"So?" Lauren didn't get her point.

"So, . . . I don't know if it's this way in California, but around these parts, any kind of underground poker playing where money is exchanged is *illegal*."

"Oooh." Lauren was like a kid in a candy shop. "You mean we can send him to jail?"

"No, I don't think anyone's going to arrest him for it, but we sure can embarrass him and a few of his cronies. See, I happen to know that Norro wants to run for sheriff next election. So if we can get evidence on him that he's doing something illegal, . . . even if half this town gambles, he won't be able to run for public office!"

"Perfect!" Lauren squealed.

"Good one!" Pam gave Stephanie a high five.

". . . I don't want to be a wet blanket, girls,

. . ." Eleanor interjected, ". . . but is this plan somethin' that would be pleasin' to God?"

A hush settled over the room. "You're right," Lauren agreed. "Let's really think about what we're doing . . . but not for too long."

Eleanor slapped her up side the head.

"OK, sorry, sorry. . . . Hey, that hurt!"

"Sorry, . . . it's a southern thing. Now let's get back to plotting."

"We've got to do something to stop Norro, but there's got to be a way not to offend God. He needs to handle this. . . ."

"Yeah," Stephanie broke in. "But I just want to be his henchman!"

Tonya had been pretty quiet until then. "Nope. I don't think God would be offended. I think it's a perfect idea. We wouldn't be doing anything wrong, and we've got to stop the guy in his tracks. He's not going to give it up just because we say 'pretty please.' As far as I'm concerned, he deserves a lot worse. The only thing we're going to be doing is keeping him out of public office, where he has no right to be anyway."

"Hear, hear," they all concurred.

"OK, so let's make a plan. The faster we get this done, the better. You said he's playing tonight?" Eleanor was in her directing seat.

"Yes, every Sunday and Thursday, but the big money night is Sunday as soon as it gets good and dark." Stephanie laughed. "Maybe they think no one'll see their cars lined up at the motel."

"Perfect. . . . I'll get the cameras. Ham has a key to the photography room, and they have all kinds of lenses and doodads."

Lauren added, excitedly, "Yeah, and I know how to use the doodads."

"Wait a sec, . . ." Pam queried, ever the logical one. "What time is everyone meeting up? Lauren and I were going to go pick up Irene at five-thirty."

"Well, this *must* be God because they all get there around seven!" Stephanie could barely contain herself.

Eleanor was curious. "Pam, why exactly are you going with Lauren to get Irene?"

"I have to talk to Irene about Chelsea. And on that note, I'm going to be needing all of you to pray for me, please. Chelsea's not doing well in counseling, . . . and that's about all I can say."

"Enough said, we'll be prayin'." Eleanor looked at the others for confirmation.

"So we're all set. Why don't we meet at the crossroads of I-76 and Wilson Pike at seven sharp."

"OK. But if for some reason Irene's plane is late, I'll call you. Everybody take their cell phones."

Again, all agreed. But as they started to disperse, Tonya intervened. "Hold on." She fervently grabbed all of their hands and pulled them to the center of the table.

"Father God, I just want to confess my confusion over my relationship with Shooter. I ask my sisters in Christ to pray for me. I ask forgiveness from Lauren for not thinking about her feelings for Brian, and I thank you for her sweet nature in realizing I meant no harm. In Jesus' name."

Then Lauren prayed, ". . . And Father God, I have to confess, as you tell us to do, that I've been feeling jealousy and confusion . . . and you're *not* about confusion, and you're certainly *not* about jealousy. I ask for forgiveness from Tonya for my fleeting thoughts of anger, having nothing to do with her. Yes, I'm muddled up about my feelings for Brian, but I'm sure it's just a momentary lapse. If there is to be anything between Brian and me again, please make that clear. And Father God, I ask you to soften Shooter's heart and let him know your will in his life, and cover my sister Tonya with peace and love. . . . And I ask that all in Jesus' name."

All the women leaned in and hugged one another, knowing that each considered the others a gift from God — their friendship, their fellowship, and the absolute knowledge that together they stood stronger than they ever could alone.

And then, before they all passed through the hallowed door of the diner, Stephanie couldn't resist challenging her circle of friends . . .

"Is God a single parent? There will be a test, girls!"

CHAPTER 16
-TRUTH BE KNOWN-

Despite her weekend of unwinding and excess, Irene looked absolutely stunning as she stepped off her plane from New York.

She wasn't expecting to find Lauren waiting at the end of the concourse since she usually picked her up outside of baggage claim, so her immediate response to her sister's wide open arms was unfortunately terse.

"What are you doing here?"

Lauren smothered her with kisses. "Nice to see you too, Rene."

"Sorry, I just thought you'd be out front."

"Well yes, but I wanted to talk to you for a minute. Come on, let's sit down."

She pulled on Irene's arm, but the woman wouldn't budge. "Lauren, we can talk in the car. I just got off a plane, and I feel like an accordion. No more economy class for this girl."

"Please, just for a minute. I have to

explain something to you."

Now Irene was concerned. "Is everything alright? Is Chelsea . . . ?"

"Everything's fine, but Pam needs to talk to you."

"What?"

"It's about Chelsea."

"What's wrong?"

"Nothing, Chelsea's fine. Pam just needs to talk to you for a few minutes."

"When?"

"Well, we thought now. We just had our meeting at Norros. Remember I told you we were having an emergency meeting; and of course, Pam was there. Not that she discusses anything with me or the others because of the patient-client privilege thing, but you're her mom and I'm only her aunt. . . ."

". . . Lauren, will you please get to the point? You're starting to give me a headache."

"OK, sorry. . . . Pam told me there're some issues with Chelsea's counseling she wanted to discuss. Now, I can be there if you want me there. We came in two cars. Pam brought hers, and she could drive you home, and you two could talk. But if you want me there, she can leave her car, and we can all go with me, and I'll come back and get . . ."

". . . Hold on. Pam is here? . . . Where?"

"She's outside baggage claim with her car, and she can take you home so you two can go over the counseling things . . . if that's what you want."

"I want to grasp what on earth you're talking about. Doesn't Chelsea have an appointment with Pam tomorrow? Maybe I should just go with Chelsea and 'discuss.' "

"No, Rene, I don't think it's something Pam can discuss with you in front of Chelsea. Not that I know all the details. I don't. And if you want me to come with you . . ."

". . . No, it's alright. I get the picture. OK, so I'll go back with Pam, and you'll go back by yourself, and I'll just see you at home."

"Right! Well, it'll probably work out just perfectly because I have to go get my truck in the parking lot, and you have to get your bag, so . . ."

". . . I'll just see you back at home then."

"Yes, perfect."

"OK, well, let's go."

"OK. . . ."

Atop a stepladder, Lauren rummaged through the shelves of her parents' closet, her voice muffled as she searched the piles of hats and sweaters.

". . . Come on, Dad! I remember you had one."

Margaret and Sam sat on their bed like two bumpkins at a bus stop. On occasion Sam got up and steadied the stepladder when Lauren would adopt an unreasonable angle trying to search higher into the closet than was safe.

"If you're talking to us, we can't hear you. You sound like a moth covered with sweaters!" Sam yelled.

Suddenly a pile of his clothes landed in a thud on the floor. "Got it! Yeah, I found it." Lauren bounced up and down on the ladder.

Sam swatted at his daughter. "Stop doing that; you're going to end up on your head."

She gleefully descended, holding a black ski hat/mask that covered one's entire head with the exception of eyes, nose, and mouth holes.

Margaret started to pick up her husband's sweaters off the floor. "I still don't understand why you want to wear that."

"First of all, Mom, . . . it's cold outside. Plus I don't want to be seen. We're on a mission. Hey, Dad, where's your flashlight?"

"Under the kitchen sink."

"And it's OK if I wear your big parka?"

"Yes, it's fine." He was beginning to get

short-tempered about his daughter's she-nanigans. "Lauren, wouldn't it be easier if all of you just talked to this Norro charac-ter?"

"There's no talking to that man. And please, don't mention a decibel of this to Irene. She should be back any minute. . . ." Lauren checked her watch, panicking. ". . . Matter of fact, she should be back by now."

Just then, lights from Pam's headlights flashed across the bedroom window. "Oh goodie, they're here."

Lauren kissed her mom and dad. "OK, so Irene's here and you don't have to worry about Chelsea. Have a good evening, and I'll let you know how it went when I get back. Everything's going to be fine."

She started to exit, but then turned back. "Oh, just so you know, Irene may be a little upset with what Pam had to tell her. I don't know anything about it. . . . Well, just a little bit. Chelsea's not doing well in her counsel-ing, but everything's going to be fine. Pam is all over it. Anyway, I'll be back in a little while. Love you, bye."

Margaret and Sam just stood there nod-ding, accustomed to their daughter's ramblings.

Flanked by William and Bingo and laden

with her father's black ski cap and parka, Lauren collided in the front foyer with Irene who had just entered, clearly upset; she dropped her suitcases where she stood and looked at Lauren.

"Well, I don't know what I'm going to do with Chelsea. I really don't. And by the way, neither does your friend Pam."

"What do you mean? What's wrong?"

"What isn't wrong? Pam says that she doesn't feel like she's making any headway with Chelsea because . . . I don't know, something about they don't have 'the same faith.' I wish she would have brought up all that before she started working with Chelsea."

"Well Rene, it's more about Pam trying to reach her on a level that she's just not accepting right now."

"Well she should carry on. I don't understand why Chelsea has to see somebody else. Everything seemed to be going along alright."

"Did it?"

"Not according to Pam. She says that Chelsea is just going to sessions to keep peace around here and that she's not honestly opening up. Oh yeah, and that she's transferred all her emotions onto Trace and Pam's concerned about their relationship.

By the way, Lauren, this is exactly why I didn't want Chelsea seeing so much of that boy."

Irene started to pull out a cigarette from her purse in frustration until she caught Lauren's stare. "OK, I'm going to stand outside by the front door and have a cigarette. Then I'm going to go talk to my daughter, and I will fill you in once we're finished."

"You'd better hurry because she thinks she's going to go out with Trace. If you want her to stay home tonight, I'd get in there fast."

Irene stuffed her cigarette back into the pack. "Oh no, she's not going out with anybody tonight."

"Rene, try to calm down before you talk to her, OK? She's been pretty sick, and she's pretty feisty."

"Well, so am I — not sick, feisty."

"Good, I love a 'matched set,' but unfortunately I've got to go."

Irene gave her a reassuring hug. "I'm fine. You go on. Pam told me you have a meeting with the girls."

"I can stay if you want me to."

"No, it's fine. This is between Chelsea and me. You go."

"I'll be back in just a little while. That'll

give you time to talk, and if you need me, I'll have my cell."

"Go, go, go."

"OK." Lauren glanced at the pack of cigarettes.

Irene slapped her hand, cigarettes and all, across her heart. "I promise I won't sneak a smoke inside, even though you make me feel like a child."

"Thank you. Of course you realize I can smell that stuff a mile away."

"I said I promise."

"Thanks, Rene."

Lauren raced down the back roads in her truck as fast as she dared go. She was running late. Finally reaching the appointed intersection, she skidded to a stop next to Eleanor, Stephanie, Pam, and Tonya, who all waited in Tonya's Chevy.

Totally dressed in black with her ski mask on, Lauren jumped out of her truck to join the girls, slinking along as if she were on some covert mission. As she piled into the backseat, she was yammering a mile a minute.

". . . Sorry, sorry. I got hung up with Irene." She pulled her flashlight out and shined it in each of the women's faces. "Where are your outfits?"

The ladies shook their heads. "What outfits?"

"We're sneaking up, aren't we? We don't want to be seen."

Eleanor couldn't help but giggle. "We're not doing *Mission Impossible* here, Lauren. Besides, if anyone sees you dressed like that, they'll call the police on the spot. All we have to do is casually walk around the motel and hope that a window is a little open so we can snap some pictures."

"Right, and that's my job, and I don't want to get recognized, OK?"

Everyone just nodded, knowing it would be easier just to let Lauren do it her way than try to argue with her.

The E-Z Motel had a neon "No Vacancy" sign flashing out front. Its rather small parking lot was packed with cars, far more than the twelve motel rooms warranted.

Tonya parked her car around the corner out of sight of the motel while Lauren assembled the camera and flash with the expertise of a professional.

"OK, so . . . once we get the pictures, . . ." Lauren adopted a husky whisper, ". . . are we going to wait to develop them to confront Norro, or are we just going to bang on the door like they did in *The Untouchables* and give this guy 'what for'?"

Eleanor considered her loony friend. "Sweet pie, maybe you should go home and take a nap. You're way over the top, here."

Meanwhile, Stephanie had ventured forth a couple of yards to check out the goings-on in the motel and returned bursting with excitement. "It couldn't be more perfect! I'm telling you, this is a God thing. Everybody's there! I can smell the cigar smoke from here, the back window is open, and the curtain is pulled away! Bullwinkle could get this picture without even trying."

"OK, let's go." Lauren started off, accidentally tripping the light meter, which tested itself directly in her face. Blinded by the flash, she fumbled about, stumbling over her man-sized black snow pants. Finally losing her balance, she bounced off the driveway surface.

Despite her fall, she saved the camera from harm, holding it high in the air at the expense of her now trashed kneecaps, which were bloodied and bruised from the impact of the gravel. The girls finally gathered her to her feet but not without some difficulty.

"I'm OK. I got it. I didn't drop the camera. I'm amazing! Did you all see that?" Steadying herself, Lauren was off and running again.

Making her way around the back of the motel, Lauren held the heavier branches back for her friends, anxious to spot her perfect shot. The girls gathered behind a nearby tree, concerned that the frost from their mouths might give away their positions.

"See," Lauren pulled her ski mask over her mouth as she spoke. "I'm the only one who can speak without fogging. Ha! And you said I was overdressed."

Stephanie put her hand over her own mouth. "Look Mom, no mask and I can speak too."

Everyone giggled at the joke except Lauren.

"Did I tell you guys that I hate being teased?" Lauren suddenly looked like she was about to cry.

"We're all on the same side, sweet pea. Lighten up." Mist poured out of Eleanor's mouth as she spoke. Panicked, Lauren slapped her hand over Eleanor's face who responded with force. "Hey, that hurt," she hissed as she slapped Lauren's hand away.

"OK, sorry, sorry. It's a Southern thing! Just don't speak, or they'll see us!"

Meanwhile, Stephanie was transfixed with her view of the players at the poker table. "Oh my, oh my, yes! Well, if we ever need any favors in this town, all we'll have to do is pull out our picture. There's Judge Barker. . . . Oh, . . . hey, isn't that the officer who arrested Irene?"

Lauren's eyes narrowed. "How does that creep know those other creeps?" Then she turned to her friends, deadpan serious. "Oh, I guess creeps hang together, don't they?"

"Lauren, everybody knows everybody in small southern towns. Oh, look, . . . there's Mr. Willard. He's the coroner. . . . Ah-ha, and Mac. He runs a tractor supply store off Highway 86. Oh, wait, wait, wait. . . ."

Emerging from the bathroom was a red-faced, wide-barreled elderly man with a cowboy hat and cascading white hair reminiscent of Colonel Sanders.

Lauren pointed excitedly. "I know that guy! Isn't that the mayor?"

Tonya was quick to correct her. "Nope. He runs the pizza parlor, and I'm sure you'll see him again at Christmas. He plays Santa Claus on the side."

"OK, girls, it looks like everyone's arrived. I'm going to go do it." Lauren was revved up for action.

"Now don't go off half-cocked," Stephanie cautioned her. "We have to see the money on the table and Norro's face. Don't worry about anybody else. Just take a couple of shots, and let's get out of here."

Nodding affirmation, Lauren pulled her flashlight out like it was a gun and started to proceed down the slope. But within a few feet she slipped. Careening downhill, she landed dangerously near the back window of the poker game. Miraculously, she stopped just short of crashing into the motel wall. Not one to be discouraged, Lauren turned back to the girls who were cringing and ducking behind the evergreens and gave them a thumbs-up.

Once Lauren recovered from her slide, she steadied herself and took a couple of photos of Norro without the flash. Then she boldly turned the flash on and took one more wide shot before running back to home base.

Stephanie could see past the curtain that the sheriff noticed some sort of ruckus outside the open window, but it was his turn to bid, so his attention quickly reverted back to the game in progress.

Chelsea's Coke can full of soda smashed against the bedroom wall. Stunned, Irene stared at her daughter and then at the mess on her sister's rug.

"You little brat." Livid, she grabbed Chelsea's arm and twirled her around to face her. She was a nanosecond away from slapping her child. The two glared at each other, neither about to back down.

Thankfully, Irene controlled her temper and let go of Chelsea, who stood her ground mere inches away from her mother's face. "I'm going out! You said if you were home I could go out! I don't care what Pam says. I don't want to go to counseling anymore anyway. I didn't do anything wrong! Why are you punishing me for something your stupid husband did to me? I'm over it. He's dead, and I'm fine."

"You're not fine. You just threw your Coke can against the wall. You're out of control, Chelsea."

Now the girl started screaming at the top of her lungs. "Because I'm a prisoner! Because you won't let me go out!"

"Chelsea, you're not going anywhere while you're behaving like this. Part of what Pam is saying is that she is concerned . . ."

". . . I *hate* her!"

"Chelsea, watch your mouth. She's just trying to help."

"What I tell her is supposed to be private."

"She's concerned about you. She's worried about your relationship with Trace."

"She doesn't know anything. Trace is the only good thing in my life! She's just some stupid old maid. She doesn't even have a boyfriend. What does she know about anything?"

"Look, if you don't like her as a counselor, that's fine. I'll find you another one. But we are going to get down to the bottom of what's really going on with you. I'm not just going to close my eyes because you want to go out. As long as you're under age and you live in this house, you will go by my rules. . . . I simply don't feel comfortable about how you're behaving."

Suddenly it was all too much for Chelsea. She was exhausted, she wasn't feeling well, and she collapsed on the floor in tears. Irene bent down to try and hold her daughter, but at her mother's touch Chelsea violently pulled away.

Spent, Irene finally acquiesced. "Do you want me to leave you alone?"

"Yes!" Chelsea sobbed, as she rolled herself up into a ball.

"Are you sick? What's wrong with you?"

Chelsea was barely audible between sobs, yet her anger was clear. "I'm going to bed . . . but you can't keep me from going to school because that's the law! So just leave me alone. I'll see Trace tomorrow, and you can't stop me."

Irene slowly stood. "OK, Chelsea. But just know that I'm putting on the house alarm.

That means I'm not stupid, and I know about your little escape route through your bedroom window. If you try that tonight, the alarm will go off, so just get some rest, and we'll work this out when you feel better."

By now Chelsea was all cried out. Defeated, she just stared off into space.

Emotions were running high on all accounts in the Patterson house that Monday morning. Lauren hadn't slept a wink in anticipation of the opening of the shelter, Irene hadn't slept all night from worrying about Chelsea, and Chelsea had spent most of the night doubled over in pain and bouts of nausea. But despite her malady, Chelsea made a good show of it as she attempted to exit through the kitchen the next morning where all members of the family, including Margaret and Sam, were gathered for breakfast.

Just as Chelsea was about to escape, Irene called her over. "I need to talk to you for a minute. Let's go to the front hall."

Chelsea rolled her eyes, barely recognizing the existence of anyone else in the kitchen except Tucker, who waved at her. She waved back as she exited with her mom.

Once Irene and Chelsea were in the hall,

Irene scrutinized her daughter. "Chelsea, you really don't look well."

"I'm OK."

"Alright, I know you're angry with me, and I don't want to fight with you. But when you get home this afternoon, we're going to sit down and calmly discuss what our options are about getting you some help. You obviously don't want to talk to me, but you've got to talk to somebody."

"Mom, I don't want to keep Trace waiting, OK?"

"Fine. But I want you to come straight home from school. Is that understood?"

"Yeah."

She started out the door when Irene grabbed her arm. Chelsea pulled back, ready for another confrontation. "Would you just please go in and take a minute to wish your aunt good luck on the opening of her shelter? It's very important to her."

"Then can I leave?"

"Yes." Irene mustered every ounce of control she could not to respond to Chelsea's rudeness as she followed her daughter back into the kitchen.

Making a perfunctory stop to give Lauren a quick hug, Chelsea mumbled, "I hope it goes good for you this morning." And with that the girl was gone.

Regardless of how terse Chelsea's well wishes were, they were more than Lauren had expected. She looked at Irene. "Wow, that was a surprise."

"Not really. That was an order from me. But she's mad at me, not at you. I know that Chelsea loves you. Whether *she* knows it or not, she does care. . . . She's just been in a terminally bad mood for the last several years."

Sam looked at his older daughter. "Did you two have a fisticuffs last night? I heard a big crash."

Irene sighed. "Yes, well we had a little run-in with Chelsea's Coke can and the wall and the rug. Which, by the way Lauren, I'm going to call a professional carpet cleaner to restore."

Irene's statement got the attention of Tucker, who was diligently eating his cereal. "How come she doesn't have to clean up, and when I make a mess, I do?"

"Well, Tuck, . . ." Lauren searched for a reasonable answer. ". . . Chelsea hasn't been feeling very well, so we're going to take care of her mess this time. OK, buddy?" She quickly changed the subject. "So I'm going to take you to school as soon as the opening's over. . . ."

". . . Is Dad going to be there?"

"No, that's why he brought you home late last night. He's got a business trip, remember?"

"Oh, yeah, he told me."

"So Mom and Dad, you're going to go with Irene. That way I can take Tucker to school, and she can just bring you right back."

"That's fine, dear. Don't worry about us."

Lauren adopted her Patton stance of authority. "And Rene, you said you'd drop off the film?"

"It would be my pleasure. I can't believe that Norro individual is the 'in-house photographer.' What a creep."

Tucker pointed his cereal spoon at his aunt. "It's not nice to call someone a creep."

"Well, Tucker, it's not nice to point; and it's the nicest thing I can think of to say about that creep."

Lauren glared at Irene, who immediately recanted. "OK, you're right, Tucker. I'm sorry. Norro is just a bad man."

Now Tucker looked at his mom. "Is it OK to call someone a 'bad man'?"

"Well, *you're* not to call adults any names, . . . but yes, Tucker, sometimes people are just plain old bad, and it's OK to challenge them about the things they're doing wrong."

"Like when Steven put that ant in my

sandwich at camp?"

"Yeah, kind of like that. That was definitely a no-no."

"That's good, because I don't want to eat ants."

"You don't have to, Tuck."

Relieved, the boy went back to finish his bowl of cereal. "That's good."

Lauren actually blinked three times hard, thinking she was seeing a mirage. Then Tucker practically leaped out of her arms as she was carrying him up the steps to the shelter when he spied his friend. Suz had made herself a comfortable seat out of the edge of a giant planter standing guard by the front door. And as she stood up to greet her godson, Tucker almost knocked her over with a body blow of sheer joy at the sight of his buddy from California.

"Oh my gosh!" Lauren squealed. "What are you doing here?!"

"Surprise, surprise! I took the red-eye."

Lauren and Suz hugged, and then all three jumped up and down like orangutans.

"What's a 'red-eye'?" Tucker tenderly touched Suz's face. "Did somebody hit you?"

"No, no! It just means that I have red eyes. . . ." Suz pointed to her beautiful blue blood-shot eyes. ". . . Like these, from flying all night and not getting a lot of sleep."

Tucker considered her explanation. "That's weird."

Meanwhile, Lauren pulled out her keys and opened the shelter's door. "How long have you been waiting here, you nut?"

"Oh, about an hour. Nope. . . . Let's see, maybe it's been an hour since I felt my toes. I thought I was in the south, as in 'warm.' "

"I don't believe you actually came! Wow!" She put her arm around her friend, and they all proceeded into the foyer. "Have I got a good cup of coffee waiting for you. . . . Cream so thick it will curl your hair and kill you in the same gulp."

Suz and Lauren spent the next half hour catching up with each other while Lauren and Tucker gave her the grand tour of the shelter. But before Suz could say, "Wow," everyone started piling in the front doors for the grand opening — assistants, Mrs. Strickland, several animal crates delivered by the local shelters to transfer some of their overflow. It was like a celebratory circus come to town.

The press conference was over in what seemed like mere moments, and the shelter's first parade of pets was ensconced in their beautiful kennels — warm, safe, fed, and loved.

Lauren had even shared a kind word with Brandon Chase, who had attended the press debut. And although she was furious with him for having secondhandedly sponsored so much press about Irene over the last months, Mrs. Strickland was quick to point out that the "press-fest" had ceased. Not only that, Lauren couldn't deny the fact that he was the one who had run her commentary about the animal chutes and ultimately put Mrs. Strickland and Lauren together.

Pam and Eleanor enjoyed kidding Lauren after the conference about Mr. Brandon Chase being a pretty good-looking gentleman with whom she'd be working closely in the future since Lauren was in charge of promoting the shelter. And even though Lauren hated to be teased, she couldn't sidestep her happiness at finding at least one other man besides Brian whom she found attractive.

"OK, yes," she admitted to her friends. "So maybe my femininity isn't dead, lost, or frozen."

What a most amazing morning it had been,

Lauren thought, as she gathered Tucker's things to take him to school before dropping Suz back at the airport. She was frustrated, however, that no matter how hard she tried, she couldn't talk her friend into staying even one night. But then again, Lauren understood that Suz had to get back to take care of her husband, Fred. Besides, what really mattered was that she had come across the country just to be there for the shelter's opening — to be there for her friend.

Lauren smiled, remembering Suz's framed cross-stitched gift for her last birthday, "A good friendship is a well-worn path between two homes." And then there was Christmas's work of art; "You don't have to change friends when you understand that friends change."

And what a joy it had been to introduce Suz to her circle of friends; of course they all felt as if they had known one another forever. And when they prayed together before Stephanie had to run back to Norros, and Pam was finally about to sit down with Mrs. Strickland over coffee to share her aspirations for the Hope School, and Eleanor had to head back to the high school, and Tonya back to her college classes, Lauren couldn't ever remember feeling such a sense of accomplishment, peace, and well-being.

Unfortunately, her tranquility would be short-lived.

CHAPTER 17
-TIMING-

Chelsea's history teacher literally carried her into Eleanor's nurse's office during mid-morning break at Greystone High. The girl was hemorrhaging profusely.

Eleanor rode along with Chelsea in the ambulance that dashed them the short distance to the local hospital a brief five minutes from the school. Chelsea was crying hysterically in response to the severe pain she was suffering and at the sight of all the blood that understandably frightened her.

In the midst of her panic, she kept calling out for Trace. And although Eleanor remained professionally calm, she was extremely concerned for the girl's health and state of mind. Eleanor told her that she had pulled Trace out of class and he was already on his way to the hospital, so she'd see him there. But she emphasized to Chelsea that she first needed to be seen by a doctor.

Lauren had just said her good-byes to Suz at the airport when she received a call on her cell phone from Ham about Chelsea's condition. Stunned at the news, she assured him she was on her way to the hospital and that she would call Irene, sure the scary news about her daughter's emergency best come from her. It was also agreed that Ham would contact Stephanie, Pam, and Tonya.

With sirens blaring, the ambulance arrived at Centennial General. Dr. Logan was standing outside the emergency doors waiting for Chelsea and Eleanor. The commotion was overwhelming as the teenager was admitted into the area. There was no time for forms to be filled out or questions to be asked. This girl was in serious trouble.

Chelsea was immediately wheeled into an examining room just as Irene arrived with her parents. And within moments the rest of the family and friends gathered.

The head nurse insisted Lauren and Irene wait in the hall while the doctor examined Chelsea. "He'll be out as soon as possible to give you an update," she stated, but Irene protested, "She's my daughter! I want to see her, and I want to see her now!"

Lauren tried to reason with her sister, knowing she was beginning to panic. "Rene, just let them do what they need to do to find out what's wrong."

"No, I have to know what's going on!"

Having returned from the front desk, Eleanor joined the women. Her voice was filled with compassion. "Irene, Chelsea was brought to my office bleedin'. I was with her in the ambulance. She was upset but conscious. Please know that I didn't leave her alone for a second."

"What do you mean she was bleeding? Bleeding from what?"

"It appeared to be vaginally. Has she been sick?"

"She's been throwing up, right?" Irene turned to Lauren for confirmation.

"Yes. She has the flu."

Irene nodded, addressing Eleanor again. "It looked like her stomach hurt, but I thought that was just from vomiting for two days. I only saw her last night, and she didn't look well, but she insisted on going to school this morning."

"Alright. . . ." Eleanor tried to ease Irene's concerns. "Before we left the school, I called my personal doctor, Dr. Logan. He's top-notch, believe me. He teaches at Vanderbilt, so rest assured, Chelsea's receivin' the very best care."

Irene suddenly looked faint. Eleanor and Lauren ushered her over to a couch near Stephanie and Trace, who were huddled next to the front doors. Stephanie was filling her son in on Chelsea's condition as best she knew.

"Is she OK, Mom?" The boy was stuttering from nerves.

"Just calm down, Trace. She's with Dr. Logan. . . . They won't even let . . ."

". . . I gotta see her, Mom!"

"Listen to me; we just have to wait." She pointed over to the ladies on the couch. "Look, . . . they won't even let Irene in to see her right now."

Inconsolable, the boy was frantic. "No, you don't understand! I have to see her!"

"No, what you have to do is calm down. I'm sure Chelsea's going to be fine, and after the doctor gets a handle on what's going on, you can go in and see her, OK?" Stephanie tried to be reasonable, but she was taken aback by her boy's intensity. In fact, Trace looked like he was about to burst into tears.

"What's wrong with you, son?"

He finally broke. "She's pregnant."

Stephanie just stared at him in shock; it took several beats before she could even mouth the word. "Pregnant?"

"She told me this morning."

Stephanie took her son by the arm and stiffly escorted him through the emergency entrance to the outside. Her voice dropped to a harried whisper. "What are you talking about?"

"She told me when I picked her up for school this morning. That's probably why she's sick. She was so upset."

Stephanie broke down. "Oh, Trace . . . Oh no. How could you do . . . How could . . . ?"

"I'm sorry, Mom, . . . I'm sorry. I messed up! I can't believe she's pregnant. We only did it one time."

Suddenly angry, Stephanie just shook her head. "It only takes *once*, Trace."

He started to pace. "Yeah, right, I guess so."

"When did this happen?"

He realized that there was no point in trying to be evasive with his mother considering everything that was going on. But more importantly, his concern for Chelsea overrode his fear of tongue-lashings or punishment for his indiscretions. And yet, when he looked at his mother's expression of disappointment in him, he was shattered.

"It happened right after she moved here. I'm not trying to blame her or anything, but . . . I don't know, Mom. Usually with the girls, I'm the one that has to make the moves, so it's a little . . ."

". . . What do you mean?" Stephanie was trying her best to control herself.

"Chelsea . . . She said she fell in love with me right off and that she wanted to be close to me. . . . And it just happened, Mom. She just . . . wanted it to happen, you know? Look, I know it's wrong, but I do love her, and she loves me."

"Really? Well that's a good thing, Trace, because you have to take responsibility for all of this."

"I know, I know." And then the reality of the situation started to hit him. "Oh, man . . . what's going to happen about college . . . basketball?"

Stephanie didn't know whether to slap him or hug him. By then she was as much a bundle of confusion as he. Finally, she put her arms around Trace, knowing she had to be careful about how she responded and what she said if she was to be of any help to her boy. "It'll all work out."

He pulled away from her, shaking his head. Stephanie had never seen him so distraught.

"Mom, I just can't believe . . . *one* time. And I told her after that . . . I told her that I wanted to wait. All the stuff we've talked about. . . . And I told her that I really cared about her and I wanted to treat her right. . . . And she said OK. She never really pushed it much again, like she just needed to know I was going to be there, that I wasn't going to leave her or anything. And that's what I've got to tell her now, Mom. I've got to tell her . . ."

He whirled around and slammed his fists onto the concrete wall. "It's all my fault she's in there. . . . She told me she was pregnant, and I just . . . I couldn't say anything. I didn't know what to say, and she got so mad. I've got to tell her that I'm going to be there for her!"

"It's alright, you'll get to tell her. It'll all be fine." Stephanie looked through the hospital windows at the others gathered inside. She could see the terror on Irene's face, and her heart just broke for her. It broke for all of them.

"Son, . . . we just have to get through this now and make sure Chelsea's OK. We'll deal with everything else later. Why don't you stay out here, and I'll go in and see if Ms. Irene's heard anything."

"OK, . . ." he muttered to himself, walking back and forth like a caged animal. But when his mom started to go, he turned around in a panic. "No! You're coming right back. . . . You're going to tell me the truth, right? I want to see her."

"I promise, Trace."

He turned and faced the wall again. After a beat Stephanie walked into the lobby just as Dr. Logan came out of the exam room. He called Irene over, who hung onto Lauren like a child. Everyone else stayed back a little to allow Irene her privacy.

"Mrs. Williams, I'm Dr. Logan. . . ."

". . . Yes, how's Chelsea?" Irene cut him off.

"She's going to be alright. We have to do a few more tests, but we've got her on IV fluids and medication to control the bleeding. It has slowed significantly."

"What is it? What's wrong with her?"

The doctor realized that Irene didn't have a clue about her daughter's condition. "Mrs. Williams, Chelsea is pregnant."

Both Lauren and Irene were flabbergasted. "Pregnant?"

"Yes, ma'am. It appears that she is miscarrying, but I can't be sure of that until we get some more test results. I just wanted to come out and tell you that we've gotten her vitals stabilized, and what I want to do next is an ultrasound to see how far along she is. She's asking for somebody called Trace, but

I can't advise that she have any visitors other than you right now."

"Rene, go on in and see her. I'll be right here if you need me." Numb, Irene just nodded. Lauren stepped back. "I'm just going to let everyone know that she's going to be alright, and leave it at that for right now." Again, Irene nodded as she accompanied the doctor into Chelsea's room.

Irene hesitated at the door to take a moment to regard her daughter. She looked like such a child, so fragile. Putting on a brave front, Irene approached, holding Chelsea's hand once she reached her side. "You're going to be alright. Everything's OK."

Chelsea burst into tears. "I don't want to lose my baby!"

Irene took a moment to digest the words coming out of her daughter's mouth. "Well . . ."

The doctor intervened. "Chelsea, what I need to do now is an ultrasound just to see how your baby's doing." Dr. Logan's voice was smooth as silk. "We're going to hook up a fetal monitor, and we'll do everything we can to see if we can stop what looks to be a miscarriage."

At his words Chelsea cried out. Irene could barely stand it as she held her daughter's hand tighter. "Sweetie, they're going to do everything they can. We just have to get you better."

"Where's Trace? I want to see Trace!"

By now Chelsea was back to her hysteria.

Dr. Logan pulled Irene away for a minute to the side of the room. "I'm going to give Chelsea a sedative. . . . She needs to calm down. Is Trace here?"

"He's outside, I think."

"Is it alright with you if she sees him? She seems very determined."

Irene sighed, "Yes, of course. Should I go get him?"

"Go on. . . . It's going to take a few minutes to get the sonogram in here, so tell him to hurry. If you want to come back in during the actual ultrasound, you're welcome." Dr. Logan gave Irene his most reassuring smile.

"Thank you so much."

"Of course, ma'am."

Irene returned to Chelsea's side as the doctor left the room. "Sweetie?" Her daughter just moaned. ". . . I'm going to get Trace now. He's right outside, alright? So you just relax. They're going to give you a little sedative. Everything's going to be alright. So, I'll go get Trace now, and I love you." Chelsea just nodded.

Irene emerged from Chelsea's room, directly to Lauren who was only steps away. Her words were whispers as she fought to control her emotions. "Would you please find Trace? Chelsea wants to see him. The doctor says it's OK for just a few minutes, and then they have to do a test."

"Is she alright?" Lauren brushed back Irene's hair to look her in the eyes.

"Yes, I think she's going to be alright."

"OK, then, I'll go get him, Rene. Just . . . wait here. Do you want Mom and Dad? Do you want anyone around you?"

Irene shook her head. "No, I'm going back in to see Chelsea after Trace, so just tell everyone that she's going to be alright."

Lauren gave her sister a hug, then made a quick pass through the group assuring all that Chelsea was doing better. Then she asked Stephanie to come along with her, and as they stepped away from the group, she regarded her friend. "Where's Trace?"

"He's just outside. Oh, Lauren, what a mess."

Lauren wasn't sure what to say, or if she should say anything. "What do you know, Steph?"

After a beat, Stephanie broke down in tears for the first time since she'd arrived at the hospital. "I know Chelsea's pregnant. She told Trace this morning. . . . Oh, my Lord. How is Irene?"

"Basically she's in shock. Look, the doctor said that Trace could see Chelsea for a few minutes, and then they have to do a test, so why don't we just get him?"

Stephanie pulled herself together. "Yes, absolutely. He wants to see her very badly."

Trace was petrified as he entered the examining room, afraid of what he'd see, unsure of what he'd say, but knowing that he wanted to be there for Chelsea. When he reached the bedside, he took her hand. "I'm really sorry, Chels," was slow to come to him but sincerely said.

Chelsea started to cry again. "I don't want to lose our baby."

"Shhh . . . Hey, the main thing is you've got to be OK."

She pulled her hand away. "Right, you probably want me to lose the baby!"

"No, that's not true. That's why I wanted to see you. I'm really sorry. I'm sorry this happened, and I'm sorry I didn't . . . I'm sorry I didn't know what to say this morning. That doesn't mean I don't care. Everything's going to be OK, Chels. You've got to get better, and I just want you to know that I'm going to be here for you."

There was a light knock at the door. A nurse entered, rolling in an ultrasound machine.

"You'll have to excuse us, young man. We're going to do a test right now, and the doctor's going to be right in."

"What test?"

"We're just going to take a little picture to see how the baby's doing."

Chelsea grabbed Trace's hand tightly. "Don't go, please!" She frantically looked at the nurse. "He's the father! Why can't he stay?"

"Oh . . . Well, let me talk to the doctor. Please don't get upset. This test isn't painful. Don't worry. You can just look at a little picture of your baby if you want to watch."

Just then, Dr. Logan returned with Irene, who nodded at Trace. The tension was riveting.

"I want Trace to stay, Mom! Don't make him go."

Irene looked at the doctor.

"This young man is the father?" Dr. Logan asked in a kind tone.

Yes, . . . and I want to stay."

"Good enough. Then let's take a look."

Chelsea settled down as the doctor pulled the bedsheets back off of her stomach and applied some gel on her lower abdomen. The nurse was careful to turn the screen so that everyone in the room could have a clear view. Then the doctor placed the medical implement on her stomach and moved it around until he found the image of the fetus on the screen.

Everyone stood in utter silence, astounded at what they were seeing. Not only that, they could hear the baby's heartbeat, and they could see the outline of the baby's body as the doctor pointed out the little head, arms, and legs. And then they watched the baby jump in the womb. Yes, it was absolutely astounding, and it was the first time Irene had heard her daughter laugh for so long. There were just no words to be said; the experience was life-changing for everyone present.

"Alright, let me go and review the tape. How are you feeling, Chelsea? A little bit more calm?" Dr. Logan smiled at the girl who actually looked dreamy eyed — not only from the sedative but from seeing her baby within her body. She grabbed the doctor's arm. "Please, don't let anything happen to my baby."

"We're going to do our best. Your baby

looks fine right now. We've given you something to stop the bleeding, but you have to stay very calm." Chelsea nodded.

Trace was totally transfixed as was Irene, who decided to give the kids another moment of private time. And as she left the room, she felt like she was floating in the middle of one of her dreams. She had actually just seen her grandbaby on the screen. Her mind raced.

Irene returned to the waiting room, her eyes scanning each friend and family member who was there praying for Chelsea. It was a sobering moment as well as a tender one; and Irene, although emotionally spent, felt the sweet sensation of loving support.

She watched Lauren approach, and as her sister reached her side, Irene laid her head on Lauren's shoulder while she whispered in her ear. "I just saw the baby. It actually has a little heartbeat and it did a flip-about."

Lauren melted at the sound of such a sweet image. And as Irene glanced away, her eyes met Stephanie's from across the room. She felt compelled to go to the woman, saying to Lauren in a small voice, "I'll be right back."

"Sure."

■ ■ ■ ■

There were no words necessary between Irene and Stephanie. They just held each other in a gesture of support and the knowledge that they had a connection now — a life connection, a grandchild to share. And within such a short duration of time, what both had considered to be stunning and disturbing news about their youngsters expecting a baby suddenly now seemed to be a miracle and a gift. Stephanie and Irene finally released each other, smiling through their tears as they nodded in silent agreement.

Irene made her way back over to her sister, pointing toward the farthest set of chairs down the hall so they could be absolutely private. And as they sat down, Lauren noted that she was having difficulty reading her sister's expression.

It took a while for Irene to begin to speak, but when she did, it seemed as if she had been waiting for this moment of confession her entire life. It wasn't a conversation she was looking forward to; it simply emerged. She needed someone to listen to her as she admitted to herself the reality of a deep, dark secret she had held deep within the recesses of her heart, locked away for decades.

Her voice was small and shaky as she spoke to Lauren in a staccato rhythm. As she opened up, she seemed to be able to watch the story unfold in her imagination. And although Irene wished she could detach herself from the pain of the experience, there was no more room for denial in her heart.

"When I was nineteen years old, I was seeing that boy that you hated . . . Jason."

"I didn't hate him, Rene, I just . . ." Irene held her hand up to silence Lauren.

". . . None of that counts. What matters is that I became pregnant by him."

Lauren tried to contain her surprise, knowing the last thing that she wanted to do was derail Irene's obvious need to confess.

"I never told anybody, not even you." She looked at her sister, managing a small smile. "Actually, that's the only thing I've ever kept from you."

"Oh, Rene . . ."

". . . Because it was nothing, Lauren. I went to the doctor, and he told me that my pregnancy was just an 'inconvenience.' I knew I couldn't get married then. I was in college, and Jason was going off to graduate school. There was no time for a baby. And, truth is, we weren't really such a big item. I hadn't even dated him that long. Anyway . . ." Her voice trailed off for a moment before she could continue. ". . . I had a few friends who had had abortions. They said it was a simple procedure, just like the doctor told me it was. The girls said I wouldn't even have to miss any of my classes. I could go into a clinic on Saturday and be back in school on Monday, and no one would know the difference. We were like a little sorority. We made a pact that we would always protect one another. . . . And once it was done, we'd never bring it up again, never think about it. . . . See, the whole thing just didn't exist."

Again, Irene paused, having difficulty continuing. ". . . And so I did it. Jason took me down to the clinic, I paid my half, and he paid his half: $350.00. By the way, it did hurt . . . The abortion hurt a lot. . . . They said it wouldn't, but it did. But then again, I figured I deserved to hurt. Something didn't feel right, but it was just easier not to think about it. Anyway, it was just a blob of tissue. The nurse and doctor said so. It wasn't even a baby yet." Suddenly, Irene wailed from her depths. "Oh, God! Lauren, I just saw Chelsea's baby. My grandchild!

She's not even showing like I was. I could hear the heartbeat. I could see the baby move." She stumbled over her words. "The baby . . . It was a baby."

Now Irene totally lost it, crumbling in her sister's arms. They rocked back and forth, silently digesting the realization of what Irene had done. All the pain, shame, and guilt that she had secretly carried for so long. And there was more coming up in Irene, more she was realizing and recognizing for the first time.

"And I never told you, I never told anyone but those girls. And every time you had a miscarriage and when you finally found out you couldn't have children, I felt so guilty that I had just gotten rid of one like it never existed. That's what I kept telling myself . . . it just never happened. And I kept it there, in that deep, dark place that I told myself wasn't real . . . until now. Oh, God, . . . it hurts *so* much!"

Lauren took her sister's face in her hands; she proceeded very carefully. "Rene, this is just the beginning. There are so many things that you're going to find out about your life that are the results of that pain. And why you did the things you did, and how you felt, and why you hurt and wanted to be numb. . . . It'll all make more sense to you

411

now. I never knew what that deep sadness and anger was about in you, but now I understand. That can be healed . . . that can be recognized, understood, and forgiven. You don't have to live with a secret anymore, with nightmares! I'll help you; we'll go through it together. Everything's going to be alright. Chelsea's going to be alright, and we'll just pray that the baby's going to be fine."

Irene started to sob again. "I was going to tell her to have an abortion. I was going to insist that she could not have a baby. I was going to make her do to herself what I did to myself because I didn't know, Lauren. I didn't know. . . . I *swear* I didn't know it was a baby."

"God can turn all things around, Rene. He's calling for you with his arms wide open. There's no condemnation in Christ!"

Irene stiffened, and Lauren realized that although her sister had opened up more than she ever had before, she still needed time, and that was OK. All Lauren needed to do was love Irene unconditionally and be there for her, and then they all needed to love Chelsea and Trace and be there for them.

And when they broke from their emotional embrace, Dr. Logan was standing there before them. "Mrs. Williams, may I speak to you alone for a moment?"

Lauren stood. "Sure, sure. I'll be over with Mom and Dad, Rene." She looked at the doctor for a minute, who thankfully had no interest in keeping Lauren in suspense. "Everything looks good."

Lauren burst into an explosive smile, gave Irene another quick hug and walked back down the hall. Irene's expression of torment softened at the doctor's assurances.

"So, are you saying the baby is alright?"

"I can't make any hard promises, but the situation is looking better than I had initially thought. Of course, most miscarriages occur during the first trimester, so the good news is that we're past that vulnerable stage."

Irene shook her head for a moment, confused. "The first trimester, which is the first three months?"

"Yes, ma'am."

"I don't understand. . . ."

The doctor felt he was giving her encouraging news, so he proceeded with enthusiasm. "Well, once we measured the baby, we know that it is at eighteen weeks gestation."

Irene was barely audible. "No, that's not possible. That's . . . four and a half months."

"Yes, ma'am."

"But we didn't move to town until September."

Now the doctor seemed confused. Irene glanced back at everyone gathered in the waiting area and then vacantly looked down the hall. A sense of panic overtook her as her mouth slowly formed the word, "Ford . . ."

To become a part of our Circle of Friends, please join us at www.jenniferoneill.com. We'd love to hear from you!

ABOUT THE AUTHOR

Jennifer O'Neill first became known as an actress starring in such films as *Rio Lobo* (with John Wayne) and *Summer of '42*. She also spent an unprecedented thirty years as a spokesperson for CoverGirl cosmetics. Today, Jennifer hosts a nationally syndicated television show and is a renowned author and inspirational speaker. She lives in Nashville, Tennessee.

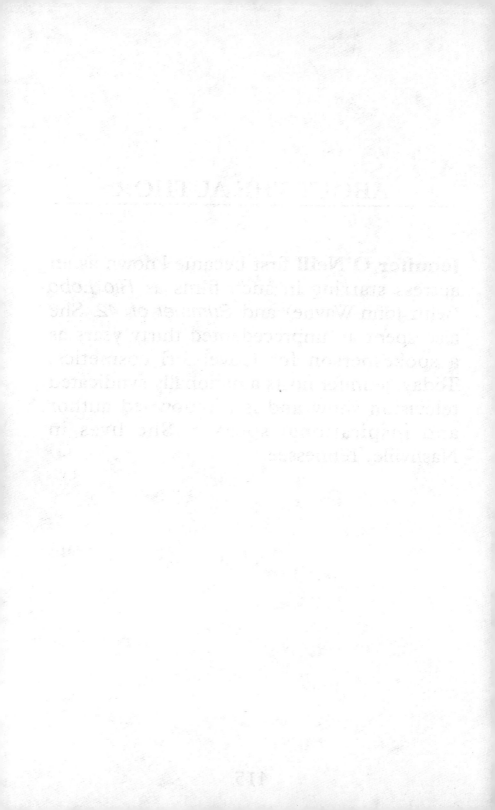